PRAISE FOR KIM LAW

"*Montana Cherries* is a heartwarming yet heart-wrenching story of the heroine's struggle to accept the truth about her mother's death—and life."

—*RT Book Reviews*, 4 stars

"An entertaining romance with a well-developed plot and believable characters. The chemistry between Vega and JP is explosive and will have you rooting for the couple's success. Readers will definitely look forward to more works by this author."

—*RT Book Reviews*, 4 stars (HOT) on *Caught on Camera*

"Kim Law pens a sexy, fast-paced romance."

—*New York Times* bestselling author Lori Wilde on
Caught on Camera

"A solid combination of sexy fun."

—*New York Times* bestselling author Carly Phillips on
Ex on the Beach

"*Sugar Springs* is a deeply emotional story about family ties and second chances. If you love heartwarming small towns, this is one place you'll definitely want to visit."

—*USA Today* bestselling author Hope Ramsay

"Filled with engaging characters, *Sugar Springs* is the typical everyone-knows-everyone's-business s̲m̲a̲l̲l̲ ̲t̲o̲w̲n̲.̲ ̲L̲a̲w̲ ̲s̲k̲i̲l̲l̲f̲u̲l̲l̲y̲ ̲p̲o̲r̲t̲r̲a̲y̲s heroine Lee Ann's doubts and fears, _____ e a better person than he believes he _____ ʒces are a delight."

_____ *ws*, 4 stars

Montana
DREAMS

Also by Kim Law

The Wildes of Birch Bay

Montana Cherries

Montana Rescue

Montana Mornings

Montana Dreams

Deep in the Heart

Hardheaded

Softhearted

Turtle Island Novels

Ex on the Beach

Hot Buttered Yum

Two Turtle Island Doves (novella)

On the Rocks

Sugar Springs Novels

Sugar Springs

Sweet Nothings

Sprinkles on Top

The Davenports

Caught on Camera

Caught in the Act

Holly Hills

"Marry Me, Cowboy" (novella), *Cowboys for Christmas*

Montana
DREAMS

Kim Law

 Montlake
Romance

Published by Montlake Romance, Seattle

www.apub.com

Amazon, the Amazon logo, and Montlake Romance are trademarks of Amazon.com, Inc., or its affiliates.

ISBN-13: 9781503902855
ISBN-10: 1503902854

Cover design by Shasti O'Leary Soudant

Printed in the United States of America

To Arsula Shumway. You know I love your name.
Thanks for the use of it!

Chapter One

"Can we just sit a minute before we go in? Catch up a little?" Jaden Wilde rested his hand on his girlfriend's forearm, halting her escape from the front seat of his rental. She paused before opening the door, and when she glanced back, he offered his signature head-tilted, you-know-you-love-me look.

"It's your brother's wedding, Jay," Megan pointed out. "And we're already *very* late."

He caressed his thumb over her arm, wishing it weren't February and they didn't have to be bundled up for the weather. He wanted to touch her skin. "But I haven't seen you in seven weeks, Meggie. I *miss* you."

Resolved, Megan reversed position and covered his hand with hers. "And I haven't seen *you* in seven weeks. I get that. It's been a while. We're not used to that." Though dating for more than three years, this was the first time they'd been separated for any real length of time. "But you're the one who didn't make it in for the rehearsal last night. You're the one who barely picked me up in time to even *make* it to the wedding tonight."

"I can't help that my flight got canceled." Jaden motioned to the falling snow outside the car. "Or that an unexpected snowstorm slowed my drive from Missoula."

"Yet you were supposed to arrive *Wednesday*, Jay. You observed your last counseling session that morning. You should have been here days ago."

"I had to meet with my professor before leaving town. You know that. And he only had yesterday afternoon available."

"And you couldn't have arranged any earlier appointment had you set it up weeks ago?"

Megan's eyes narrowed with annoyance, and Jaden blew out a frustrated breath. It seemed all they did lately was argue. Ever since Megan had stayed in Birch Bay after Christmas. He was tired of fighting with his girlfriend. Tired of not having his girlfriend at his side.

And if she'd been in Seattle, *she'd* likely have reminded him to make that appointment weeks ago.

"Can't we just . . . *be* for a minute?" He tried again. "Just enjoy each other's company?"

He didn't want to go into the surprise he had planned for later by starting the evening off like this.

"We're already here," he went on. "We're sitting in the church parking lot." He looked at his watch. "And the wedding doesn't start for another ten minutes. We have time to say hello to each other. To smile at each other."

The annoyance in her eyes shifted, but instead of the pleasure he'd hoped to see, thinly veiled anger shone back. "That's exactly my point." She enunciated her words a little too clearly. "The wedding starts in *ten* minutes. We *don't* have time to say hello to each other. Not right now. You're in the wedding party, and you haven't even *met* the woman you have to walk down the aisle."

She once again reached for her door handle.

2

"Then tell me you'll come home with me after this weekend," Jaden hurried to say. He gripped her hand when she looked back. "You've been here helping out for weeks. My family appreciates it. They've told me so. They love you, and The Cherry Basket needed you when Sarah first left." He gave her a pleading smile. "But it's time to come home now. *I* need you now."

Her lack of opening the door didn't exactly reassure him. "Are you aware we found out this week that Sarah isn't coming back to work at all now? She's staying in Bozeman to take care of her mother indefinitely. Which means the store is no longer only temporarily without a manager. It's *completely* without one."

"But you're not even *in* retail, Megan. Both of your degrees are in technology." It was becoming increasingly difficult to remain calm about this whole situation. "That's it." He sliced his hands through the air as if calling a batter safe at home. "I'm drawing the line. It's not like it's the busy season right now, anyway. Someone else can handle things until a new manager is hired. They'll be fine without you."

Megan's glare turned to ice. "First of all, Jaden Wilde, you don't draw lines. Not for me. *Ever.* And second . . . quit being a selfish ass for once in your life, and think about your family."

"Selfish ass?" He reared back. "Are you kidding me? I always think about my family."

"You only think about how you can help them *emotionally.*"

He clenched his jaw. The accusation was unfair.

"You know that's not true." He took a calming breath and brought his voice back to a normal volume. This argument was rapidly getting out of control. "I think about a lot more than that, and you know it. I care about all of them. About the orchard, the store. I only want us all to be happy and healthy for once in our lives."

"And together," Megan said softly. "You want all of you to be together."

He wasn't sure what her point was. "Of course I do."

He didn't talk about his family a lot, but Megan was aware of their history. He and his five siblings hadn't had the best childhoods in the world. Their mother had been narcissistic, and her manipulations had affected all of them. It had even played into their relationships with their father, because Max Wilde had done more dodging and hiding from his wife than having a backbone and helping his children.

But they were on the path to healing now. At least, some of them were. His sister, Dani, and their dad had both been through counseling after the past had reared its head three years before. Dani still kept weekly appointments, and she was happier now than Jaden had ever seen her. She was also firmly rooted in Birch Bay. As was Nick.

Nick and Nate were twins, only two years older than Jaden's twenty-five, and though Nate still roamed the world like a nomad, Nick had come back home and settled down as well. Gabe was about to get remarried—this time to a wonderful woman. And Cord, though probably as messed up as any of them had ever been, hid his issues well via his work. He was a medical doctor and partner in a private practice down in Billings.

Some of them were good, and some of them weren't. But was it so bad of him to want to be able to help if he could? To hold out hope that they might someday be the family he'd always dreamed they could be?

"Let's not fight, Megan." He took her hand again. "I love you. I hate fighting with you."

"And I hate fighting with you." She squeezed his hand in return and offered a tentative smile. "But tell me just how you think the store's going to run itself? They need me here, Jaden. And I want to be there for them. I think a lot of your family. Plus, I *like* doing this. I'm actually pretty good at it."

He knew she was. Dani raved about her every time they spoke. The business, thanks to its increased online sales, had cleared more in the past few weeks than it averaged during their high-tourist months.

"And what's three more months, anyway?" she continued, though she no longer looked at him.

They planned to move to Birch Bay for good three months from now, once he finished his practicum and earned his master's degree in counseling psychology. He had a job lined up for the following year, working under a local psychologist in order to earn his counseling certification, and he planned to eventually open his own practice here in town. His focus would be children and families.

Megan would work as a freelance app developer, they'd buy a house . . . have babies . . .

"Fine," he relented. And though Megan once again turned for the door, a sharp blast of air whipping inside the second she cracked it open, Jaden only reached into his coat pocket. "But then we're going to do this now, instead of waiting until tonight as I'd planned."

Megan looked back once again, her original annoyance making a reappearance. "Do what now?"

Then her gaze landed on the jeweler's box in Jaden's hand.

"Oh, Jay." She shook her head. "*No.* Don't do that now."

"*Yes.*" He reached across her and closed the door. "*Now.* I miss you, Meggie. I love you. I want to—"

"Not. Now." Megan stressed the words with a soft voice, and something about the way she said them finally registered. She was serious.

"Why not now?" He straightened in his seat.

"Today is about Gabe and Erica. It's their wedding." She shook her head again. "This isn't about us."

"And we don't have to make it about us. That's not what I'm trying to do." He forced a smile, wishing they could have one single conversation like they used to. Where they didn't have to argue.

He opened the box to the ring he'd had designed for her.

He also had the passing thought that the day *could* be a little about him. It was his birthday, after all.

"I love you, Megan." He held the ring up between them. Was it so wrong to want his ring on her finger for his birthday? "And you love me. This isn't about making it our day, it's just about making it official. Is that such a bad thing? I'm tired of waiting, Meggie. I love you. I want my ring on your finger."

But as his words ran out—and as she remained as silent as she'd been throughout the length of his monologue—he began to clue in to what it was he *really* saw in her eyes. And it wasn't respect for another person's nuptials that had her stalling.

Panic suddenly threatened to close off his air. "You don't *want* to marry me?"

He pulled back. He knew he'd been rushing the engagement—the plan had been to wait until after his graduation. But as she'd just pointed out, that was only three months away.

Megan's lips tightened the slightest amount, and then her trim shoulders lifted in a shrug beneath her wool coat. "I just think we need to talk about things first. And we *don't* have time to talk right now."

"What do we need to talk about?" His heart rate remained out of control. This was Meg. This was the woman who loved him. She couldn't be changing her mind about that.

She'd sworn she wouldn't.

"We've dated a long time, Jay."

He nodded. "Yes, we have. And people typically follow that with marriage."

"Or . . . maybe they realize that marriage may *not* be the right next move?"

The expression of apology that appeared with her question had the airport sandwich he'd wolfed down threatening to make a rapid comeback.

He realized he looked like an idiot sitting there with the ring still held up between them, so he lowered his hand. "What's going on here,

Megan?" Fear licked at his insides. "I don't understand. Did you meet someone else?"

"No," she hurriedly assured him. "Not at all. I've simply been thinking . . ."

Her shoulders gave another small shrug, and her face crumpled even more.

"Have you really missed me as much as you thought you would, Jay?"

"Yes." Was that all this was about? He'd been too busy to call as often as he should have. Their conversations had been short. He'd do better. "I've missed you like crazy. How can you even ask that?"

"Or have you missed me because me moving here before you wasn't our plan?"

"What are you talking about? I've missed you because you weren't there."

She reached over and took his hand, but he noticed that she chose the hand that *didn't* hold the ring. "I've missed you, too," she assured him. "But the thing is . . . I've been feeling like I should be missing you more."

Jaden felt as if a hole had opened in the pit of his gut.

He looked out the windshield, at the small church waiting for them to enter. At the happiness he knew they would find inside.

And he suddenly got it.

He turned back to his girlfriend. "You're having cold feet."

"Cold feet happens before a wedding," she argued. "Not before an engagement."

"But don't you see." He nodded toward the church. "This *is* a wedding. And it's got you thinking."

"No, Jaden. I've been thinking it for a while now."

The hole in his gut stretched wider. "It's only been a few weeks, Megan."

How long could she possibly have been thinking that she didn't miss him?

"I'm aware of that," she answered almost under her breath.

"Then . . ."

The front door of the church opened, and his sister peeked out. When her gaze landed on them, Dani waved in a quick, beckoning motion.

Jaden ignored her. "I don't understand." And he truly didn't. They loved each other.

They *missed* each other.

"It was only an inkling at first," Megan explained. "It started a couple of weeks into the new year."

So one month ago. He wiped any emotion from his face. "And what pushed it from an inkling to more?"

Guilt entered her features, and anger once again fired through him.

"You said you hadn't met anyone else," he accused.

"I haven't." She held her hands up in front of her. "I swear. It's just that"—she glanced away from him, and her throat convulsed as she swallowed—"I had a dream."

Jaden merely stared at her, unable to fathom where she might be going with her statement.

"And there's this woman in town." Megan glanced back.

"A *woman*? So . . . what are you saying?" He grasped for her reasoning. "You and she are . . . experimenting?"

She actually rolled her eyes at him. "Don't be ridiculous, Jaden. I said there wasn't anyone, and I meant it. That means male *or* female."

"Then what's the deal with this woman?"

He didn't look back at the church, but from his peripheral vision, he now caught both Dani and Cord standing at the open door.

"She interpreted my dream," Megan answered. And still, all Jaden could do was stare.

Some woman had interpreted his girlfriend's dream?

Interpreted?

He blinked as her words began to sink in. Megan was the smartest woman he knew. She'd finished her master's program in record time, had hired on as an off-site consultant with a Fortune 500 company the week after receiving her degree, and had continued to pull full-time hours for that very company even while managing his family's store. She could do it all.

Yet she was sitting in front of him now, telling him that she'd gone to a woman who'd read her dream?

And that she planned to base *their* future on whatever had come from *that* reading?

He forced his jaw to unclench. "And what, exactly, did this *woman* tell you?"

Megan wasn't a large person. In fact, she was only an inch over five feet. Yet she suddenly looked even tinier. She stared back at him. "She said I'm with the wrong man."

Jaden didn't so much as blink.

"And I think she might be right," she rushed to add.

"You *think*?"

She nodded, her composure rebounding in front of him. "I *know*, Jay. And I'm sorry about that. We're good together. We always have been. But . . . maybe we were more of a college thing."

"We're a *hell* of a lot more than a college thing." A headache had started behind his eyes. Hadn't they just been sitting there talking about their future?

"But don't you worry that the sizzle might have gone out a bit? We used to be so—"

"We still sizzle," he gritted out. She was the best damned sex he'd ever had. They had sizzle!

"We've barely said more to each other than 'how's the weather' since I moved here. Something isn't right about that, Jay."

"We're both busy." He shoved the ring into his pants pocket. "And you're wrong. We are not basing our lives on something some woman who's never met me, *nor* seen the two of us together, tells you." He shook his head, his anger now at a full boil. "It's just cold feet. Like I told you. We'll talk about this again later."

He opened his door and climbed from the seat, suddenly ready to get his wedding duties over with. To *forget* that this conversation had even happened. But the finality of Megan's voice stopped him before he could slam the door.

"It's not cold feet."

He ducked his head and glared in at her. She couldn't really mean—

"It's the end."

Her tone was so decisive that he'd swear he literally felt his heart crack down the middle. "Meg." He shook his head. "Don't do this."

"I am sorry, Jay." She climbed from the other side of the car, and the wind howled as if understanding the very pain he felt. "I still care for you," she went on. "I always will. But I think we just got comfortable. I don't want either of us to settle, and I fear if we stay together, that's what we'll be doing."

He was not settling. Megan was his world.

Jaden looked at the church again. His siblings had disappeared back inside, but he took in the snow gathering on the eaves and the golden light cast from the Victorian-style sconces. This was the oldest church in Birch Bay. It was the church his sister had started taking him to after their mother died.

He'd planned to suggest that he and Megan marry here.

"I can't believe you're choosing *now* to do this to me," he said, still not looking at her. How the hell was he supposed to go in there and act like nothing was wrong?

"I didn't *choose* now," Megan corrected. "I didn't know you planned to pull out a ring."

"But you've been thinking it." He felt like such an idiot. "For weeks you've been thinking that you didn't want me anymore. That you don't—"

He snapped off his words, refusing to sound any more pathetic than he already did.

She didn't love him. End of story.

He didn't know why it came as such a surprise.

"We've grown apart, Jay. That happens to people. But it doesn't take away from what we once had. It doesn't mean I don't still care for you."

His mind whirled as he tried to make sense of her words. Of a world where his girlfriend would no longer be his girlfriend. He couldn't picture it.

He stared down at the car, his thoughts tripping over each other. And then the logistics of the moment occurred to him. "I brought you here tonight," he mumbled. Dammit, what was he supposed to do now? "As my *date*."

Should he offer to take her home first? Ask them to wait to start the wedding?

Would she be willing to sit in the car until he'd done his part?

"I'm also a friend of your family and of the bride," she replied, her tone gentle. Her hand touched his arm, and he realized that she'd rounded the car and now stood beside him. "I want to stay for the wedding, Jay. I think a lot of both Gabe and Erica, so I want to be here for them. But I won't say anything about us. Not tonight. We'll just . . ."

She trailed off, so he finished her thought for her. "Pretend."

They'd pretend. As if he could do that while his heart was shattering.

"I don't want to draw attention," she added. "I'll slip out and call a cab when I'm ready to go. And I won't stay long. I'll go back to the house to pack my bags, and—"

"No," he interrupted. He closed his hand over hers. She was beautiful. Brilliant. The only person he'd ever loved. And she cared for his family as much as he did. "You don't have to move out of the house."

She'd been staying with his dad and Gloria due to the retail store being across the street. "I'll go to a hotel tonight. And I'll leave"—his voice cracked on the word—"tomorrow. Stay at the house. Help out all you want." He nodded as if he were okay with the words. "I'll go back to Seattle."

And he'd try to figure out a way to convince her she was wrong.

Megan studied him for a moment, as if weighing the sincerity behind his words, then she lifted to her toes and pressed a kiss to his cheek. "You're a good person," she whispered. "And this is for the best. Once you have time to think about it, you'll realize it, too."

Chapter Two

S weet mother of pearl."
Arsula Moretti faked a cough at the murmured words, her hand camouflaging her instant grin, but instead of looking over at her friend, she kept her gaze locked on the reason for the comment. "They do make quite the picture, don't they?"

Four brothers standing shoulder to shoulder, each with dark, thick hair and sculpted features that would capture any woman's attention, and all over six feet—with the exception of Jaden, who was only a few inches shorter.

Yep. Photo worthy. Without a doubt. And the fact that they were all currently wearing tuxes only enhanced the image.

"They make the kind of picture that has my clothes suddenly feeling too loose," Maggie replied. Maggie taught with Erica at the elementary school and had also been in the wedding. "So loose they might just slip right off."

Arsula snickered. "Right here while Gabe and Erica are having their first dance?"

"Right here . . . in the coat closet . . . upstairs in a hotel room . . ."

"Outside, in the middle of the freaking snowstorm," Arsula added, getting in on the game. She didn't really want to shed her clothes with any of them, though. First of all, they were all brothers of the woman she worked for. They were also brothers of her friend's brand-new husband. And both of those situations could make clothes-shedding somewhat awkward.

But also, one of them was married, another was a bit of a recluse, the third was a player, and the fourth . . . she sighed. The fourth was downright grumpy. He was also the one who'd "walked" her down the aisle.

She scowled at the mere thought of the youngest Wilde. Jaden had been mentally absent since the moment he'd stepped inside the church's vestibule.

The wedding planner, who'd been about two seconds from becoming unglued by that point, had caught sight of him and immediately directed him to Arsula's side. She'd then signaled the processional to start. And while Arsula and Jaden had been awaiting their turn, Arsula had quickly stuck out a hand and offered a smile to the remaining sibling she'd yet to meet.

Neither gesture had been returned.

Instead, she and Jaden had made their way to the front of the church, and after Gabe and Erica exchanged vows, one of Jaden's brothers had had to nudge the moron when it was his turn to escort his assigned bridesmaid back down the aisle.

Arsula's scowl grew deeper. It had been mortifying.

"Champagne?" a server in black and white asked, jolting her back to the present and reminding her that Gabe's brothers were about to toast the bride and groom.

"Thank you." She accepted the flute. But then she returned her attention to the man whose passive blue eyes were framed behind the retro round lenses of his glasses. The mere fact that Jaden had never once acknowledged her existence should totally tick her off. He'd been more than rude.

However, while he'd been ignoring her, she'd been paying attention to him. And she'd picked up on one very vital piece of information. Though he'd been MIA from most moments throughout the wedding, the taking of the pictures, *and* the sit-down dinner . . . he *had* spent a fair amount of time tossing glances at his girlfriend.

Or was she now his ex-girlfriend?

Arsula had to wonder, because while Jaden had been looking at Megan, Megan had been looking at *anything* but him. And whether the deal had actually gone down or not, Megan *definitely* intended to break things off with him.

"Erica seems so happy," Maggie said, and Arsula forced herself to once again return to the present—and this time to stay there. She'd check in on Megan before the night was over. She wanted to make sure the other woman was okay. See if she needed to talk.

"She and Gabe are adorable together." Arsula's gaze returned to Erica's heart-patterned wedding gown. She, Maggie, and Erica had spotted it at the same time the day they'd gone dress shopping, sealing the deal for a Valentine's Day wedding.

"I hope we find someone who makes *us* that happy someday." Maggie's words came out wistful, and Arsula slipped an arm through her friend's.

"Are you kidding me? That's not even in question. I mean . . . how could we not? We're awesome."

Maggie chuckled in agreement and dropped her head to Arsula's shoulder, while Arsula's mind once again spun. She didn't actually *know* what the future would hold, of course. That would be a gift well beyond the one she *had* been born with. But she did know that deserving people had a habit of having things work out. Especially if they were willing to look inside themselves and to listen with their gut.

The dance ended, and Erica and Gabe, each as smitten as the other, remained wrapped in each other's arms. Erica rested her head on her groom's chest, and they both smiled at Cord as he took the microphone and cleared his throat over the speaker.

"To the bride and groom," Cord began.

As the Wilde brothers took turns offering good wishes and the hope for a healthy life, Arsula took in the explosion of shimmering red décor. The ballroom had been transformed into Cupid's paradise, and though Arsula wasn't necessarily looking for love at that point in her life, she had to agree with Maggie. She, too, hoped she'd one day find this kind of bliss. It was too beautiful a thing not to want.

Nick and Nate finished up the toasts, both pulling chuckles from the crowd, and the DJ in the corner once again started up the music. Guests began mingling, some heading straight for the candy bar—which consisted of a wide variety of assorted chocolates to commemorate the day on the calendar—and Arsula decided to weave her way through the crowd. She'd come without a date, so she didn't need to stick close to anyone in particular, which would allow her to chat with lots of people. And *that* was one of her favorite pastimes.

She'd lived in Birch Bay for five months now, having moved to the town she'd never even heard of after waking one morning and knowing there was somewhere she needed to be. She'd packed up her car, said goodbye to her parents and three older brothers, and hadn't looked back. She also hadn't regretted her decision. Not even when she'd gone home for Christmas and her dad had laid into her.

But also, it had been five months, and whoever the person was she'd moved here to help had yet to reveal themselves. And that *was* beginning to weigh on her. *Especially* after she'd gone home for Christmas and her dad had laid into her.

"Arsula Moretti."

She stopped moving at the sound of her name.

"You. Look. Amazing."

Arsula broke into a grin as she turned and found Jewel Brandon beaming at her. Jewel had been one of her first clients after moving to town. She'd come into the office one day, having hired Dani to roll out a marketing campaign for her bull-riding stock contracting business, and she and Arsula had ended up going to lunch.

"Thank you." Arsula reached out for a hug.

"That dress was made for you," Jewel continued. She took Arsula's hands as they separated, holding them out to their sides. "Red is your color, girlfriend."

Arsula looked down at the floor-length velvet dress, and though she didn't say it out loud, she knew the dress complemented her dark hair as well as her part Native American, part Italian features. "I will admit that I didn't complain when Erica chose this for the wedding," she teased.

"I can see why."

They both laughed and then spent a couple of minutes catching up. Jewel had been eight months postpartum when they'd met, and over lunch that first day, Arsula had learned that, though thrilled to be a first-time parent, Jewel had struggled more than she'd expected. She'd gone through a bout of depression and had recently begun experiencing dreams that left her in a state of anxiety.

"How's the baby?" Arsula asked. "And Bobby." She glanced around, hoping to catch sight of the woman's husband and child.

"They're both amazing. Leah started walking last month, and we already can't keep up with her." She waved a hand toward the crowd behind her. "We left her at home today, but Bobby's around here somewhere. He saw a high school buddy he wanted to catch up with, so I headed to find you."

"I'm so glad you did."

They talked for a few more minutes before Jewel declared it was time for her husband to dance with her, then Arsula continued her trek through the crowd. She caught sight of Jewel's sister Harper on the other side of the room.

Harper was married to Nick Wilde, and after Jewel had raved about working with Arsula, Harper had ended up seeking her out as well. Harper and Nick had a happy marriage, but that didn't keep her from continuing to suffer occasional guilt over the loss of her first husband.

"Dance with me, beautiful lady?"

As she once again stopped in the middle of the dance floor, this time she didn't have to see the person before knowing who went with the voice. "Max Wilde," she said as she turned. "Just the person I'd hoped to dance with."

The patriarch of the Wilde family gave a deep laugh and placed an arm at her waist. "You clean up nice. Anyone ever tell you that?"

She chuckled. Max could be as big a charmer as his sons. She'd met him at the same Labor Day party where she'd first been introduced to Cord, Nick, and Gabe. That was also where she'd met Erica. "And you, sir, could make any woman in this room swoon."

She tucked her head into his shoulder as they danced, and feelings of gratitude washed over her. She'd never had trouble fitting in, yet that hadn't kept her from being uneasy at the thought when she'd first driven into Birch Bay.

"How's Gloria?" she asked, referring to his wife of two years. His first wife had been gone almost two decades.

"She's right as rain. Treats me like a king."

Arsula smiled. "And the farm?"

Max ran the family cherry orchard, having come back to the job after stepping aside for several years, and though she'd been out at the house only one time, it hadn't taken more than that to understand the love the man carried for the place.

"It's . . . good," he answered, and at his hesitation, she pulled back. "You sound worried."

"Nah." He shook his head. "No need to worry. Not yet. Just a feeling . . . or *something*."

She hadn't meant to, but she realized she'd stopped dancing. "About what?" She always listened to feelings.

"Some trees we planted back in the fall." He waved a hand, clearly hoping to dismiss the conversation. "A pick-your-own field we hoped to grow. No big deal."

"And it's not doing well?"

"I . . ." His shoulders sank as he looked at her. "I actually won't know until spring, and honestly, there's no reason to believe there will be a problem. It's been a cold winter, but not cold enough to do harm. I just . . ."

"*Feel* that there are going to be issues?"

He nodded as if not wanting to accept it. "I can't help but fear we're going to lose them."

"So you replant," she offered. As always, leaning toward the bright side.

"Yeah." He nodded again. Then he restarted them dancing.

"And if those don't take," she added, "you replant again."

Max didn't reply, just nodded his head a third time, and another sort of worry started to build inside Arsula. She couldn't pinpoint it, but tracing her gaze over the lines of the man's face had her own gut speaking.

"Are *you* okay, Max?"

He pulled his gaze back to hers. "Sure. What's not to be okay about?"

"I don't know," she murmured. "Just . . ."

"Life is good," he said, his voice ringing a tad too upbeat. "Couldn't be better." But when he no longer made direct eye contact, Arsula's concerns grew.

She nodded, not ready to push the issue, but told herself to check in on him later.

The song ended, and she thanked Max for the dance, but as the next song began, her gaze landed on another member of the Wilde family.

This time it was Jaden. He stood at the bar set up on the other side of the room, an empty tumbler in hand, but unlike previous instances when she'd caught sight of him, his attention was no longer on Megan. It was on *her*.

And this time . . . her gut told her something entirely different.

"Crap on a cracker," she muttered to herself.

When Jaden didn't look away, a hint of nausea began to swell.

Really? she asked herself. *Him?*

Well, that's irony for you. She'd been waiting five months to find out who her subconscious had sent her here to help, and now she finally knew. It was the man whose girlfriend she'd recently suggested would do well to accept that he wasn't the person for her.

The man whose girlfriend now stopped *directly* in front of Arsula.

"Do you have a minute?" Megan asked. "I could use a quick boost of support."

"Of course." Arsula ignored Jaden. "Do you want to step out of the room?"

"No." Megan shook her head, and then she motioned in the opposite direction from where Jaden stood. "Maybe just off to the side of the crowd?"

They slipped to the periphery, but before Arsula could say anything, Megan began.

"I ended things in the parking lot tonight. And I feel *horrible*."

Arsula barely kept her jaw from dropping. "In the parking lot?"

No wonder Jaden had been absent all evening.

"I couldn't help it. He had a *ring*."

"An engagement ring?" Arsula asked, for clarity.

"*Yes*. And he showed up so late today that I didn't have time to talk to him beforehand. He just . . . *pushed*. And I . . ." She trailed off with a quick glance toward the bar.

"You did what you know in your heart was *right*," Arsula reminded her. When Megan had first sought her out, Arsula had seen immediately

20

that she'd outgrown the relationship. As much as anything, Megan had needed someone to tell her it was okay to feel what she was feeling. "You did what you'd planned to do, anyway."

"I know. Yes." Megan nodded, as if trying to refortify herself. "It was the right thing to do. I *do* know that. Stringing it out wouldn't have helped anything. I just . . ." Sadness filled her eyes as she stared back at Arsula. "I still care for him, Arsula. He's my *friend*. Or he *was* my friend. Long before we ever started dating. And I hurt him tonight."

"Of course you still care for him." She took the other woman's hands in hers. "And we both know the last thing you wanted was to hurt him."

They'd talked multiple times after the initial conversation concerning Megan's dreams, and though Arsula felt bad that their discussion had led to the other woman ending what had once been a promising relationship, she'd never once considered retracting anything she'd said. She trusted her gift. Always.

Even if she did hate the pain it sometimes inflicted.

"But as you just said"—Arsula didn't break eye contact—"delaying wouldn't have helped anything. For either of you."

"Right."

Arsula hated the helpless look marring the other woman's face.

"And yes, I know that this *was* the right thing to do," Megan went on. "He needs"—she shrugged—"a different kind of love than I can give him now."

Arsula squeezed her hands. "He *needs* his soul mate."

"Exactly." Megan squeezed back. "And though I hate that that's not me . . ."

She trailed off again, but this time it was Arsula who glanced toward the bar. Only, Jaden no longer stood there. "You'll both be better off with the decision having been made," Arsula finished for her.

Megan nodded, the guilt covering her face beginning to lift. "We will."

She looked out over the crowd then, not seeming to land on any one person as her eyes tracked the partygoers, and before long, the confident woman Arsula had come to know returned.

"We will," Megan said again, this time without hesitation, and then she pulled Arsula in for a hug. "Thank you," she whispered into her ear. "Both for helping me to see things before and for giving me the reminder I needed tonight."

As Megan returned to the throng of people, Arsula remained where she stood. And she reminded herself that playing a part in hurting him or not, her reason for moving to Birch Bay was *Jaden*. And Jaden would soon be heading back to Seattle.

Therefore, she had to talk to him tonight.

The problem with that lay in the fact that she didn't quite know how to start. She had no clue what demons might keep him awake at night, and neither did she expect him to be open to talking with her. From the little she knew about the guy, he was more of a by-the-book type than one willing to embrace his feelings.

Additionally, and this was pure speculation on her part, she'd guess Jaden Wilde to be the type to mock her beliefs instead of being open to them. Or heck, maybe she'd been obtuse for the last ten years and *everyone* had been mocking her. Laughing at her behind her back.

After all, if that's what her dad had been doing . . .

She swallowed past her hurt and pushed the negative thoughts aside. She wouldn't let herself believe that. She'd helped many people, and they were thankful for it.

The women on her mother's side of the family were born with a gift. At least, everyone but her mother had been. A gift meant for helping others, and one to be treated with respect. So help Jaden Wilde she would. And maybe by doing so . . . she'd find a way to prove herself to her father once and for all.

And if she didn't?

Her chest grew tight. Then maybe she'd agree that her father was *right* once and for all.

"Are you going to marry Megan someday?"

Jaden jerked his attention from the woman who'd not only been dancing with his father earlier, but who'd also just shared a private conversation with his girlfriend.

He stared down at the seven-year-old in his arms. "What?"

Had Megan said something to her?

"Because if you are," Jenna went on, "I could be your flower girl. I have experience now."

Relief rushed him at his niece's words. Hopefully no one was feeling sorry for him yet.

"I see that you do." He nodded toward her pink-and-red dress as they danced, then extended one arm, the movement encouraging her to do her "signature twirl." "You did an excellent job being the flower girl tonight."

Jenna slanted her lips accusingly. "You didn't even see me do it, Uncle Jaden. You were late, remember? We were all waiting on you." She twirled under his arm once more and, after retaking his free hand, peered up. "What were you doing sitting outside in your car for so long, anyway?"

"I was . . ." He searched for Megan—who'd steadfastly been keeping a minimum of thirty feet between them since finishing dinner. He found her in lively discussion with yet another group of people. "Megan and I had something to talk about," he answered absentmindedly.

When had his girlfriend become acquainted with so many people in town? He'd swear she knew more residents than he did, and she'd only been around for a few weeks.

"Was it about getting married?" Jenna asked, and once again, he brought his gaze back to hers. "'Cause I heard Pops and Gramma talking about it last week," she explained. "They said that weddings were running in the family and that you and Megan would probably be next."

Weddings definitely seemed to be running in the family. First his dad and Gloria, then Dani and Ben, then Nick and Harper, and now Gabe and Erica.

And dammit, he *should* be next.

"I don't know," he finally answered. "Maybe." He refused to state out loud that there was even a chance he wouldn't be marrying Megan. The more he'd thought about their conversation in the car, the more he'd decided he'd been right. It was cold feet. She couldn't really dump him so easily and just move on with her life. Not after all the years they'd been together.

He glanced at her again, and annoyance returned. She couldn't just dump him, no matter *how* easy she might currently be making it seem.

The song came to an end, and before he could ask if Jenna would like to dance again, she let go of his hands. "Thank you for the dance. You were a lovely partner." She offered a curtsy, and her dimples winked, even though she tried to keep a straight face.

He tilted his head. "I can't talk you into another?"

Dancing with her would be better than stewing over Megan. Or wondering about the woman he'd seen *talking* with Megan.

Who was that woman, anyway? Clearly a bridesmaid, based on her dress—but he didn't remember seeing her earlier. And what had she and Megan talked about? She'd even held Megan's hands at one point.

Jenna gave him a look that went well beyond her years, while also crossing her arms over her thin chest. "I was just trying to be nice when I said you were a lovely partner, Uncle Jaden. You stepped on my feet three times. I think maybe it was because you weren't exactly *into* the dance. You kept looking around at everything else."

He grimaced. Called out by a seven-year-old.

"I did do that," he confessed. "And I'm sorry." He kissed the back of her hand and offered an apologetic pout. "Forgive me?"

"Maybe." She returned another beyond-her-years look, and he could see her thoughts churning. "But only if you promise to let me be your flower girl."

He loved that she didn't immediately cave. "What about Haley?"

Haley was Ben's daughter. She was the same age as Jenna.

Jenna seemed to consider her options, her gaze seeking out her cousin as she grew quiet and contemplative, and then she gave Jaden a decisive nod. "Two flower girls. Twice the rose petals. We can each go up one side of the aisle, and your wedding will be twice as beautiful."

Jaden grinned despite the giant crack that remained in his heart. He loved spending time with his nieces, and once he moved back home, he intended to make that a priority.

"Deal," he said.

They shook on it, and as Jenna moved off, she zeroed in on Nate. At the same time, Haley went after Nick. Another song swelled under the tulle and twinkle lights as the dancing continued, and Jaden allowed his eyes to once again scan over the crowd. But this time it wasn't solely Megan he sought.

Someone bumped into him before he could locate either his girl-friend or the mystery bridesmaid, and he decided it was time to get off the dance floor.

Heading back to the bar, he ordered another whiskey and sent the amber liquid along the same path several had forged before it—and that was when his gaze landed on Megan. She sat with his dad and Gloria now, *still* acting as if there wasn't a thing in the world wrong, and he reminded himself he could be just as casual as she was. In fact, he was pretty sure he'd perfected the pose over the last couple of hours. Hadn't he spent the evening doing a fair amount of laughing and talking of his own? Just two people working the room. That's all they were.

Not two people on the brink of collapse.

He ordered one more drink, this one on the rocks since that last one had kicked his buzz into high gear, and he waded back into the dancers. He had to get Megan alone. There was no way he would just accept her dumping him, and certainly not due to some dream. She had too solid a head on her shoulders for that. It had to be that she was going through something she hadn't told him about. A stressor of some sort. He'd get her alone, make her talk through whatever it was, and they'd be fine.

A whisper of a laugh sounded to his left, and he glanced over to find his sister gently swaying in the arms of her husband. Their three-month-old had been bundled up and taken off to bed after dinner, and Dani now only had eyes for the man in front of her. The sight had Jaden stopping. His sister's happiness still managed to astound him. If anyone deserved it, it was her.

He fingered the ring in his pocket and restarted his path, and when he emerged from the crowd, he positioned himself two tables from Megan. He nodded hello to a couple of neighbors he hadn't seen in a while and made a show of nursing his drink. But Megan rose within seconds of his arrival. She pressed quick kisses to his dad's and then to Gloria's cheeks, and Jaden kept an even expression as he eyed her departing back. This was not how he'd seen the evening going.

His girlfriend made another round on the dance floor, speaking briefly to Gabe and Erica, before laughing at whatever Nate said as he and Jenna sidled up behind her. She turned to the two of them, her smile wide and welcoming, and allowed herself to be pulled into the dance.

Jaden's irritation grew as he watched. He didn't like seeing the woman who was supposed to be his girlfriend wrapped in the arms of another man. Even if it was one of his brothers.

Thankfully, the song ended sooner rather than later, but Jaden had barely risen to his feet before Megan headed for the door. And just like that, she was gone.

Without so much as a glance at him.

He dropped back to his seat, dumbfounded. *Dammit.* He deserved better than that.

He also acknowledged that the pain that had been swelling steadily behind his breastbone all night suddenly exploded.

Dani's gaze met his from over Ben's shoulder, and Jaden couldn't miss the sympathy in the slant to her mouth. And without words, he knew that *she* knew. And dammit to hell, he didn't need his sister feeling sorry for him tonight.

Thumping the pad of his thumb against the side of his now-empty glass, he turned away from Dani's prying eyes. He also reapplied his it's-all-good face. He didn't know how many people had picked up on the fact that his supposed girlfriend hadn't spoken to him all evening, but he determined that if he acted as if all was right with the world, no one would ask him about it. Because talking about it might just make it clear how pissed off he really was.

He eyed the bar, calculated how long it would take to work his way back to it, and then two hands appeared in his view. One hand held a double shot of whiskey—long, tapered fingers gripping the small glass from the top—while the other encircled a tumbler of water.

He looked up at the bearer of drinks, for some reason unsurprised to find the bridesmaid standing before him. And realized just how drop-dead gorgeous she was.

"Drink?" she asked. Lashes as dark as her hair surrounded brown eyes.

"Which can I have?" He eyed her high cheekbones.

"Whichever you want."

Jaden took the shot glass, then he squinted at the woman as he gulped down half the liquid. He really wished he'd paid more attention when introductions had been made earlier.

Or *if* introductions had been made. He couldn't say for sure that they had been.

"I'm Arsula," she eventually told him.

She pronounced her name in a way as if to indicate he should already know that.

"The woman you walked down the aisle earlier tonight?" she added in a questioning tone.

His squint turned into a frown. That had been *her*?

How the hell had he not noticed what she looked like then?

"You don't say," he muttered. He tossed back the rest of the drink, then he let himself take a careful look at what he'd missed earlier.

His eyes trailed over her, taking in the deep red of the dress that was cinched at a high waist before it draped smoothly over her hips. The amount and cut of material didn't necessarily scream sexy—and other than the V neckline, her hands and fingers, and the peekaboo hints of tanned flesh displayed at the curve of each shoulder, no other skin showed. Yet the dress didn't have to hug her for him to understand it hid curves. Especially since she now had a hip cocked to one side and a hand at her waist.

"You about finished there, Romeo?"

He dragged his eyes back up her body. It was possible he'd had a shot or two too many. "Just about," he told her. Screw Megan. If she could dump him the way she had, then he could certainly flirt with a bridesmaid at his brother's wedding. "But if you wanted to twirl in place"—he did a little spinning motion with one finger—"I'd be more than happy to check out the back side as well."

"Good grief." She rolled her eyes at him, then pulled out a chair. "I should have given you the water," she muttered as she plopped ungracefully into the seat.

"No one needs water tonight." Jaden took the glass from her as she lifted it to her mouth and replaced it with a flute of champagne he snatched from a passing server. "Drink up, lovely bridesmaid." He nodded toward the fizzing bubbles. "You're already behind."

She had the thickest bottom lip he'd ever seen.

"I'll drink it"—she eyed him critically—"but trust me, I have no intention of *catching up*."

"No?" Jaden watched as she drank. "Then what *are* your intentions?"

This time she eyed *him* while she downed the alcohol.

When the glass was half-empty, she dabbed a napkin at the corner of her lips and folded her hands in her lap. "I actually have *no* intentions," she informed him. "I'm good at reading people, so I came over because you looked like you could use a friend."

Her words deflated his budding mood. "My friend ratio is fine," he grumbled. Then he glanced toward the door where Megan had disappeared.

"That why you're sitting over here pouting?"

He jerked his gaze back to hers. "I'm not pouting."

"No?" She finished the champagne, licking her lips with a smacking noise. "Could have fooled me." She eyed the same door he'd just been scowling at. "Want to talk about it?"

Who the hell was this woman? *No.* He studied her a moment longer. "I do *not* want to talk about it."

Nor did he care that he'd had too much to drink in too short a time, that he would likely drink a heck of a lot more before the night was over, and that if she would humor him, he'd bring the bridesmaid a drink every time he got one for himself.

Because to hell with it. There was a party going on around them, and he hadn't flown in from Seattle to do nothing but sit at a table and stew. It was Valentine's Day. The day for "love."

His freaking *birthday*. He frowned.

He would deal with what might or might not be left of his and Megan's relationship tomorrow, but tonight he intended to forget there was an issue.

He rose from his chair, proud of himself for weaving only marginally, and held out a hand to the lady in red. "Can I interest you in a . . ."

He frowned again as his words stalled. "What did you say your name was?" It had been something weird.

"Ar*su*la."

"Right." He nodded, noticing that her eyes were too pretty to simply be referred to as brown. "Ar*su*la." Definitely a weird name.

And definitely gorgeous eyes.

He inched his hand closer to hers. He liked gorgeous eyes. "Will you dance with me, Arsula?"

Chapter Three

They'd done way more than dance the night before.

At least, Arsula thought they had.

She blinked open her eyes, her mouth dry and her thoughts a mixture of Jaden and the dream she'd awakened from, and she stared at the aqua blue of her bedroom ceiling. But what, exactly, *had* they done? What had been real, and what was a product of her subconscious?

She closed her eyes and tried to remember. They'd danced, definitely. *Several* times.

And they'd drunk.

A groan slipped out. They'd drunk *way* too much.

And as if getting soused at the wedding hadn't been bad enough, when the last guest had departed the hotel's ballroom, they'd taken their "two-person party"—Jaden's words, not hers—to the bar down the street. Where they'd continued to drink.

Why *she* had continued, she had no idea. She could barely remain on her feet with a measly three drinks in her. Plus, she'd only gone over to Jaden in the first place to try to figure out how she was supposed to help him. Yet for some reason, as the night had slipped closer to today, and as they'd found themselves routinely falling into fits of giggles over even the most inappropriate of things, she'd declared herself fully able to keep up with him. And then she'd set out to prove it.

Covering her face now, she simultaneously blocked the sunlight from stabbing holes through her eyelids and continued to sort through the events of the previous evening. Aunt Sul popped into her mind, as well as her father. The two of them had been playing cards and telling her it was her time to put in a bid.

She shook her head. That was clearly part of her dream. Her mother's aunt had been dead for nine years, and her dad remained in Cheyenne with the rest of her family.

But what did the dream mean?

She pushed thoughts of it to the side. She'd figure that part out later. Right now, she needed to remember the night before.

There'd been more dancing at the bar. More talking, with the conversations being surprisingly easy. Jaden had actually turned out to be a lot of fun. And then Jaden had . . .

She sucked in a breath as she remembered. *Poor Jaden.*

Reopening her eyes, she once again stared at the ceiling. He had accidentally called her Megan.

Arsula's heart hurt for him. His slipup had flipped the mood of the evening and sent him spiraling into sadness. They'd left the bar soon after, intending to take a walk and sober up. Only, it had been so cold. She shivered as she recalled the frigid chill that had seeped into her skin. She'd still been in her dress from the wedding, and though she'd also had on her long coat, it had been no match for the February Montana night. Jaden had been cold as well. He'd left his jacket at the hotel, so she'd drunkenly offered to share hers.

A smile curved her lips as she pictured the two of them struggling to fit into her coat together. Their actions reminded her of the old Three Stooges shows she'd routinely watched with her father. She'd have to ask Jaden if he'd ever watched the Three Stooges. He'd no doubt see the humor as well.

Before she could ask herself when she might even see Jaden again, however, she remembered what had come *after* the coat.

And how she'd pointed out that her apartment was just across the street.

Oh shit.

She cringed at the silent curse word. *Sorry, Aunt Sul. Sorry, Jesus.*

Then she scowled and came very near to cursing again. Because though she'd love to believe that what had come *after* the coat had all been part of her convoluted dream . . . she couldn't quite convince herself it was true.

Cautiously, she turned her head. And gulped.

Yep. Jaden Wilde was in bed with her.

She blinked at his sleeping form, taking in the whisker-stubbled man with his hair flopped into his eyes, and she racked her brain trying to remember what had come next. Surely they hadn't . . .

They'd kissed. She remembered that much.

She closed her eyes as she replayed additional moments. They'd kissed, and then they'd made it to her building and stumbled up the single flight of stairs. And not only had the kissing continued all the way across the snowy street *and* up the stairs—but their hands had also been all over each other as they'd done both.

And then they'd . . .

Horror mixed with guilt as the next memory barreled through her, and she lifted her head to peer across the room. Son of a biscuit eater. Why couldn't *that* have been part of the dream?

Her red panties lay in a tangle just inside the bedroom door, with Jaden's trousers and underwear dropped haphazardly next to them. Outside the bedroom door was her bra, one of his shoes, both of his socks, and the red garter belt she'd thought would make her feel sexy the night before. And all items, she knew, had been shed via a drunken striptease performed by the both of them.

She dropped her head back to the pillow. *Double shit.*

Aunt Sul would likely reach down from heaven with a bar of soap any minute, but she couldn't seem to clean up her thoughts. What was she supposed to do now? And how in the world would she ever be able to look Megan in the eye again?

She looked back at the man lying beside her. This was *not* what was supposed to have happened between her and Jaden. She'd come here to help the man. Not to sleep with him!

Plowing her fingers through her hair, she once again closed her eyes and groaned. Her thoughts immediately ceased, however, as she became aware of another minor detail. And then everything inside of her clenched tight.

Withdrawing her hands from her hair, she stretched out her left arm and carefully turned her hand palm down. Then she bent at the wrist, lifting her fingers toward the ceiling . . . and her stomach very nearly heaved out the liquor from the night before.

She was wearing the two-carat ring Jaden had intended for Megan!

Arsula's mouth grew even drier, and she told herself not to panic. They weren't engaged, of course. It was just a ring. One she had no intention of keeping.

But why in the world had she let him put it on her? It had been meant for Megan!

And she *did* recall him putting it on her. He'd suggested she keep it since his girlfriend didn't want it.

She tugged the ring off before Jaden could wake and catch her wearing it, and when he shifted beside her, groaning with the move, she quickly shoved it under her hip. He groaned once more, his face now buried in the pillow, and Arsula hurriedly propped herself up against the headboard. She tucked the sheet securely around her breasts, and then she waited.

"Uhhhhh . . ." Jaden expelled yet another sound, this one coming out more as disgust than simple disgruntlement, and he turned his face back toward her. His eyes remained closed, however, so Arsula mustered up the courage to fake a smile. Her heart pounded as if trying to break free of her chest, and five seconds later, Jaden's eyelids finally began to twitch.

She held her smile, wishing she'd had the foresight to get *out* of bed before he'd woken up. At least then she could have put on clothes.

It was too late for that now, though. Because Jaden's eyelids opened. Nothing else about him moved at first. He licked his lips, the move producing a dry, sticky sound. And then he yawned wide and began to roll to his back.

Arsula gripped the sheet to her side to keep it from going with him, and when he got stuck mid roll, his dark brows scrunched together. He tugged at the sheet, using only his shoulder as leverage, but she held tight. So he tugged again.

That's when she knew he'd finally seen her. His gaze landed on her fingertips where they clenched the sheet at her hip, then his eyes trailed up her arm.

Their gazes connected, and not knowing what else to do, she ratcheted up her smile.

"Good morning," she finally said into the silence. Her cheeks were starting to ache from all the smiling.

Jaden didn't reply.

He took in the room instead, a frown tugging at his lips as he found his glasses on the bedside table, and then he let his eyes rove over every inch of her bedroom. He squinted at the sunshine streaming through the dreamcatcher hanging inside her bedroom window. Then he brought his gaze back to her face. Then to her bare shoulders.

"What . . ."

His scratchy voice trailed off as he roamed over the sheet covering her bare body, and he finally seemed to catch on. Because he was up and out of the bed in record time. *Naked.*

"What the hell?" he barked out.

Her smile dropped. "What do you mean, what the hell?"

"I mean what"—he jabbed a finger in her direction—"the *hell* is going on here?"

Now *she* frowned. And narrowed her eyes at him. It's not like the situation was ideal for her, either.

Her annoyance apparently revived her full memory as well as got her blood pressure inching up, because she now had a complete replay of exactly what *had* happened in that room last night and what had *not.* And Mr. What-the-Hell needed to *back* the hell off.

She also found herself more than a little relieved this wasn't as bad as it looked.

Forcing herself to remain calmly on the bed, she couldn't keep from pushing back at the man whose finger remained pointed at her. "Are you referring to the fact that I politely gave you a place to sleep last night?" Her artificially sweet voice only seemed to irritate Jaden more. "Or to the fact that you performed a striptease before *going* to sleep?"

He scowled as if confused by her question, and then apparently caught on—at least to part of it. Because he looked down at himself. She looked down, too.

"What the—"

"Hell?" she finished for him. She gave him another smile when he looked back up, this one not at all polite. "We've covered that already."

She considered tossing him the crocheted blanket from the foot of her bed, but then she decided his arrogance didn't deserve modesty.

"I can't believe . . ." Jaden's words once again trailed off as he went for his slacks and underwear, and she allowed herself a parting peek. It may not be the most ethical thing, to take in a man's backside as he bent to retrieve his clothing, but at the same time, she knew few women who'd look away when presented with the same opportunity.

Especially when his backside looked like that.

As his superb rear disappeared beneath a pair of navy boxer briefs—Jaden muttering under his breath the entire time he tugged at the material—she decided the prudent thing would be for her to get out of the bed. Only, she wasn't about to offer the blockhead another look at *her* goods.

Forcing herself to avert her gaze, she climbed from her position at the headboard and tugged the sheet out with her. After wrapping it around her toga-style, she pulled her shoulders back, making herself look as formidable as possible, and prepared to confess that this wasn't *actually* what it seemed.

Before she could get a word out, though, angry blue eyes once again accosted hers.

"What happened here last night?" he demanded. "And where the hell *am* I?"

"You're in my apartment." She glanced out the double windows overlooking Main Street. "And we're above your sister's office. I work for her."

He eyed her with suspicion. "You work for Dani?"

"Correct. I'm her office manager." She'd initially been hired only as the receptionist, but with Dani's maternity leave, she'd taken on additional tasks.

"And you brought me to . . ." Jaden weaved in place as he scanned every inch of the room once again, and Arsula had the thought that she should probably move closer in order to catch him if he fell. Clearly, he still had more than a fair amount of liquor sloshing through his veins. She might have declared herself able to keep up with him the night before, but the reality was that she'd failed. The man had drunk her under the table.

She didn't move closer, though. She wasn't sure she'd try to catch him if he *did* fall.

"What . . . *exactly* . . . happened here last night?" he asked again, his ire still clearly running high, but his voice now oddly subdued. "Because this"—he waved a hand in a circle, taking in both her and her bed—"*isn't* me. You must have . . ." His jaw clenched instead of finishing his thought out loud, and Arsula's brows rose high on her forehead.

"I must have *what*?" She crossed her arms over her chest. The idiot wasn't really going to stand there and accuse her of slipping him a roofie, was he?

Like she'd *need* to roofie a man to get him into her bed.

He held his ground. "I couldn't have agreed to this. I have a girlfriend."

"No, actually. You do not."

He flinched at her announcement.

"That's right." She reminded herself to remain calm, but she feared it wasn't going to play out that way. Too many years of being picked on by three older brothers wouldn't allow her to simply back off from an argument. Especially one where she wasn't in the wrong. "She broke up with you, remember? You told me *all* about it last night." She didn't bother pointing out that she'd already been aware of the facts before he'd shared them. "*Before* you came to my place. Of your own free will."

With a growled "I shouldn't have told you anything," he suddenly stomped from the room.

Arsula trailed after him, one hand holding the sheet snug at her breasts and the other gathering up the extra material to keep from tripping on it, and she continued her barrage. "In fact"—she didn't pause as he snatched up his socks and shoes—"you told me she said *no* when you proposed to her."

Heated eyes glared at her. "She only said no because I caught her off guard." He tugged on his shoes, cramming his socks into his pants pockets instead of putting them on his feet. "We weren't supposed to get engaged until I finished my master's program."

"Then why did you ask her last night?" She really should back off, but this way was more fun.

Jaden snatched up his shirt. "It's none of—"

"Why did you have a ring made for her?"

That one made him pause, and she held up her left hand when he turned back.

"That's right." She wiggled her bare finger as if the ring were still wrapped securely around it. "You told me all about the ring, too. Even put it on my finger." She didn't offer to retrieve it for him. Her mother would be highly disappointed in her lack of control. "It's pretty enough," she went on, "but a tad *gaudy* for my tastes."

He glared at her. "I can't believe I'd *ever* sleep with someone like you."

"And I can't believe I'd lower my standards enough to *allow* you to!"

He jerked open the outer door, and a dusting of snowflakes whipped inside. He hadn't yet buttoned his shirt, and he held his tux jacket and bow tie in his hand, but he seemed intent on getting out of there as fast as possible. He stood in the open doorway, his face now hot with rage, and made the mistake of jabbing a finger in her direction once more. "*You* are the devil."

She threw a vase at him.

He ducked, and the vase shattered on the concrete stoop behind him. "What the—"

"Hell," she finished. "I know. We keep covering that. And Jesus hates cussing, by the way. You shouldn't do it so much." She threw the TV remote, and it bounced off his shoulder.

"You're insane."

"And you're an idiot. Get out of my apartment." She fired a book and got him square in the cheek before he could get out of the way, then she cringed as the hardback clattered to the floor. Her concern was for the book. Not for him.

Jaden didn't waste any more time sticking around. He stepped out onto the stoop, the soles of his shoes crunching on the shattered ceramic of the vase, but the moron made one final mistake. He turned back.

"This is *your* fault," he snarled, "and you'd better not breathe a word of it to anyone."

"*My* fault?" Her eyes dropped to his crotch. "So you're implying that you're not in control of your own dick?"

"I'm saying that—" He bit off his initial reply, his jaw twitching as if trying to get control of his words, and he ended by holding one finger up in front of him. "Just stay the fuck away from me."

He turned to go, and she finished with, *"My pleasure!"*

The lamp from the end table hurtled through the air before she realized she'd even picked it up, and as if in slow motion, Jaden's foot lowered for the first step. Only, the lamp clipped the back of his head before he could find his footing, and with bile rising in her throat, Arsula stood frozen as the sickening thuds of Jaden Wilde's body tumbling down the narrow metal stairs echoed up to her.

Chapter Four

Arsula rose from the vinyl padded chair for the third time in the last ten minutes and paced the twenty feet to the opposite side of the room. There were only two other people in the emergency room waiting area, and their eyes tracked her as she methodically moved back and forth. She counted her steps as she marched across the tiled floor, turned, and putting one foot precisely in front of the other, made her way back.

Pivoting, she headed the other way once again, but before she could make it half the distance, a commotion at the entrance had her turning her head. The woman behind the registration desk looked up as at least six Wildes barreled into the room.

"Jaden." Cord was the first one to speak.

His eyes landed on Arsula before the registration lady could utter a word, and with long strides, he reached her in seconds. Additional family members followed behind him—as well as Megan.

"How is he?" Cord demanded. "*Where* is he?"

Arsula pointed at the door that led to the patient area. "They took him back right after we got here." She wet her dry lips and kept going. "He hasn't gone into surgery yet, though. He . . ."

Her voice cracked as she took in the faces staring back at her, and as she had since the first dull thud had rung out from her steps, she silently beat herself up for her part in this.

Cord reached out and took her hand. "It's okay." His hand patted hers. "Just tell us what you know. He . . . *what?*"

She licked her lips again. "He has to have emergency surgery." Her heart thundered, due to both nervousness at standing in front of so many members of Jaden's family—all looking to her for answers—and the memory of seeing Jaden sprawled at the bottom of her steps. "His bone . . . his *ankle*. He broke it." She swallowed her guilt and finished in a whisper. "The bone was sticking out of his skin."

That brought Cord up straight, and before Arsula could manage another word, he'd turned and was speaking with someone at one of the two check-in counters. The patient door opened two seconds later, and Cord disappeared behind it.

Arsula stared at the door as it swung closed and wished she could go back with him. It wasn't her place to do that, though. She was just the woman Jaden had woken up with that morning.

Not to mention he hadn't exactly calmed down before the ambulance had arrived at her apartment.

Turning back to his family, she noted that even more people had shown up, and with the exception of Gabe and Erica, all of them were now there. Also, more than one of them wore a perplexed expression mixed in with their worry, and at least three pairs of eyes tracked the bag of clothes she held clutched tightly to her chest.

"He's going to be okay," Arsula said, hurrying to comfort them.

She didn't know this for a fact, but someone had said that to her the last time she'd asked, so she felt emboldened to pass it along. She thrust the bag toward Dani—a nurse had brought Jaden's belongings out after they'd prepped him for surgery—before it occurred to her that Dani already had her arms full with her daughter. So she turned to Jaden's dad. But Max had one arm through his wife's, and he seemed to be focused on something beyond Arsula.

She glanced behind her but didn't see what might have caught Max's attention.

"I'll take his stuff." The words came from Megan, spoken with a quiet resignation, and Arsula turned back. Guilt squeezed at her throat as the other woman stepped forward, her eyes not quite meeting Arsula's.

"Megan, I . . ." Arsula began in a whisper, but she cut off her words when Megan's chin inched higher. The woman was as mortified to be standing there as Arsula was.

Instead of trying to explain, Arsula simply handed over the clothing.

"I also have . . ." She shoved her hands into her jacket pockets as she spoke, before realizing the inappropriateness of her actions. Pressing her lips together, she tugged out the pair of socks. They'd fallen from Jaden's pockets as he'd tumbled down the stairs.

As she handed them over, it was now *she* who couldn't make eye contact. She looked at the other woman's hands instead. If being the cause of a man falling down a flight of icy stairs wasn't enough to sink her into a pit of guilt and shame, passing over last night's clothing to his girlfriend—even his *ex*-girlfriend—finished her off.

"I really am sorry," she said, forcing herself to speak. She had to say *something*. Megan might be fine with the breakup, but that wouldn't make the moment any easier. "This isn't what it looks like. We had some drinks after the wedding. He was . . ."

She shook her head as silence surrounded her. Because it was *almost* what it looked like.

"I gave him a place to sleep it off," she continued in a whisper. "Nothing happened."

Once again, she became aware of her blood pounding at a too-fast rate. If she didn't get out of there soon, she might be the next patient to be wheeled away on a gurney. Either due to succumbing to a panic attack, or because she might just have a full-out heart attack.

"Thank you for staying with him until we got here." This came from Dani, and Arsula forced herself to look up. Dani smiled gently and reached out to pat Arsula's forearm.

"Of course," Arsula answered. She wished she didn't have to go. She wanted to stay to make sure Jaden was okay. But she did understand that leaving would be for the best. Jaden needed his family around him now. And he didn't need the risk of getting upset again if he happened to see her. "I also have . . ."

She stopped speaking once again as her fingers dug into her jeans pocket and brushed the ring. She'd grabbed it as she'd raced back into her apartment to hurry into clothes before the ambulance arrived. She wouldn't hand the ring to Jaden's sister, though. And certainly not in front of Megan. She'd come back later and give it to Jaden.

"I have great belief that he'll pull through this okay," she finished instead of mentioning the ring, and Dani gave her arm a squeeze.

"Thank you again," Dani said.

Arsula left, avoiding making additional eye contact with anyone. She knew most of Jaden's family, and she didn't want to see them thinking badly of her. But also, she *liked* Megan. And she'd hate to make Megan even more uncomfortable than she already was.

And seeing potential evidence that her ex had gotten naked with another woman . . . *on the night of the breakup?*

Definitely uncomfortable. For anyone.

But especially if he'd gotten naked with the woman who—however minutely—had played a role *in* the breakup.

"Ah geez. You again?" Jaden scowled at the sixty-something nurse who'd just entered his hospital room. She'd been in to check on him three times since midnight, and stupidly, when the door had begun to swing open that time, he'd hoped it would be another woman coming to see him. Like his *girlfriend*.

"You likely won't catch a better sight than me before seven in the morning." The nurse winked at him behind purple-rimmed glasses. "Unless it's what's in this little paper cup you're staring at so intently."

She rattled the pills she held in her hand and, after passing the paper dispenser off to him, poured a cup of water from the pitcher beside his bed.

"More pain medicine, I presume?" Jaden stared down at the two tablets, one orange and one white, and twisted his mouth into a frown.

"Don't you think you need it?"

Sadly, he did. Not that he wanted to admit it. Nor did he actually want to take anything that would make him high off his ass before his family showed back up. He still had to figure out where he could go to recuperate, how to keep from falling behind on his practicum since he needed to be in Seattle for the required counseling sessions, how quickly he could *get* back to Seattle . . . and then there was the little matter of Megan. Who apparently wasn't even speaking to him now.

"Take the pills, Jaden." The nurse patted his arm. "You had major surgery not twenty-four hours ago. You'll have plenty of time to play too-tough-for-pills later." She lifted his hand toward his mouth, her eyes warm with concern. "But right now, your body needs to heal. And to do that, *you* need to take your medication."

He scowled at her once again. He really did need to keep his wits about him.

But he'd also been sitting there in near unbearable pain for the last thirty minutes.

He swallowed both pills with one gulp of water . . . and *without* looking at the nurse. He hated the admission that he needed them, but he decided to be thankful the IV morphine from the night before had already been stopped instead. That way, he should at least have a few minutes before he became too loopy to think straight. Maybe by then, Megan would either come by or at least return his texts.

"Did you have a good visit with your brother this morning?" the nurse asked as she investigated his propped-up foot. "I'll tell you, that man had everyone on the floor buzzing."

Cord had stopped by while it was still dark outside. He'd had to get back to Billings in time for his first patient of the day, but he'd stuck around overnight to make sure there'd been no complications.

"My brother always has everyone buzzing," Jaden grumped. Cord could crook his little finger and get no fewer than five girls instantly tittering over him.

"He's a good-looking one, that's for sure."

"And what do I look like? Chopped liver?"

The nurse chuckled and repositioned the covers over his foot. "You're right. You're good-looking, too. I didn't mean to imply otherwise."

She gave him another wink and a pat, and as he'd done while swallowing the pain meds, he looked away. How embarrassing to have begged for a compliment. Especially one to show that he was as good as his brother.

"In fact," the nurse went on, "I'd say that girlfriend of yours is lucky to have you."

Thinking about Megan made him growl. "That girlfriend doesn't even like me right now. She won't come see me or even text to ask how I'm doing."

Not that he could really blame her. He *had* spent the night with another woman.

She had shown up when his family first got the call, though. He'd learned that after waking from surgery. She'd come to the hospital along with everyone else, but then she'd had to stand there and accept his clothing from the very woman he'd just spent the night with.

He growled again, and the nurse shoved a thermometer into his mouth.

"You're wrong." After noting his temperature, she wrapped her fingers around his wrist. "She *did* come to see you. You were just asleep."

Megan had been there?

"When?"

She didn't reply until she released his wrist. "Right after I started my shift." She wrote in his chart. "The poor thing. She seemed so worried. I let her come on back even though visiting hours had been over for a while."

Jaden hung on her words. Megan *did* care. He'd known it. No stupid dream was going to change that.

Now he just had to convince her that what had happened the night of the wedding meant nothing.

"She brought you those." The nurse nodded toward his bedside table, and when he looked over, his head already swimming with the effects of the drugs, his gaze landed on a slim vase bursting with brightly colored flowers.

The sight dumbfounded him. Megan had brought him flowers? That wasn't like her.

Normally she was too practical for flowers.

"Want me to read the card to you?" the nurse asked, and Jaden immediately nodded.

"Please."

He couldn't take his eyes off the bouquet, and for the first time in the last thirty-six hours, true hope began to flow. His life, as he knew it, *wasn't* over.

"Dear Jaden," the nurse began, and Jaden shifted his gaze so that he now watched her as she spoke. "I'm so very sorry about . . . *everything*"—she glanced up, a question in her eyes, but he didn't fill her in on what "everything" meant—"and I absolutely hate the role I played in it. I would never in a million years want to cause anyone the kind of pain"—she flipped the card over—"that I know you must be suffering. Please don't hesitate to let me know how I can help. Just say the word, and I'll be there."

Jaden stared at the card in the woman's hand. Megan was sorry.

They were okay.

His heart began to beat again. All he had to do was say the word.

He reached for his cell to text her for the third time since waking up. Maybe she hadn't heard the first two since she'd been by the hospital so late the night before. That would account for her lack of reply.

"She seems like a sweetheart," the nurse said as she tucked the card back into its envelope. "Of course, I knew that well before last night. I met her at the gym back in December and ended up having a long conversation with her."

Confusion tickled at the back of his mind. How had she met Megan at the gym in December?

Oh yeah, Megan hadn't gone back to Seattle with him after Christmas. She must have joined the local gym.

He went back to his text, his head bent forward, and noted that focusing was becoming a bit of a struggle. The pain meds were definitely kicking in.

"And here she is now." The nurse's voice seemed to come from a hundred feet away, and it was all Jaden could do to lift his gaze to see what she was talking about. Who was here now?

The nurse was ushering someone into the room. "Come on in, honey. He's awake."

Jaden clued in to her words and realized that Megan must be there. Only, when he got his gaze to focus enough to shift it to the person who'd just entered his room, it wasn't his girlfriend who now stood awkwardly at the foot of his bed.

It was the woman he'd woken up beside the morning before.

Chapter Five

Arsula twisted her hands together as Jaden's blue eyes stared blankly back at her. She doubted he'd forgotten who she was in the last twenty-four hours; therefore, she assumed his glazed look stemmed from painkillers. That fact made her wonder if now had been a good time to drop by to give him his ring back.

"Hi," she eventually said, unsure how else to start or even how he might react to her being there.

"You're not Megan."

She blinked. Definitely not how she might have guessed he'd react. Then he turned to the nurse.

"She's not Megan," he said to Susan, the woman Arsula had first met in Erica's exercise class.

"Who's Megan?" Susan asked.

"You said my girlfriend was here." Jaden pointed at Arsula. "But that isn't my girlfriend. She's just the woman I slept with before she knocked me down the stairs."

Arsula's eyes went wide. *"No."*

She shook her head as she tried to take in both Jaden and Susan. "No," she repeated. "I did neither. I *didn't* sleep with him, and I didn't knock him down the stairs. It was an accident."

"We woke up naked together, and you threw a lamp at me."

She grimaced. "Well, yes. Both of those things technically *did* happen. But I only threw the lamp because you made me mad when you called me the devil."

"But you are the devil. You talked me out of my clothes even though I have a girlfriend."

"I . . ." Arsula momentarily closed her eyes. This was not at all how she'd envisioned the morning going. She'd hoped to slip in and out without causing so much as a stir. Not to be gossip fodder before she'd even had her second cup of coffee.

"I'll leave you two to it," Susan murmured, patting Arsula on the shoulder before ducking out of the room. When just the two of them remained, Arsula inched around to the side of Jaden's bed.

Anxiety clawed at the back of her neck. "I'm sorry about throwing the lamp at you."

Jaden didn't reply. He just peered at her through thinly slit eyes, and then he dropped his head to the pillow as if unable to hold it up a second longer.

"Do you want me to go?" She motioned toward the door. "I could just—"

"You brought me flowers."

She glanced at the bouquet sitting beside his bed. "I did."

"Why did you bring me flowers?"

She gave a little shrug. "Because you're in the hospital. And because I felt bad about my part in your falling."

"You threw a lamp at me."

She sighed. She knew she had. But really, it hadn't been that large a lamp. A ten-dollar purchase from a big-box store shouldn't have been heavy enough to knock him down the stairs. "I really am sorry," she told him. And she truly was. "I don't usually lose my temper like that."

Her last statement could be considered a tiny fib if the right person were to be asked. She'd been sent to detention far too many times during her teen years to ever be able to say she didn't *usually* lose her temper when someone goaded her. But the good news was, it was more of a heat-of-the-moment thing. Her outrage rarely lasted beyond the argument itself.

"I like the flowers," Jaden said, his eyes now closed and his words running together. "Nobody's ever brought me flowers before."

"I'm glad you like them. My mom sent them to me for Valentine's Day, but I thought you needed them more." Her mother always sent her flowers for Valentine's Day. Even when she'd still been living at home.

Jaden nodded. "I did need them. I didn't even get a birthday present."

A birthday present? "Was it your birthday recently?"

"Saturday."

This made Arsula smile. She loved birthdays. "You were born on Valentine's Day?"

His eyelids fluttered, but they didn't open. A half smile touched his mouth, though. "I'm a Valentine's baby. Shouldn't be so hard to love me then, right?"

Once again, Arsula was taken aback. He'd been like that Saturday night after he'd accidentally called her Megan. He'd grown melancholy and skated right along the edge of sad.

"I would guess you're quite easy to love," she replied honestly. Until the hours following the wedding, she would've had no basis to make that statement. After spending time with him, though, she'd seen that though he might present a hard front—and really, all his brothers did that—Jaden Wilde had a good dose of squishy on the inside.

He didn't reply to her statement, and as Arsula stood there, taking in the steady in and out of his breaths, she assumed he'd fallen asleep. Which meant . . . she should probably leave.

She didn't immediately move toward the door, though. There was something soothing about watching this man sleep.

The lines of pain that had been carved around his mouth and eyes as they'd waited for the ambulance the day before were gone now, and in their place was a peace that too often seemed rare in the world today. Everyone was always stressed or in a hurry. *Or* had their guard up and didn't want to let anyone in. Arsula was good at reading people, even when they tried to shield themselves, but when their shell was completely down, it often felt as if she were looking directly into their souls.

And in Jaden's soul, she saw the little boy he would have been when he'd lost his mother.

Was that how she was supposed to help him? To overcome something relating to his mother's death?

She remained uncertain. She had little knowledge of the details surrounding his mother's passing. Only that she'd been involved in a car accident and that Dani had come home from college to help finish raising him and the twins. Nick, Nate, and Jaden had all been under ten at the time, while the older brothers had both been in high school and nearing graduation, and from what Arsula had learned over the past months, her death had been hard on all of them. Only, for some reason, she'd always sensed there was more to their struggles than solely the fact that they'd *lost* their mother.

Maybe if she knew more about Max's first wife, that would clue her in to how she might be able to help Jaden? Or about what his life had been like *after* his mother's death?

She wouldn't get answers standing there watching him sleep, though. And she *did* need to get to work.

Retrieving the engagement ring from her purse, she moved to place it on the bedside table, intending to leave it so he'd see it when he woke up. As her fingers hovered over the small table, however, it occurred to her that anyone could happen into the room and lay eyes on it before he did. And if that were to be the case, there would be questions about *why* it was there. Which could become embarrassing.

She wouldn't want to do that to him, so she tucked the ring back into her purse. She'd find another time to return it.

Taking one final peek at the silent form sleeping under the covers, she made herself turn to go. But his fingers closed around her wrist.

"Don't leave," he murmured, and she looked down to find his eyes once again open and looking directly at her. "I don't want to be alone. Will you stay and talk to me?"

She swallowed. Whatever kind of pain meds they had him on, she wanted to know. Maybe she could slip one into her father's brandy if she ever got up the nerve to tell him she wouldn't be moving back home.

"Sit." Jaden patted the mattress. "Tell me about you. How do I know you?"

This made her smile again. The man was out of it.

She sat, and his eyes drifted closed. But they immediately popped back open. "I danced with you at Gabe's wedding."

Arsula nodded. "You did."

"You're a really great dancer." He laughed out loud, his lips curving in the midst of his scrubby whiskers and the sound a little too loud. "You looked hot in that dress, too. I wanted to take it off you."

She didn't remind him that he *had* taken it off her.

He lifted his head from the pillow and squinted. "What did you say your name is?"

"Arsula."

He grinned again, his eyes closing more the wider his smile got. "That's right. It's a funny name."

"I like it. I'm named after my great-aunt, who was named after her grandmother."

"*Yee-ah?*" he slurred. "That's nice, carrying on a family name. Do you have a niece?"

"Not yet, but I have three nephews."

His shook his head, his eyes fully closed once again and his head cushioned on the pillow. "Boys shouldn't be named Arsula. Just girls. You need a niece. Or a daughter. A daughter would be fun."

She smiled at his rambling. It reminded her of Saturday night. Their discussions had bounced around, covering a number of topics, yet in the end it had felt as if they'd had one cohesive conversation. "Someday I hope to have both," she admitted. All three of her brothers were married, with Boyd, the youngest, expecting his first child in a matter of weeks. A child who could potentially be the first girl of the family. And possibly her namesake.

And as for having a daughter . . . she had no current prospects.

"I have a niece," Jaden told her. He removed his continuing hold on her wrist and held two fingers up between them. "Two of them. They're the best. And they love me, too. For real, I think." He squinted at her again. "Do you like your family, Arsula?"

"I do." Her heartbeat seemed to slow as her internal radar blipped over the comment about his nieces loving him. "My family is terrific."

Had that simply been the medication talking?

Or had it been *him* talking *because* of the medication?

"Do you like *your* family?" she asked.

"Sure. They're great."

His hand lowered, and he once again reached for her. Only this time when he made contact, it wasn't to snag her by the wrist. He rested his hand beside her leg instead. And then he caressed the backs of his fingers over her thigh.

She dropped her eyes to his fingers.

"Do you know Megan?" His question had Arsula dragging her gaze back up and doing her best to ignore the paths of heat now winding their way along her legs. "Because I saw you talking to her at the wedding."

"I do know her." She also noticed that Jaden no longer looked at her.

Not only did she know Megan through their meetings to discuss the other woman's dreams and to help her understand how to trust in her own intuition, but Megan had offered to work up a website for her. Arsula hadn't been sold on the idea—sticking with local clients and having people seek her out via word of mouth had always been enough for her. Why change things? But over dinner one evening, she'd shared an idea that had rarely gone beyond a flicker, and before they'd parted ways for the night, an initial website concept had been scratched out.

"Then will you tell her that I'm sorry?" All inflection left Jaden's voice. "I'm sure you were nice to sleep with and all, and I apologize for not remembering it." He swallowed, and his eyes remained downcast. Dark crescents of eyelashes framed the top of each cheek. "I . . . also apologize for accusing you of drugging me."

The movements on her thigh stilled, and when she didn't say anything, he finally lifted his gaze. He must have missed her telling Susan that they hadn't slept together.

"You're nice," he confessed. "I could tell that while we were hanging out. *Before* I couldn't remember what else happened. And I don't think you'd do something like that."

She appreciated his apology. And his belief in her.

She also appreciated the fact that she hadn't had to bring up the subject in order for him to offer it.

"Thank you." She covered his hand and let sincerity ring through. "You're forgiven for that."

His eyelids began to droop again. "Then will you tell Megan I'm sorry? Because I shouldn't have done that to her."

She squeezed his hand. "You're fine there, too. Because we didn't actually *have* sex."

His brows pulled together. "We didn't?" His disbelief was obvious. "But you were naked. And I was, too."

"Yes, we were both naked."

"*And* we were in bed together."

"Yes," she answered patiently. "But we *didn't* have sex."

She didn't know whether to admit that they'd *intended* to, or whether to just let him think their nakedness had been a strange by-product of climbing into the same bed together.

"Why didn't we?" he demanded. His words were slurred, but she could see him fighting to stay alert. "Did we not have a condom?" Then his face cleared as if a light bulb had come on inside his head. "I don't carry condoms."

"Lack of a condom wasn't the issue."

"Then . . ." He frowned again, but then another knowing look came into his eyes, and he nodded as if with sudden understanding. "You're on birth control."

"I—"

"But I'm clean," he interrupted. "Did I forget to tell you that? It's just been me and Megan for years."

"You . . ." She blew out a breath and found herself wishing the meds would go ahead and pull him under. She really would prefer to skirt the issue altogether. Not only would she not have to be talking about having sex with him if she hadn't drunk so much, but also . . . most men wouldn't take the information she possessed especially well.

At this point, though, she had the feeling he didn't intend to stop until he got an answer that made sense. So heck, why not have a little fun with it? She liked Jaden best when they were laughing, anyway.

"You actually *did* tell me that," she confessed. "And I *am* on birth control."

She didn't know why she'd just shared that.

"Then why didn't we have sex?"

Because one plus one didn't always equal two, she thought. But instead of confusing him more with her convoluted logic, she glanced surreptitiously at his lap. "Because someone drank too much whiskey before making it to the bed."

He studied her, clearly not catching on, then glanced to where she'd been looking at his lap.

"Are you saying that I passed out?" he finally asked. "That after getting you naked *and* getting into bed with you"—his gaze lowered to trail over her—"I just passed out?"

His disbelief stroked her ego. "You eventually did. First, though . . ."

She glanced at his lap again, this time more pointedly, and he finally seemed to understand. Then she laughed at the look of horror that passed over him. Her chuckles grew even more pronounced when he lifted the sheet covering his body and gawked at whatever he discovered underneath.

"Oh geez," he mumbled, and he dropped the sheet. "Are you saying I couldn't get it up?"

"I'm afraid so."

He looked under the sheet again, and disgust lined his features. "That's bullshit. I *can* get it up. I never have that problem." He looked at her. "Do you want me to show you?"

"No." Arsula laughed again and reached out to push the sheet back down to his chest. Painkillers made him hilarious.

"But I can," he argued again.

"I'm sure you can."

"Don't patronize me." He narrowed his eyes at her. "I recognize the tone. If you patronize me, I'll show you right now."

He made a face of concentration then, his gaze glued to that particular area of the sheet, and Arsula couldn't help but watch.

Only . . . nothing moved.

He finally groaned and collapsed with exhaustion. "Dammit," he growled out. "Why isn't my dick working?"

Arsula snickered. "I'd say right now that's thanks to the quantity of pain medication coursing through you."

This brought his gaze back to hers. "You can tell they've given me something?"

"Yeah, Jaden. A little bit."

"*Great.* I thought I was acting normal."

He went back to glaring at his unresponsive member, and Arsula shifted farther onto the bed. She hiked a knee up onto the mattress and ended up watching what he watched—but there remained no movement. She knew she should get out of there and let him sleep. He'd be released later today, and from what she'd gathered by talking to Susan, he had a long road to recovery ahead of him. He'd no doubt need all the energy he could muster just to be wheeled out of the hospital and transferred to his own bed.

However, she couldn't bring herself to go. She liked hanging out with him.

"Arsula?" He finally spoke again, and she shifted her gaze to his.

"Yes?" The lightheartedness of the previous moments disappeared.

"Thank you for coming to see me."

She offered a tight smile. That was the sweetest thing he could have said.

He rested his head back against his pillow, both of them seeming to sink into their own thoughts, before he once again reached out a hand to her. This time his palm slid over her knee, and she instinctively knew that whatever he was about to say, it was important.

"Will you do me a favor?" The deep timbre of his voice made the hairs on her arms stand.

"If I can."

"Will you let me stay with you when I leave here?"

Her features dropped. *Stay with her?*

They'd only met two days ago!

"I . . ." She shook her head, unable to utter another word.

"I won't be able to go back to Seattle immediately," he explained. "And I don't want to go to the house. I don't like it there."

"But"—she swallowed—"I don't think staying with me would be appropriate, Jaden."

"But you said you'd help." He nodded his head toward the flowers she'd brought in. "You said all I had to do was say the word."

"Yes, but—"

"Word," Jaden whispered, and she heard so much in that one syllable.

She saw even more in his haunted look.

He didn't like staying at the house he'd grown up in . . . Why not?

Did it have to do with the house itself? The orchard?

Or simply the fact that Megan was currently living there?

She bit down on the inside of her lip as her thoughts continued to churn. Jaden had said he didn't "like it there," which was more than being uncomfortable with Megan's living arrangements. So it had to be something else.

His mother? According to Erica, Jaden's mother had been a manipulative person. She'd also mentioned that Gabe still suffered some lingering issues due to his childhood.

Had whatever affected Gabe had an impact upon Jaden as well?

It was possible. If their mother had been that manipulative a person.

So was that it, then? Her heart began to race. Was Jaden's problem that he had deep-rooted issues concerning his mother?

"I can't be there like this." Jaden spoke again before she remembered to reply. "I don't want to be a burden to anybody. I don't want to have to ask." The last part barely whispered out, and his gaze once again shifted away.

Arsula waited to see if he'd say more, and when he didn't, she forced herself to speak. She had to say something. But what came out floored her. "I have all those stairs."

Would she really consider taking him in if she didn't?

"I forgot about the stairs," he mumbled, and sadness seemed to pin him to the bed. "Maybe I can just stay here then. I'll talk to that nurse. See if she can make that happen."

"That nurse's name is Susan."

Blue eyes flickered back to hers. "Yeah?"

Arsula nodded and once again bit her lip. She wanted to comfort him with a hug.

"She seems nice," he went on. "Do you think she'll let me stay?"

"I . . . *doubt* your insurance company will let you."

Dejection covered his face. "Oh yeah. I forgot about that. It's not like this place is a hotel, is it?"

He lifted his head and peered toward the door then, his head bobbing drunkenly as he kept his gaze locked on it. Then he swung his eyes to the cell phone lying on the bed beside him. He picked it up and stared at it before putting it down and turning back to Arsula.

"Then will you do me a different favor?"

She nodded. "Whatever you need."

Insecurity filled Jaden's eyes. "Will you tell Megan that we didn't sleep together? Tell her . . ." He gulped, and it was a moment before he finished. "Just ask her to still love me?"

The plea ripped her heart out. Because she couldn't do that, either. At least, not the last part.

She *could* speak with Megan, however. And she probably should do that much, anyway. Because whether a relationship had reached its ending or not, thinking an ex had slept with someone else the very night it ended would hurt anyone.

"I can't lose her." Jaden's eyes were closed now, and his words had slowed. But his thumb began to move over her knee. "Don't tell her I sent you, though. I don't want her to see me as weak."

Jaden's deep breathing indicated he'd once again fallen asleep, and against her better judgment, Arsula still didn't get up. She'd figured out the source of his hurt, she was certain. His mother. Now all she had to do was figure out how to get him to open up so she could determine the specifics. And then help him to overcome it.

The door opened behind her, and she glanced over her shoulder, moving almost as if she were as lethargic as Jaden. She expected to find Susan looking back at her from the doorway, but instead she found Dani, Nick, and Nate. Three siblings come to check on their little brother.

Three siblings shocked to find their little brother with a woman sitting on his bed.

Chapter Six

Embarrassment flooded Arsula when she realized that Jaden's siblings all simultaneously readjusted their gazes to Jaden's hand on her knee.

"It's . . ." She hurried to stand, *not* allowing herself to once again voice the "it's not what it looks like" argument, and faced them, guilt heating her cheeks. Because it *had* been what it looked like.

It had been Jaden needing the comfort of another person's touch.

It had been *her* sitting on his bed next to him. Way too close for someone he'd just met.

And it had been her, understanding that she was the person he needed to connect with. And her willingness to be that for him.

"How's he doing this morning?" Dani spoke while her brothers remained mute. All three of them filed into the room, and each took up a spot around Jaden's bed.

Arsula stepped out of their way. "I think he was hurting pretty badly before I got here. He was awake and talking until just a few minutes ago, but a lot of it was slurred as the pain medicine kicked in."

"And what was he talking about?" Nate looked at her from the other side of the bed, his gaze unreadable.

She fidgeted with the zipper of her purse. Nate made her nervous. She knew Nick fairly well, having met him shortly after arriving in town, but until Friday night, she'd never seen nor spoken to the other twin. And though he might be physically identical to his brother, the two men were entirely different creatures. Nate struck her as someone walking around inside a six-inch impenetrable shell.

"He was talking about when he's released from the hospital," she shared.

"Good." Nick gave a nod, and the move had the ability to ease Arsula's nerves. "Maybe he's come around. He refused every suggestion we offered last night."

Arsula chewed on the corner of her lip and studied Jaden's sleeping form. "Something tells me he's still going to refuse them," she finally admitted. Then she lifted her eyes back to his siblings. "He suggested he'd rather stay *here* instead of going to your family home."

She didn't know where she'd gotten the chutzpah to say that to the three of them, but it wasn't as if Jaden could do it for himself.

"Staying here is out of the question," Dani stated.

"I know. I pointed that out to him."

"So he has to come home," Nate announced.

"He . . . *uhmmm*"—she glanced from sibling to sibling—"and *Megan* . . ." She really didn't want to be the one to share that he and Megan had broken up if they didn't already know. That didn't feel her place.

At the same time, if Megan was still at the house . . .

"We know about the breakup." Dani came around to stand beside her. She touched a hand to Arsula's arm. "She filled us in yesterday. And though she's going to keep helping out at the store until we can find a new manager, she's already looking for another place to live."

Good. Arsula didn't voice her thought, but she was glad Megan would be leaving the house. It would be healthiest for both of them.

"The thing is, though," Arsula continued out loud, "I don't think that Megan being there is Jaden's *only* issue."

"Is that so?" Nate's voice remained unemotional. "And how long is it that you've known our brother?"

Embarrassment once again heated Arsula's cheeks, because he was spot-on. She hadn't known Jaden long enough to be speaking for him. That wouldn't stop her, though.

She turned to Dani. "I know it seems weird, but do you remember what I told you when I first moved here? About knowing that Birch Bay was where I needed to be?"

Out of the corner of her eye, she caught Nate crossing his arms over his chest. Dani nodded. Dani had become a friend as well as a boss, and though she might not fully believe in Arsula's gift, she did seem to entertain the idea that Arsula carried a deep ability to understand people.

"What about it?" Dani cautiously asked.

"He's"—Arsula nodded toward Jaden without looking at him—"the reason."

She wished they weren't having this conversation in front of two of Jaden's brothers, but given that she'd already plunged in headfirst, she might as well finish. "I might have only met him a couple of days ago, but I get that I can *help* him."

"What the hell are you talking about?" Nate bit out. Irritation rolled off him, while Nick exhibited more interest than confusion. Arsula attributed Nick's reaction to the fact that she'd spent several evenings working on very personal issues with his own wife.

"It's not exactly explainable"—she tried to explain anyway—"but I knew at the reception that I could help him in some way. *Emotionally.*"

"This is ridiculous." Nate began to move in the small space. "As is the idea of Jaden going anywhere but to our home when he's discharged.

65

I'm staying at the house as well, and I can stick around however long he needs me." He skewered Arsula with a look. "And *you're* going to stay away from him. Because what he doesn't need in his life right now is a full-fledged wacko."

"Stop it, Nate," Dani chastised her brother, but Arsula just ignored the wacko comment. She'd heard it before.

"I can't stay away," she informed him. "Whether I want to or not, our paths will cross." And the sooner she allowed that to happen, the sooner she could ease whatever hurts Jaden held inside. She turned back to Dani. "He said he doesn't like it at the house. He doesn't want to go there."

"He's going to be laid up for weeks." Nate hadn't lowered his arms. "Did he happen to mention that? Unable to put weight on his foot and looking at months of physical therapy. And we haven't even talked about how he'll get around until he can drive again."

"He's not going to be able to return to Seattle," Nick added. "At least, no time soon."

"He mentioned that, too. Would it be possible for him to finish his degree from here, do you think?" Arsula wasn't certain how much he had to finish up.

"He's in the middle of his practicum," Dani explained. "It's similar to an internship, but it's only a few hours each week. He has to observe individual and group counseling sessions, as well as occasionally work directly with clients."

"And if he doesn't finish this semester," Nick continued, "he doesn't receive his degree."

Arsula studied Jaden again. She felt bad for him. She could understand how upsetting it would be to be this close and not to be able to finish on schedule. If only she hadn't thrown that lamp.

But then, maybe *that* had been part of their paths crossing. She'd been *meant* to throw the lamp.

She considered the thought. She'd heard crazier.

"I've spoken with a local psychologist who practices here in town," Dani told her. "A friend of mine. Jaden had already arranged to spend a year practicing under her, starting in May. That would allow him to earn his license. Since this has happened, though, Janette's open to the idea of him finishing out his practicum with her first. Assuming we can get everything sorted out with the head of his degree program."

"I can get him back and forth to her office," Nate said. "That won't be a problem."

"But I still don't want to stay at the house."

All eyes turned when Jaden spoke. And seeing his clear gaze, Arsula wondered how long he'd been awake.

"Jaden." Dani moved to his side. "It's just not practical for you to be on your own right now. And where would you go, anyway?"

"I'll go back to Seattle as soon as I can."

She gave him the kind of look that only an older sibling can pull off with the baby of the family. A look Arsula had witnessed more times than she wanted to count. "You'll need help getting around. At least for several weeks." Outwardly, Dani remained patient, but her voice changed to an I'm-the-oldest-so-I'm-in-charge tone. "So you *can't* go back to Seattle. Not for a while. It's simply implausible."

A muscle twitched in Jaden's jaw.

"And you have plenty of people right here willing to help you out," Nick added.

Jaden didn't so much as glance at his brother. "I have school to finish."

"I think we can make that happen from here, too. I've already talked to Janette, and she's on board to help you out. The thought is that you can log your remaining hours with her."

Again, a muscle twitched. "I also have my thesis, a class to finish up—"

"I know all of that, Jaden, but we can work it out. I promise." Frustration slipped into Dani's voice, along with a stiffness to her shoulders. "I'll make some calls to the school tomorrow. I'll—"

"*I'll* make the calls."

Dani gripped her hands in front of her. "Fine. You make the calls."

"Because I can handle my own life."

"Of course you can. No one doubts that."

Arsula snuck a glance at Jaden's brothers, wondering if they were growing as concerned as she. Jaden seemed so different now than before his family had come in. So much more distant.

"That's enough." Nate nudged Dani to the side and took her place next to Jaden. Because, *clearly*, he remained clueless to his brother's distress. "This isn't an argument worth having. You'll be discharged today, and you have to go somewhere. We're taking you to the house."

Arsula whipped her gaze back to Jaden's.

"I am *not* staying at the house," he repeated. He'd gritted his teeth, and his lips barely moved as he spoke. He then sought out his sister. *"No."*

The word came out deadly quiet.

Dani elbowed Nate and once again took pole position at her youngest brother's side, then she leaned in and took his hand. "It's not the same anymore. Gloria has changed a lot. She—"

"And Gloria doesn't need me underfoot."

"Jaden," Dani pleaded. Her gaze clung to his. "Be reasonable. If not there, then—"

"Enough." Nate let out a long sigh. "Listen to what I've been trying to tell you all this time, idiot. You won't have to be a bother to Gloria. *I* can stay. *I'll* help you out."

Jaden smirked. "What? Are you looking to take on a charity case these days? Trying to make up for past sins?"

"For the love of—"

"Just shut up," Jaden told him. "You have your own life. You don't even want to be here. Go back to wherever that life is." He turned to Dani. "And I won't stay with any of the rest of you, either, so don't bring it up again. You have a new baby. A whole world you've worked hard for and created for yourself. Gabe has a new wife and a daughter who needs him to concentrate on *her*. And he certainly doesn't need me there in the way. And Nick . . ."

He turned to his other brother, and Nick straightened where he stood.

"What about me?" Nick had remained quiet throughout the exchange. "I have two spare bedrooms, and like I told you already, you're welcome to either or both. Whatever you need."

"While lying there listening to you trying to get your own wife pregnant?"

Nick jolted. "What makes you say that?"

Jaden made a face. "Are you saying that's not what you're doing most nights?"

"Well, no." A hint of embarrassment passed over his brother's face. "I *am* doing that. But we can be discreet about it."

"You won't have to be discreet, because I won't be there."

"Come on, Jaden." Nick held his hands out to his sides. "Quit being a child about this. You're just making excuses. We all have space. We're all willing to help you out."

When the argument had first started, Arsula had considered slipping into the hall to give them privacy. It hadn't seemed like a scene she needed to be involved in. Now, however, she was glad she'd stayed. Because now she felt that if she weren't there, Jaden would have no one on his side. Even though she'd yet to figure out why they needed sides.

"I'll go to a hotel," Jaden announced. "And I'll call Uber to take me to appointments."

All three of his siblings began to argue, so Arsula stepped forward. "I have a suggestion," she offered, lifting her voice to be heard above theirs.

The arguing stopped.

"You?" Nate shook his head with derision. "You don't have a dog in this race."

"What is it?" Dani ignored her brother.

Jaden didn't say anything. He just watched her, his gaze steady.

"The sitting area in Dani's office," she began slowly. The idea had come to her a few minutes earlier, but she'd initially tossed it aside. "It's large enough for Jaden to be comfortable in, and it's rarely used. There's even a full bathroom right outside the room."

"Are you kidding me?" Nate raised his voice. "In an office?"

She turned to Dani. "I could keep an eye on him during the days. Maybe transfer the office phone to my cell whenever he needs to go to the doctor."

"*I'm* taking him to his doctor's appointments," Nate roared.

"Or when I need to observe a therapy session," Jaden added, ignoring his brother, and Arsula glanced back at him. They exchanged an almost imperceptible smile. "It wouldn't have to be for forever," he went on. "Just until I can get back to Seattle."

Nate sighed as if the entire idea were ludicrous, but Nick spoke up, his attention on Arsula. "Why would you offer to do that?"

She gave a small shrug. "I *did* throw a lamp at him."

"That's right," Jaden crowed. He grinned as if his point had just been made. "It was her fault that I broke my ankle."

"*Partially* my fault."

"Therefore, she *should* be the one to take care of me." This time it was Jaden crossing his arms over his chest, and when he caught Arsula looking at him, he winked. As if the two of them had just shared a secret.

The vibe of the room suddenly righted itself, the tension of the prior moments all but gone, and she knew she'd done the right thing.

"In the office," Dani mused.

"I'll be right upstairs in the evenings." Only one other person worked out of the office. Tim had been hired as point man for a number of their clients, as well as to bring in new accounts. He only spent a couple of days a week there, however, because he had a similar setup at home. "I can leave the door to the inside stairs open, so I'll know if he needs me. *And* I'll give him a bell. Just in case I don't hear if he calls out."

Nate grunted, but Dani studied her youngest brother.

Arsula could see her considering it. "I really don't mind," she assured the group of them. "In fact, I'd like to do it."

She hadn't come to Birch Bay to help Jaden *physically* heal, she knew, but what better way to help him get to the bottom of his issues than having him living below her?

Nate gave another grunt, Nick tilted his head as he watched Dani work through the idea from every angle, and Jaden didn't take his eyes off Arsula.

Finally, Dani gave a nod. "I'll talk to Tim. He can work at home if Jaden's being there proves too disruptive. But I'm okay with it if Jaden is."

Jaden grinned, and suddenly, it wasn't his mental well-being Arsula was thinking about. Instead, she was remembering how he'd grinned exactly like that just before he leaned in and put his mouth to hers.

Chapter Seven

The car hit another pothole, and Jaden gritted his teeth. *"Please . . . avoid . . . the potholes,"* he said for the third time. He stared at the roof of the car from his horizontal position in the back seat as his pain level inched another notch higher.

"He's trying, Uncle Jaden." Jenna peered at him from the front passenger seat, her eyes heavy with concern. "I promise. I'm watching him to be sure. But he's being super careful."

"There's just holes all over the place," Haley added from beside Jenna. The two girls were buckled in together in the front seat since Jaden took up the full length of the back.

Given that her dad and Erica were off for a quick honeymoon, Jenna was spending a couple of nights with her grandparents, and additionally, Haley had been invited to stay over. Therefore, as Nate had left the house to shuttle Jaden from the hospital to Dani's office building, both girls had begged to ride along. Nate remained quiet in the driver's seat as their dad's car took another small dip, and after Jaden grunted once again, he silently conceded that it was possible Nate *was* being careful. It had been a cold winter in the northwest part of the state, and the roads weren't in the best shape.

However, that *didn't* mean he had to be rational in his thinking.

"Then if you can't avoid the potholes," Jaden gritted out, nausea from the pain now churning inside him, *"go . . . faster!"*

The hospital was only fifteen minutes from the small downtown area, and Jaden was ready to be there.

"Or you could just take your pain meds," Nate suggested, his tone mild.

"Or you could just learn to drive for once. You've been doing it for over a decade."

Nate hit another pothole—one Jaden was sure had been intentional—and Jaden reached toward his ankle with a loud groan. His foot was in a splint up to his knee, propped on a pillow on the other end of the seat, and beads of sweat covered his brow. Probably he *should* take his pain meds, but the last time he'd seen Arsula, he'd been higher than a kite and had literally begged her to take care of him. And that made no sense.

He didn't beg anyone to play nursemaid for him, so why would he ask a virtual stranger?

And *why* did the fact that he was heading her way right now *not* bother him?

He wanted to be lucid enough to try to figure it all out, but if the pain got much worse, he'd be looking for a white flag to wave instead.

The car slowed and made a right, and Jaden could see that they'd turned onto Main Street. He blew out a shaky breath.

"We're almost there, Uncle Jaden," Jenna reported from the front seat. Her brows remained drawn with worry. "And the sidewalks have all been scraped, so you don't have to worry about falling on the ice."

Thank heaven for small favors.

He leaned his head to the side, his cheek resting against the back of the seat, and closed his eyes. He just needed to get into the building, make it to whatever bed situation Arsula had set up for him, ask her why in the world she'd agreed to do this in the first place, and then he could medicate.

"We're here, Uncle Jaden." It was Haley who spoke that time. She kept her voice low, as if a quieter tone might help ease his pain. "Arsula is already waiting for you."

He forced his eyes to open, and sure enough, standing just inside the door to his sister's office was Arsula Moretti. She still wore the jeans and boots she'd had on at the hospital earlier, but she'd changed into an oversize sweater that hung almost to her knees. It looked to be thick, and its bulk rounded over her hips before narrowing to a few inches above her boots. The color was such a bright yellow that he squinted as if to block the shine.

"I love her clothes," Jenna whispered to Haley as the two of them scrambled out of the car. They hit the ground, bundled in their heavy coats and hats, and made a dash toward the front door.

"And I love that I seem to be the only one in this family who has any sense at all," Nate grumbled from where he remained in the front seat. The girls disappeared inside the building, and Nate readjusted the rearview to meet Jaden's eyes.

"Let me guess," Jaden cracked. "You don't like Arsula."

Nate's foul mood from that morning had carried on into the afternoon, and Jaden had picked up some of it himself.

"I don't *know* Arsula," Nate corrected. "Nor do you."

Jaden shifted his gaze to the woman at the center of their conversation. Nate was correct. He *didn't* know her. Yet . . . here he was.

He took in the fact that her hair seemed to defy gravity this afternoon. It was twisted into a knot on the top of her head and stood what seemed to be six inches high. And she was gorgeous. "I don't know," he murmured, as much to himself as anything. There was something unique about her. Something . . . *special.* "A person could do worse."

"What the fuck are you talking about?"

He looked back at Nate, realizing what he'd just said—*and* what he'd been thinking—and attempted to recover. "I'm just saying, maybe you should give her a chance." He nodded toward the woman in question. "Look at her. I say consider it. She could be just your type."

Nate's look turned to one of incredulity. "Are you suggesting that I like sloppy seconds?"

"I did *not* sleep with her," Jaden gritted out. They'd covered this multiple times already.

"Sure you didn't. That's what she claims, too."

"Because that's the truth."

"Yet you fell down her steps at eight o'clock in the morning. Dressed in your tuxedo from the night before."

"I got drunk. I couldn't go to the house after Megan had broken up with me."

"But you *could* have stayed at the hotel."

The two of them stared at each other, their eyes locked in the rearview mirror, until Jaden finally nodded. "Yes." He could have done that. He *should* have done that. And he didn't know why he hadn't.

Instead, he'd come back here and taken Arsula's clothes off.

He remembered that now. He also remembered kissing her. He'd been the one to start it.

And he'd liked it.

The details remained sketchy concerning what she'd looked like once that red dress had been removed. As well as how far things had progressed before they'd . . . stopped. But *had* he been able to get it up . . .

He forced himself to look away. He wouldn't have been able to forgive himself if that had happened. He wanted Megan. He was committed to Megan.

"What are you doing, Jaden?" Nate remained in the car, the door closed and his tone solemn. He still hadn't turned around. "Do you intend to sleep with her now? Is that what's going on?"

"*No.* I *intend* to get my girlfriend back." He just had to figure out how. "I love Megan. You know that."

"Yet you think staying with another woman while you recuperate will . . . what? *Help* win Megan back?"

They both looked at Arsula again, who now watched the two of them with an unwavering stare that Jaden innately understood to mean she was aware they were talking about her.

"There's nothing between me and Arsula," Jaden stated without taking his eyes off her. He didn't understand why he was here any more than Nate did, but he was okay with his decision. He tried his best to explain. "I needed a place to stay. Someone to help me out until I can handle things on my own."

And it wasn't as if his girlfriend had shown up to do it.

Nate finally turned in his seat. "Seriously. That's your reasoning? Then why not let *me* help?"

Jaden had never heard so much as a hint of need come from his brother before, and Nate would probably go to his grave denying it ever happened. Yet in that one question, need had been overflowing. "Like I told you at the hospital, I know your life isn't here. You never stick around. And I won't ask you to do that for me."

"But I offered."

"And yet aren't you already jonesing to be back on a crab boat?"

Nate had left home after graduating high school, and he'd made Alaska his base. He was a crab fisherman in the winter, and who knew what he did the rest of the year. And until the last couple of years, he'd rarely returned home at all.

Jaden understood why. Just as he also understood why it was *now* easier for him to be there. Only one other brother knew the full story about what had really kept him away.

Recent changes in the family dynamics hadn't changed Nate all that much, though.

"I was surprised to see that you'd made it in for the wedding," Jaden continued, "but I know sticking around isn't for you. You'll feel the need to go soon, and that's fine. I understand. And I don't judge. But I won't be the one who keeps you tied somewhere you don't want to be."

Nate wore an expression indicating he had more to say, but in the end, he shook his head, mumbled something about the absurdity of little brothers, and exited the car. He circled the hood, heading for the back passenger door, while Jaden quickly lifted his crutches from the floor. The second the door opened, he jabbed them out, rubber bottoms first, and clamped down on the pain as he maneuvered himself forward. He got to the edge of the seat, foot still straight out in front of him and still hurting like a mother, and thrust the vase of flowers he'd brought from the hospital toward Nate.

"Carry these, will you?"

"The flowers the woman with whom you *didn't* sleep brought you?"

Jaden scowled. "And try to be nice when we get in there."

"Nice is overrated." Arsula's voice came from behind Nate, and both brothers shifted so they could see her.

She hadn't put on a jacket before coming out, and her teeth chattered as she took the vase out of Nate's hands. Without a word, she turned and led the two of them into the much-warmer building. Once inside, Jaden could see Jenna and Haley waiting in the back room, and with sweat making a slow trek down the middle of his back, he forced himself to keep moving. Nate stayed close by, but as if in unspoken agreement, he didn't physically offer to help.

Once they reached the room, Jaden stopped just inside the open french doors and literally hung on his crutches. He should have taken the advice of the discharge nurse and let Nate bring him home in a wheelchair.

He also should have taken his pain meds.

"Let me help you into the bed," Arsula said, and Jaden didn't have the energy to refuse.

With her help, he shrugged out of his coat, then together, she and Nate worked to get him situated on the small sheet-covered mattress. It was only after he was once again horizontal—his breaths coming out in pants and his right foot throbbing like a son of a bitch—that Jaden realized they'd put him in a hospital bed.

He lifted his head and took in the room.

"Where'd you get the bed?" he croaked out in exhaustion.

Arsula handed him a glass of water, and Nate passed over a couple of pills.

Jaden took them.

"I spoke with a friend before leaving the hospital," she answered. "She made some calls and got the medical equipment place to deliver today."

A small fridge served as a bedside table, a TV hung from a mount on the ceiling, and a dark-brown couch had been pushed against the wall, positioned underneath the TV.

"I figured I'd be on a couch." He lowered his head back to the pillow.

"You need to get plenty of rest while also keeping your foot elevated." Arsula arranged a blanket over his legs. "That'll be easier done in a bed than on a couch."

"And we brought you pillows from the house," Jenna informed him. "They're the ones with the feathers inside. Megan said they're your favorite."

Jenna and Haley stood at the side of the bed, both looking as hopeful as they did worried, and Jaden reached out a hand to them. He ignored the flare of hope that threatened to ignite at the mention of Megan caring enough to make sure he got the type of pillows he preferred. She still hadn't returned any of his texts, nor had she stopped by the hospital before he'd left.

"Thank you for helping me," he said to both girls. "The feather pillows are definitely my favorite."

78

The girls smiled, and he squeezed each of their hands, but his energy was dropping fast.

"How about you two help me get Uncle Jaden's things," Nate said, and the three of them disappeared from the room. The bell on the front door tinkled as they went back outside, and Jaden watched as Arsula cringed at the noise.

"I'll take the bell down," she assured him. "I wouldn't want it to wake you every time it rings."

His sister had started and now ran a public relations firm that had both local and nationwide clients. It was wildly successful, but she'd originally begun the company out of the house. Most business was done via phone or on location with the paying customer. He couldn't imagine the bell on the front door of her office would be ringing all that often.

"I'm sure I'll be fine," Jaden assured her. Then he closed his eyes.

He woke a few minutes later to the sound of low voices coming from the front room. He couldn't see them, but he heard Nate and Arsula talking.

"My number is on there in case of an emergency," Nate was saying. "Along with Gabe's, Nick's, and the landline at the house."

"And I already have Dani's," Arsula added. "Here's mine." There was silence for a moment, and then Arsula said, "I'll let you know how he's doing."

Nate laughed without humor. "Don't worry. I'll be checking up on him."

As they'd come to agreement at the hospital about where Jaden would stay, Nate had continued to insist he'd remain in Birch Bay. Therefore, *he'd* be the one to ferry Jaden to and from appointments.

Jaden hadn't argued.

The rattle of pills could be heard, as well as Jenna and Haley laughing from a room farther away, and even without seeing the exchange, Jaden could sense the awkwardness between the two adults.

"Nate," he called out, suddenly not ready for his brother to leave.

Nate poked his head into the room. He held up both hands as he stepped across the threshold, a suitcase hanging from each. "The girls and I grabbed your bag from the rental—which Nick and I returned to the airport, by the way—and we also packed some clothing that Gloria ran out and picked up for you."

Jaden stared at the suitcases. "She didn't have to do that."

"She knows that." He set everything down. "But you're going to need more than a couple of changes of clothes, so take them and say thank you."

"Thank you," Jaden murmured. He could barely keep his eyes open, but at least the pain had started to fade.

He also had no idea what he'd just said thank you for.

"Nate?" he asked again. He had no clue if his brother was still there, given that he could no longer hold his eyes open. *Or* how much time had passed.

"Still here," Nate assured him.

"Will you ask Megan to call me?"

There was a pause before he answered. "I'll pass along the request."

"Or can she at least text me?" Jaden pleaded.

"I'll pass that along as well."

His heart felt too heavy. "Is she even still at the house?"

"For now."

He nodded. They'd told him she intended to leave. "Tell her to stay. There's no reason for her to go. Dad and Gloria like having her there."

Nate didn't reply, or if he did, Jaden didn't hear him.

"Nate?" Jaden called in a panic, managing to lift his head from the pillow. He forced his eyes to open and found Nate standing at his side. He could also see Arsula and the girls sitting behind the reception desk in the other room, their heads bent together.

He swung his gaze back to his brother's.

"What?" Nate said.

"I know you don't understand"—he looked at Arsula again—"*this*. And to tell you the truth, I don't, either." His words were slurring badly, but he pushed on. "But I didn't want to be at the house. Not like this."

It was bad enough to have to be dependent on anyone, but he certainly didn't want to be sitting around the house he'd grown up in as if he were seven again, waiting for his mother to take care of him.

Nate gave a nod and finally didn't look as angry as he had all day. "I'll always understand the ghosts that exist in that house."

Jaden fell back to the bed and caught his breath as if he'd been running instead of merely talking, and as he did, he watched Nate turn to take in Arsula himself. "And I may not understand it," Nate said in agreement, "but I'm here to tell you that that one's got more than one screw loose. *However* . . . I also can't say that I'm immune to the draw of staying here."

Jaden watched Arsula. Best he could tell, if she wasn't throwing things at people, she was smiling. "It's not like that," he insisted.

"Right." Nate patted him on the shoulder. "Then might I suggest that if you ever do want a chance at getting Megan back, you'd better make sure it doesn't turn *into* that."

Chapter Eight

Jaden opened his eyes later that night, his brain foggy, without a clue where he was. An antique floor lamp in the far corner of the room cast a small circle of light over scratched wood flooring and one end of a dark couch. Drapes were drawn over windows on the adjacent wall, a small chest of drawers sitting between the windows, and a set of glass-paneled doors were pulled almost closed on the wall opposite the chest. From the blue-tinted glow beyond the doors, he assumed a computer monitor must be on in the next room, but nothing else indicated there might be a person *at* the computer.

The kind of silence that permeated the room made him think it must be snowing outside, and sitting there all alone, he had a brief moment of panic.

"Hello?" he said into the void. Then his eyes landed on a small bell sitting atop a stack of books, all piled neatly on the mini fridge beside the bed.

Mini fridge.

A bed.

He took in a vase of flowers, a glass of water, a cupcake with a single candle protruding from it, the diamond engagement ring he'd attempted to give Megan, and two small prescription bottles sitting within reach. And suddenly, everything—except the cupcake—made sense.

He'd broken his ankle.

And he was in his sister's office, being taken care of by a woman he'd almost slept with.

He stared at the ceiling. *Damn.* He'd made a mess of everything.

He needed to heal up, get Megan to take him back, and get the hell back to Seattle. But at the same time, he knew that at least two of those things were *not* going to be smooth sailing. He currently had all kinds of hardware holding his ankle together, and according to his surgeon, he was looking at months before a full recovery. The surgeon also claimed it would be six weeks before he could put any weight on it.

Grunting with the movement, he reached for the bell. He couldn't stand to be trapped in a room all alone.

Holding the old-fashioned bell out to the side, he rang it as if his life depended on it. A noise sounded from above, but he didn't stop ringing, and by the time Arsula rushed into his room, wide-eyed and panicked, he almost felt better.

"What's wrong?" She flipped on the overhead light and quickly crossed to the bed. "What can I do?"

"I like this bell," he told her, speaking above the still-clattering noise. He knew he was acting like a child by continuing the ringing, but he couldn't seem to help it.

Confusion crossed her features as she caught the lip of the noise-maker, and she jammed three fingers inside the opening to silence the noise. Once the clanging stopped, she lowered his hand to the bed. "What do you need me to do?"

He tugged to free the bell. "I need you to give me back my bell."

"Jaden." She snapped out his name, and he finally quit pulling against her.

"What?" he snapped back just as abruptly.

"What's *wrong*?" she asked again. She returned the bell to the stack of books and moved as if intending to take a look at his ankle.

"Stop." He pulled back, even though she had yet to lift the cover. "I'm fine. I just woke up and didn't know where I was." Which was only partially true. He didn't want to admit, though, that he'd woken up and just felt like throwing a tantrum. Grown men didn't throw tantrums.

And he wasn't even sure why he was.

Thankfully, she left his foot alone, and when she didn't immediately exit the room, he admitted to himself that he'd rung the bell because he'd wanted her in there with him.

He took in her dark hair, random strands making a soft fluff around her face, while the remainder of it fell halfway down her back. She was also barefaced and in pajamas. Red-and-green plaid bottoms, and a red cotton shirt. He looked down at his similar attire. He'd left the hospital in blue-and-green plaid with a long-sleeve navy T-shirt.

"How long have I been asleep?" he asked, and she glanced at the wall behind his head.

"Ten hours."

His eyes bulged. "Are you kidding me?"

"I am not." She moved back up to stand at his side and tilted her head as she looked down. Concern colored her eyes, and he remembered thinking how pretty a brown they were when he'd first met her.

"How's the pain?" she asked.

"I'm not currently covered in sweat."

"Good to hear." She glanced at the clock again. "I've come down twice and given you more painkillers, but it's not quite time for you to take another if you can hold out. Nate said you should take them regularly the first few days, though, since pretty much all you can do is sit here and hurt."

She pursed her lips in sympathy, then waved a remote in the air. "You can also watch TV."

"Or read, apparently."

Her eyes flicked to the stack of books. "I didn't know what you might like, so I brought down a selection."

"I doubt I'll feel like reading." He was still in the mood to act like a juvenile, so he didn't bother perusing the titles. Nor did he take the remote. He just lay there.

But he did wonder why a cupcake now sat beside his bed.

"Can I get you some food?" She placed the remote beside the bell. "And a trip to the bathroom, perhaps?"

He frowned at the thought. He had to pee like a racehorse, but he had no idea how that was supposed to happen. Nor had he thought that through when he'd begged her to take care of him. At some point he'd need a shower as well.

Christ. How was he going to handle a shower when he could barely stand on one foot?

She seemed to understand his current need without him having to say it, and since he was at her mercy, he allowed himself to be coerced from the bed. With crutches in place and his leg bent behind him, he hobbled out a side door and into a small hallway.

"This building was originally a house," she shared as she pushed open a dark paneled door. "It had already been converted before your sister bought it, but whoever did the renovations left this restroom equipped with a walk-in shower instead of just making it a powder room."

"Maybe they could see into the future," Jaden grumbled.

And know that an invalid would one day live here.

He stopped at the threshold, out of breath and his mood remaining sour, and took in the dimensions of the miniscule room. It would be tight, but he should be able to maneuver inside by himself. *Thank goodness.* Nothing like having to ask for help just to do his business.

"One of your brothers will stop by every couple of days to help you shower."

"Too bad. I was looking forward to you giving me sponge baths."

He hobbled into the room before she could reply and slammed the door in her face, and when he reemerged, he found her waiting in the same spot. She didn't mention sponge baths, and he pretended he hadn't been an ass and made that crack. She was going out of her way to help him out. He shouldn't be a jerk.

Additionally, he *should* apologize. But he wasn't in the mood.

She helped him back into bed and, after loosening his splint, retrieved a bag of ice and positioned it over his ankle. She then hit the button to raise the top portion of his bed. Once he was upright, she disappeared from the room a second time, returning with a tray containing a sandwich, a steaming mug of vegetable soup, a glass of ice, and a banana.

He tossed a quick glance at the cupcake, still sitting beside his bed like some sort of trophy, but he made no comment.

"There's an assortment of drinks in the fridge." She pulled several out, offering him a choice, and he accepted a Coke. Then he just stared at the tray in front of him. How had he gone from coming home and proposing to his girlfriend . . . to being bedbound and cared for by a woman he barely knew?

And *why* was this woman willing to care for him?

He picked up the banana, his mind whirling with a dozen questions. "I don't understand why you agreed to this." He returned his gaze to hers, trying not to peer upon her as if she were some sort of fairy godmother. "Who *are* you, exactly?"

Her sudden look of concern indicated a fear that he might have a mental disorder. "I'm Erica's friend," she said slowly. "I was in the wedding."

"I remember *that*."

"*Ooookay* . . . Then my name is—"

"I know what your name is, too," he gritted out. "*And* I remember that we woke up in bed together yesterday morning. I called you the devil, you threw a vase at me, and I got the pleasure of seeing my bone sticking out of my ankle. Which currently has me in this pisser of a mood, by the way. But, Arsula, who *are* you? You work for Dani, but where did you come from? You're not from around here, right?"

He knew he'd never seen her before Saturday night. Nor had he heard of her.

"Oh." She finally smiled, and the move turned her features into a beam of light. He liked it when she smiled. "I moved to town last fall. I'm originally from Cheyenne—which is the only other place I've ever lived—and I landed in Birch Bay after waking one morning and knowing I was needed somewhere else. So I packed up my car . . . and *voilà!*"

She smiled again, but he only frowned. Her reply provided more questions than answers.

And a lot of concern.

"You . . . *knew* you were needed somewhere else?" he said.

"Exactly."

"And where were you needed?"

She spread her arms to her sides. "Here."

He just stared at her. She made little sense. And Nate *had* said she had a couple of screws loose.

Maybe he should have listened to his brother.

He tried not to show his concern for the state of *her* well-being, and spoke in as casual a manner as he could muster. "Why were you needed here, Arsula?"

There was no time like the present to put his counseling skills to use.

She smiled again, her teeth white against her honeyed complexion, and he temporarily set aside the fact that she might be crazy. He couldn't look away from her.

"For you," she said simply, and his budding fascination deflated.

He returned his banana to the tray. "Say again?"

She fluffed his pillows instead of immediately answering, the scent of soap and what was likely some sort of girly face cream circling him as she leaned in, and given that he had to sit up in order for her to fidget with the pillows, he took an experimental sip of the soup. Its smell was as enticing as hers.

"Gloria sent the food over," she informed him. "And that's fresh-baked bread on the sandwich."

He eyed the sandwich, and his stomach growled. There was roast beef piled high between the two slices of sourdough. "Back to *you*." He ignored the meal as he leaned onto the freshly plumped pillows. "I'm quite certain you didn't come to Birch Bay for *me*. As I wasn't even here."

"I'm aware of that. And it took me until the wedding to figure out who I *was* here for." She pulled a straight-backed chair over from the corner and plopped down in it. "But to be honest, when I drove away from Cheyenne, I didn't even know in what city—or *state*—I would end up."

He was starting to feel like a character in a Stephen King novel. Trapped in a bed . . . being taken care of by a madwoman . . . one ankle was *already* broken . . .

He ignored the visual of the character Kathy Bates had played in the movie and swallowed a spoonful of soup. He also ran through a list of potential responses if he called Nate in the middle of the night and requested an immediate pickup. Nate would show up, for sure. But he'd also be spouting an "I told you so"—or more—which Jaden wouldn't want to hear.

"So you just woke up one morning and left?" He returned to the conversation at hand. "Because you had somewhere else to be? You were *needed* somewhere?"

"Correct."

She was coming across as crazier by the second.

He peeked at her while spooning another bite. "And what did your family think of that?"

She gave an unconcerned shrug. "My family is rarely surprised by anything I do."

"So that means . . . what? That they're all as nuts as you?" He said the words jokingly, but he watched closely for her response. After all, the woman thought she was there to help *him*. And he was the last person who needed any help.

The light that had been in her eyes dimmed. "My three older brothers are all doctors," she stated in a bored tone. "As is my dad. They're all married, with very normal wives and lives, and my mother is a retired elementary school teacher. She works for the State Museum now, and she and Dad plan to retire within the next ten years and travel around, helping out those in poverty-stricken areas who don't have easy access to medical personnel."

Jaden waited—impressed by the rundown on her family—but also guessing there was more to the story. After another minute, she made a face.

"And I'm the only crazy one of the bunch, okay? Is that what you're waiting to hear?"

She crossed her arms and stared back at him, and though there was no doubt she was coming across as mentally disturbed, he also picked up on a flare of intelligence in her eyes. As if daring him to a game of chess, all the while knowing she held a world title.

Or maybe daring him to ask her to prove her stability.

Something about the challenge intrigued him. He wasn't sold on her sanity, that was for sure. But he also seemed to be okay with her level of *insanity*.

Did that make *him* the crazy one?

"Why would you think I need help?" He asked his question with care.

Did he need help?

And how was it that a simple conversation with her suddenly had him questioning himself?

"I don't just think it." The challenge disappeared from her eyes and was replaced with silent understanding. "I *know* it."

He pulled in a slow breath. "What kind of help?"

She looked away from him then, her gaze making a pass over every item in the room. She took in the bags his brother had dropped off, his mangled ankle, his crutches, and everything else that had likely been brought in just for him. And when their eyes reconnected, a new level of tenderness glowed back. "Why are you here, Jaden?" she asked softly. "Why would you ask someone you barely know to help you out, fully aware of how little you're going to be able to do on your own, when you have multiple family members living within a handful of miles? All of whom are willing to do anything you ask."

He didn't immediately reply.

"What has you so afraid to stay in the house you grew up in?"

"Nothing has me *afraid*." Irritation flared at the assumption. "I stay at the house all the time."

"Okay. When?"

He scowled. How had this conversation turned into him defending *his* actions? "We come in for harvest every July. All of us stay there for a couple of weeks. Then there's Christmas. Weddings." He shot her a smirk.

"Then why not now?"

Before he could say anything, she went on.

"Why not stay with Dani or Nick if it's the house you have a problem with?"

"I don't—"

"Or is your issue with your whole family?" She watched him, and the way she seemed to see inside his thoughts made him fidget where he sat. "Maybe you refused their offers because the situation is different this time. You're not the soon-to-be counselor coming home to impart your wisdom"—tenderness once again seeped into her eyes—"but *you're* the one needing help?"

His jaw dropped at the suggestion. "You don't have a clue what you're talking about."

And he couldn't believe he was sitting there listening to this.

He had the thought to push up. To get out of the bed and get the hell out of the building. But the irony of the situation hit him. He was exactly where he'd asked to be, and he *couldn't* leave. Even if he wanted to.

"Maybe I don't," she conceded. "But I do believe I'm on the right track."

She went quiet for a moment, her eyes studying him with an intensity that made every nerve ending in his body attempt to scream at once, and he didn't know if he wanted to hear *what* she was thinking or if he wanted to start ringing the bell again, making it so loud he couldn't hear his own thoughts.

"Does it have to do with your mom?" she asked, and his pulse pounded in his neck.

Didn't everything have to do with his mom?

"Do you want me to leave?" he ground out instead of giving credence to her question. "Is that what you're hinting at? You've changed your mind, and you don't want me here after all?"

"I'm not hinting at anything. I'm perfectly fine with you being here. I wouldn't have suggested it if I wasn't."

He glared at her. "Then what's the problem?"

"*I* don't have a problem."

"Neither do *I*." His temper shot higher.

"Yet still"—she looked around the room once again—"here you are, aren't you?"

Anger burned hot, but instead of being ticked at her directness, he found that he was more annoyed with her comprehension. What did she know about his mother? And who had told her?

91

Had Dani shared things about their childhoods? About *him?*

He mentally shook his head. He didn't think she'd do that. Not with an employee.

Erica could have, though. She and Arsula were clearly good enough friends that she'd had her in the wedding. Except Erica didn't know all that much herself. Not about him, at least. She'd only moved to Birch Bay last fall, and they'd met just the one time over Christmas. Of course, he had no idea what Gabe might have shared with her.

He studied Arsula, trying to see more than the woman who claimed she'd come to Birch Bay for him, and he decided it was time to turn the tables. "Why don't *you* tell me why I'm here? You're the one who thinks she knows so much. Why am I here, Arsula? Why would I rather ask you to play nursemaid, a woman I just met—and who we both agree might be a tad unstable—instead of going home and staying with my dad?"

"I never agreed to any instability."

"Fine." He found himself on the verge of a smile at her instant rebuttal. "We'll leave that open for discussion. But why you? What is it about *you*"—his tone grew both serious and soft—"that makes *me* so comfortable I'd ask this of you?"

He really did want an answer to that question.

"It's because of my great-aunt Sul," she stated simply. Then she stood from the chair and began fiddling with the bag of ice on his foot.

"The woman you're named after?" He recalled her mentioning an aunt at the hospital.

"One of the women I'm named after." She removed the ice and refastened his splint, all without looking at him. "She was also named after her grandmother, and there were a handful more before her."

He had the feeling this conversation was about to dip into crazy again. "And what about your great-aunt Sul makes me want to be here with you?"

Dark eyes once again met his, and he'd swear an added level of quietness suddenly infiltrated the room. Or maybe it was calmness.

Whatever it was, it made the back of his neck itch.

"Many generations down my mother's side of the family," she began, "our relatives were full Navajo. Only a small percentage remains in our blood today, but something other than blood has continued to be passed down to the women in the family."

"Something other than your name?"

"Exactly."

He wished he could stand up. Lying there like this put him at a disadvantage. "And what is that?"

Her expression was one of both pride and hesitation. "Gifts."

He didn't say anything for a moment. Instead, he thought about the Native Americans he'd known over the years. Birch Bay butted up against a reservation, and he knew of many people who were highly spiritual. Some even created powders and balms for medicinal purposes. But he wasn't sure about "gifts."

"I assume you're not talking about old trunks and quilts," he said, and a smile touched her mouth.

"Those, too, actually. I have a one-hundred-year-old trunk in my bedroom that once belonged to my great-great-grandmother, and in it are several quilts handed down over the years."

He recalled seeing the trunk as he'd rushed to get dressed. "And your great-aunt has a gift?"

"*Had* a gift." A wistful look passed over her. "We lost her several years ago."

"I'm sorry." He could tell her aunt had meant a lot to her.

"Thank you."

"So what was Great-Aunt Sul's gift?" he asked after a moment of silence.

"One of comfort. Dozens of people would stop in to see her every day. They wanted to be around her. To talk with her. And they always left in a more positive state of mind."

He could buy that. He'd met similar people with an ability to put others at ease. Heck, that was partially the point of counseling. *Still* . . . he wouldn't refer to that as a gift. "And you think that's why I asked you to let me stay here?" he hedged. "Because you, *too*, have this gift?"

"No." She gathered the tray he'd forgotten about, and he realized he'd plowed through the entire meal. After setting the tray by the door, Arsula returned and pushed the button to lower the head of his bed. "I didn't get Aunt Sul's gift. Typically, each woman is born with a unique ability. But what Aunt Sul *did* do for me was to teach me to respect *my* gift. As well as to expand upon it." She closed her eyes as she continued to talk and laid her hands over her heart. "If you listen, all answers can be found inside you."

Jaden just watched. Apparently, Aunt Sul was where the crazy had come from.

"Everyone is born with the ability to intuit things," she continued, opening her eyes once again. "Some more than others, but we all have it. Even you. Only, most people quit listening to the whispers as they pass their childhood years. They're too busy being taught facts and science instead."

"There's a lot to be said for facts and science."

"True. But there's also nothing wrong with listening to your inner self."

Yep. Nate had been right. Screws loose.

"And one of the things *I* do is to help others reconnect with that ability," she told him.

"To listen to their . . . *inner selves?*"

The peace that had seemed to transfix her only moments before evaporated the instant disbelief slipped into his voice. "Yes. And do not make fun of me. I don't appreciate it, nor will I tolerate it."

"Fair enough." He'd keep those particular thoughts to himself. "So is that your gift then? To teach others to listen to their intuition?"

"No, that's my *skill*, and I'm very good at it. I also picked up a few tips from the time I spent with Aunt Sul, and though I don't come close to what she was capable of, I'm pretty darn good at comforting people as well."

He could agree with that. Because although she stood there talking crazy, and although she apparently thought she carried some sort of magical power inside her . . . this was *still* where he wanted to be. And not solely because he didn't want to go home. "Then what is your gift?"

He couldn't believe he'd even asked that question, but as her features once again morphed, he once again wished he wasn't horizontal. Because something warned him he wasn't going to like her answer.

"My gift is the ability to read dreams."

Yep. It didn't take him long at all to put two and two together.

"Read dreams?"

Arsula watched as Jaden pushed back in the bed, as if desperate to get away from her.

"*You're* the nutjob Megan talked to?"

"Well, I've never really considered putting 'nutjob' on a business card." Arsula didn't blink. Nutjob wasn't even a unique term.

"You told her to leave me," Jaden accused.

"I never *told* her to do anything."

"That's right." His disgust filled the room. "You just told her that I wasn't the right person for her."

She did her best to remain calm. "I only helped her to understand what her subconscious was already saying."

"You don't have a *clue* what her subconscious was saying, lady." He scraped his gaze down her, the intent clearly meant as derogatory. "Who do you think you are, anyway? Talking to me about *gifts* and *intuition*."

She grasped her hands loosely in front of her. Otherwise she might be tempted to throw something else at him. "Are you seriously going to tell me that you don't believe in intuition, Jaden? Not even a little bit? Or that you haven't studied dreams in any of your psychology classes?"

"Of course I've studied dreams."

"Then you must know that dreams are your subconscious's way of speaking to you."

He remained jammed into the bed's far corner. "That's one theory."

"And what are others?"

She could see his anger ratchet up at the mere fact she'd questioned him. "Don't talk to me as if you have any real knowledge on the subject," he fired back. "I'll bet you don't even have a day of education."

His ability to lob a bullet and land on the bone of contention between her and her father annoyed her. "I assume you're referring to formal education?"

"I'm certainly not referring to 'Lessons from Aunt Sul.'"

Now *her* anger rose. And she quit clasping her hands together.

"Do *not* go there, Jaden. I have three older brothers, and I know how to fight dirty." She dragged her gaze over the length of him, same as he'd done to her, and made sure to linger on his obvious incapacitation. "You don't want to know how uncomfortable I could make you tonight."

His mouth hung open. "So now you're threatening me?"

"Did you hear a threat?" She picked up his pain pills and rattled them in the air. "All I'd have to do is flush these babies down the toilet and take your crutches upstairs with me." Her eyes flicked to the fridge beside his bed. "I could also take your cell phone. Make sure you can't even call one of your big brothers for help."

Hatred stared back at her. "You knocked me down the stairs intentionally, didn't you?"

"Oh, *please*." She was done with this conversation. Just as she was done trying to explain herself to those too set in their ways to understand it. She put the pills back on the fridge, turned out the overhead light, and picked up the tray she'd left by the door. "Ring the bell whenever someone shows up to get you. It'll be my pleasure to let them in."

Chapter Nine

He hadn't called anyone to come get him. And he'd wanted to regret that fact for the last four days.

He hadn't regretted it, though. Nor had he figured out *why* he hadn't called.

But he also hadn't caved and offered Arsula so much as a polite word.

The woman was a damned lunatic who didn't have a clue what she was talking about. He *was* the right person for Megan. He always had been, and he always would be. He just had to get Megan to talk to him again so he could remind her of that.

And there was nothing whatsoever that *he* needed help with.

Jaden's back teeth ground together at the very thought. Yes, he had mommy issues. So what? Or, he'd *had* mommy issues. But he'd gone to counseling throughout college—with a *real* counselor—and he'd overcome those issues. He was totally healthy now. Both mentally and . . .

He glared at his foot midway through his thought. He was *almost* physically healthy.

But that wasn't anything Arsula could help him with. Just like his emotional well-being wasn't.

She was a flake. Period. End of story.

He scowled at the television as he flipped from one soap opera to the next, before he thumbed the "Off" button and threw the remote across the room. His aim was off, however, and instead of making a resounding smack against the wall, the remote landed unimpressively on a blanket draped over the back of the couch. Which only irritated him more.

He growled under his breath. Days of being laid up in his sister's office, with only pity visits from his brothers, and he was nearing stark-raving mad. It was bad enough to be immobile, but immobile *and* hours on end of being alone could make a man do irrational things.

He glanced through the open doors to the woman sitting twenty feet away from him.

Like consider making up excuses for the very person who'd ruined his life to have to do more than bring him food and grudgingly show up when he rang her damned bell.

He swung his legs out of the bed and reached for his crutches. Thankfully, he was mostly off the heavy pain meds, and from the looks of things, the majority of the swelling had gone down. His ankle still hurt like a mother on occasion. Especially if he tried to do much more than hobble to the bathroom and back. But at least he could now get through a portion of each day with his eyes open instead of closed.

Of course, that only meant he had more time to sit there and stare at Arsula.

He made it into the hallway, ignoring the sound of yet another person entering the office and greeting his nemesis, then slammed the bathroom door behind him. Scowling into the mirror, he scrubbed a hand over his jaw. He needed a shave as well as a shower—he'd refused to take one when Nate had stopped by the day before.

And possibly, he needed to quit doing his best to ensure that Arsula didn't *want* to spend any extra time around him. He'd stayed. That had been his choice. So now he could either stay and spend every moment of every night sitting alone in his room. Or he could attempt to foster some sort of truce.

But dammit, she'd told Megan to break up with him.

He frowned into the mirror and asked himself why he was still there. Why was he letting what she'd done be okay?

Then he answered his own question. Because he still didn't want to sit around the house he'd grown up in, having to depend on someone to take care of him. He still didn't want to ask his siblings to take care of him.

And he was furious at Megan for *not* taking care of him.

Damn her for dumping him.

Turning from the mirror, he took care of business and washed his hands, and when he started back out of the room, one of his crutches caught on the edge of an uneven floorboard. He stumbled, slamming his shoulder into the door facing while his head whacked against the frame. Then he caught himself on his other crutch. Forward momentum didn't cease as he spun around, the top half of him tilting precariously, and then he hopped, dropping both worthless pieces of sticks as he windmilled. Until he crashed face-first into the opposite wall.

Stars swam above him as he clenched his jaw, and all talking in the front room ceased.

"Jaden?"

He didn't respond.

He couldn't see who else might be with Arsula, but he knew that whoever it was, *both* of them were looking in his direction. That's another thing he hadn't thought through before committing to staying here. That he would be little more than a monkey in a cage. With Arsula's work area right off his makeshift bedroom, every single person who entered the building spent a good amount of time looking at *him*.

And a lot of people had entered the building in the last four days.

Arsula's face appeared in the doorway. "You okay?"

She had on a pale-pink sweater today and a dainty scarf tied around her neck, and the way she'd made up her eyes with thick liner made him think of movie stars from the 1950s.

"I'm fine." He refused to be the invalid he was. "Just making sure you're paying attention."

Her lips pursed as if silently calling him the moron that he was, and she retrieved his fallen crutches. "Do you want me to help you back into bed?"

"No." He smirked, and after another two seconds of her seeming to contemplate a reply, she silently turned and left. It had been like that all week.

Conversation picked back up the second she was out of sight—some woman telling her about the date she'd been on the night before and how she never would have gotten the man's attention if Arsula hadn't gone shopping with her to help revamp her wardrobe—and Jaden began to slowly make his way back to his room. His ankle throbbed once again, and he would love to take a pain pill. Instead, he grabbed his laptop and hauled it over to the couch. He'd made the needed calls and gotten permission to continue his practicum with Dr. Wangler until he could get back to Seattle, so he'd contacted a neighbor to pack up his computer and overnight it.

In order to complete his degree, he had one class to finish—which he'd already been taking online—the therapy sessions to both observe and participate in, as well as the required paperwork and a weekly discussion associated with the sessions. Then there was his thesis. And all of that would now have to be completed with his foot either in this stupid splint, in a cast—which apparently came next—or in an eventual walking boot. Which, funnily enough, didn't mean he'd be walking. At least not at first.

He eyed the crutches propped next to him. He suspected the three of them were going to become excellent friends over the next few weeks.

Flipping open his laptop, he decided anything school-related could wait. He couldn't very well take care of the work he had to complete without a desk, could he? So he'd order one . . . which he'd then make Arsula help him put together.

A baby's laughter came from the front of the building, and he leaned forward to see into the other room. Some woman who looked to be about his age had just come in, baby on her hip, and Jaden watched as the baby cooed at whatever Arsula said. She took the baby, jostling it in front of her as the child's mother began to relay a story about how things were going much better between her and the baby's father, and Jaden leaned back against the couch. When did she manage to get any work done around here?

It seemed half the town had come through the place in the span of a few days. And though he assumed some of it had to do with him—likely trying to figure out why he was there, maybe even *why* he'd been at Arsula's place Sunday morning to begin with—there was no way all of them were merely seeking gossip. Arsula Moretti was an enchantress, reeling them in. And from what he could tell, all they wanted to do was talk. Meaning, they were *not* stopping by for his sister's services.

Yet, half the town seeking Arsula out or not, he refused to believe the foot traffic had anything to do with any sort of "gift." That was just ludicrous.

He listened for another minute as the two women continued chattering about the current state of the mother's love life, then realizing that his ankle still throbbed, he inched forward on the cushion until he could prop his foot on the end of his bed. Except, that left his head the only part of his anatomy still touching the back of the couch. He couldn't sit like that, so he got up and hopped on one foot as he tugged against the sofa. The darned thing was heavy, and he'd barely made any progress when the PR executive who worked alongside Dani stuck his head through the hallway door.

"Making a lot of noise out here today," Tim observed. He glanced at the activity going on out front before stepping farther into the room. "Need some help?"

"I'm sorry about that, man." Jaden had met Tim earlier in the week. He didn't come into the office every day, and now Jaden felt bad that he'd disturbed him. "I just need to—" He motioned to the problematic piece of furniture, then let his hands drop in defeat. "I'm trying to scoot this over so I can prop up my foot while sitting."

"Not a problem." Tim helped him move the couch, angling it so Jaden and his crutches could still get between it and the bed, but shifting the far end so the bed's footboard could do double duty as a footrest.

"That'll work," Jaden told him. With the couch now repositioned, he tried it out again, and this time he could both sit upright *and* prop his foot.

He could also see Arsula.

Tim stood at his side, seeming in no hurry to get back to his own work, and it took only a matter of seconds for Jaden to understand why.

"She may not be the most efficient office manager in the world," Tim mused, his eyes never leaving Arsula as she continued to play with the baby, "but I'll tell you, she certainly gives life to the place."

Jaden wasn't sure the place needed life given to it. "Aren't you married, Tim?"

Tim cut a look at him, accompanied by a half smile. "Happily. With three kids, two dogs, and a substantial mortgage."

"Then maybe you should get back to work so you can make payments on that mortgage."

Tim chuckled. "Maybe I should."

He lowered to sit on the arm of the couch.

Arsula laughed at the same time the baby did, the sounds filling the space and her entire face transforming into the type of beauty Jaden suspected women might kill for. With her dark eyes shining as bright as her smile and the soft curves of her jawline giving her, at the same time, the look of innocence and youth as well as that of a sultry vixen, he couldn't peel his eyes off her.

The way she looked when she smiled was probably why so many people stopped in to see her all the time. Even the women were awestruck.

When she leaned forward and handed the baby across the bar-height portion of the reception desk, her body stretching out as she did, both Jaden and Tim held their breath. Her sweater rode up, exposing a couple of inches of bronze skin, and her black slacks showcased a perfectly rounded rear.

"*Damn,*" Tim muttered. He headed for his office. "I need to go call my wife."

And Jaden needed to text his girlfriend.

The office door on the other side of the hallway closed, and the baby and its mother left the building . . . and then Arsula whipped around. She pinned him with a stare.

"Did you need something back there?"

He shook his head. He just needed his girlfriend back.

"Then quit staring at my behind."

"Oh my gawd." Maggie Crowder stopped five feet from the table Friday night, arms out in front of her and hands pressed palms out, and she looked like someone about to break into song. "It's an Arsula miracle. Coming out of hiding after a full week of captivity."

Arsula smirked. "Funny. But you know I haven't been hiding."

"I *know.*" Maggie slid into the booth, giving Erica a "hey, hon" as she settled in beside their other friend, and snagged a tortilla chip from the bowl in the middle of the table. Instead of eating it, though, she pointed it at Arsula. "Apparently you've been shacked up with Jaden Wilde all week."

Arsula glared at her friend. "Shut up. I have not."

"Hey. I'm just repeating what I've heard."

"I've heard it, too," Erica confirmed. She grabbed her own chip and scooped out a bite of salsa. "I hadn't been in the gym for two minutes last night before three different people accosted me and asked if it was true that Jaden had dumped Megan and hooked up with you."

"What?" Horror filled Arsula. That wasn't at all what had happened!

"Don't worry." Erica reached across the table and patted her hand. "I told them they had it wrong. That you've just gone into the adult babysitting business now, as well as that of dream interpretation."

"And I told them that the real truth was even fatter and juicier than they thought." Maggie waggled her brows, and Arsula kicked her under the table.

"You'd better not have said anything like that." This was the first time the three of them had been able to get together since the wedding, and she wouldn't be there tonight if Gabe and Jenna hadn't promised to stay with Jaden until she got back.

Not that she spent evenings sitting by Jaden's side. The jerk was still acting jerky—remaining sullen throughout the days, while ringing that blasted bell in the middle of the night . . . *every single night*—but that didn't mean she would leave him on his own until it was safe to do so.

"Did one of you stand up for Megan, at least? This was her decision. *She* did the breaking up."

"Of course we did." Maggie munched on another chip. "But that doesn't mean we can't have some fun with you as well."

Her friends had asked about the night of the wedding, of course, and along with skimming over the breakup, she'd relayed the same watered-down version of why Jaden had been at her place that she'd originally offered at the hospital. She didn't make a habit of keeping things from her friends, but she had no idea what Jaden might have shared with his family. She'd also been unsure if she wanted to admit how far things had really gone with him. At least not over the phone or while sitting at her desk with Jaden looking on.

A server showed up with three margaritas, this not being the first time they'd visited the establishment on a Friday night, and asked if they wanted their regular entrees. After they were alone once again, Arsula turned to Erica. She was about to send the conversation into a full 180, but the longer she'd sat around that week, *not* talking to Jaden, the more she'd known she had to ask.

"What can you tell me about Jaden's mother?" she said, and Erica froze in the act of bringing her straw to her mouth.

"What do you want to know?"

Everything, Arsula thought. The more she learned, the better she could help.

"Everything" was too broad, though.

Maggie sipped at her drink as Arsula rephrased her question. "What was she like as a mother?"

She already knew a little. When Erica and Gabe had first been dating, his ex-wife had come back into the picture, and apparently the woman had been a lot like Gabe's mother. Meaning, manipulative and selfish. That had been the gist of what Erica had shared—along with the fact that Gabe continued to suffer hang-ups from his childhood.

But what kind of hang-ups, and *why,* Arsula could only guess.

"I wasn't around then," Erica stalled. "I didn't meet Gabe for the first time until after she was gone and we were in college."

Erica often dodged when the subject of Carol Wilde came up, and though that act alone piqued Arsula's interest, she'd always let it drop. She'd seen no need to push a subject her friend obviously didn't want to discuss.

Only, Jaden was in the picture now. And she suspected that Carol Wilde's behavior had affected him as well.

"But you have to know something about her," Arsula pressed. "You're married to her oldest son."

"I am."

Maggie watched with interest now, her drink forgotten.

"Then, other than being a self-centered witch," Arsula continued, "what do you know about her? What was she like? And just what kind of lasting impact did she leave on Gabe?"

"I always thought of her as being well put together and doting on her family," Maggie offered when the pause between Arsula's question and an answer from Erica went on too long.

Erica's response was a sarcastic grunt.

"So she really wasn't?" Maggie asked. Maggie had been there before and heard the same information as Arsula, but Arsula suspected she struggled with balancing the image formed years ago with what little info Erica had provided.

"She . . ." Erica looked pained. "The family doesn't like to talk about her," she explained. "And certainly not publicly. And honestly, I really don't know all that much." Worry creased the space between her eyes. "Why do you want to know, anyway? Did something happen that night that you aren't telling us about? Are you interested in Jaden?"

"No," Arsula immediately responded, but then she offered a slight grimace. "Okay, *yes*. Something happened that I haven't shared. But *no*, I'm not interested in Jaden. Not like that."

"Then how are you interested in him?"

"And what *did* happen?" Maggie added.

"One question at a time." Arsula turned to Maggie first, and even before she began, a weight lifted from her chest. She'd been needing to talk about this with her girls. "I might have *slightly* exaggerated the simplicity of him being at my place Saturday night."

Maggie slapped a hand on the table, and a wide smile appeared. "I knew it. You *did* sleep with him."

"*Shhhh.*" Arsula leaned in and prayed no one had heard that. "*No. I didn't. I just . . . tried to.*"

The other two leaned in as well. "You what?" they asked simultaneously.

Guilt continued to weigh on her. Sleeping with a client's ex wasn't exactly her norm, and the excuse of too much alcohol only went so far. She still couldn't understand how she'd let herself end up there. "There was a lot of alcohol that night," she attempted to explain. "Some laughing . . . some kissing . . ."

Neither of them said anything, clearly waiting for the rest of the story, so Arsula scrunched up her nose and finished. "And if he hadn't had too much to drink, we *would* have had sex."

"Would have?" Maggie questioned.

"He . . . *ummm*"—Arsula cast a quick glance around but found no one paying obvious attention—"couldn't finish."

Both women snorted and then fell into a fit of giggles.

"I know." Arsula attempted to shush them again. "But really, it wasn't funny. It *still* isn't funny."

"He couldn't get it up," Maggie choked out, this time pulling the attention of a couple of nearby diners, and she reached for her purse. "How is that possibly not funny?"

"Stop it," Arsula pleaded. "You know how men can be. A little too much, and . . ."

"Gabe isn't like that."

Arsula rolled her eyes at her friend. "I doubt 'Gabe-the-stud' has ever come close to drinking the amount of liquor Jaden put away."

"Possibly." Erica took a large gulp of her drink. "And if that's the result, I won't ever encourage it."

"I wouldn't recommend it," Arsula replied wryly. "I mean, don't get me wrong. I'm glad the evening didn't end the *other* way. But man, too much alcohol can certainly leave a girl wanting." And honestly, she *was* glad they hadn't had sex. She'd just gotten worked up, and then . . . *hadn't* gotten to finish.

Maggie snorted again, then she put a twenty into Erica's now-waiting hand, and Arsula sat back in her seat. She gaped at her friends. "Oh my God. Did you two bet on me?"

"Of course we did," Maggie answered. "We knew you were holding back."

"What was the bet?" She looked from friend to friend.

"I bet that you *did* sleep with him," Maggie answered.

"And I bet that you started to, but that you changed your mind and stopped before it went all the way."

"Well then, it seems you both lost." She reached over and plucked the twenty away from Erica. "Because though I didn't sleep with him, it also wasn't that I *changed* my mind. Therefore, I claim the money." She made a production of folding the bill and tucking it into her jeans, and as her fingers slipped free of her front pocket, she became aware that several people had turned to look in their direction.

A server arrived with their food, and while Maggie and Erica offered smiles of thanks, Arsula clued in to why they were now being looked at. Or rather, why *she* was.

"Ah, crap," she murmured.

"What?" Maggie peered up from her steaming skillet of fajitas, then glanced around when she realized Arsula was watching someone. Erica followed suit.

They both quit scanning the crowd as their gazes landed on Megan.

"We're both being talked about," Arsula whispered. "And I hate that. I didn't think about how helping out Jaden might affect her."

"Don't worry about it," Erica soothed. She reached over and patted Arsula's hand. "Some people always have to have something to talk about. There's nothing you'll ever be able to do to stop that."

"Well, I wish they'd talk about the weather instead of me."

"There's snow on the ground," Maggie droned in a monotone, still keeping her eyes on the crowd and on Megan. "It's cold outside. The end."

All three of them chuckled, and then Erica and Maggie both silently faced her.

"What?" she asked, suddenly feeling an itch running the length of her spine.

"You didn't finish your story," Erica explained.

"Yes, I did. We tried, he failed, the end."

"Nice try," Maggie acknowledged. She pointed her fork at Arsula, a bite of chicken speared on the tines. "But we need to know the rest. He couldn't finish, we can assume he either passed out or fell asleep, but *how* did the man break his ankle?"

"And *why* did you take him in?"

Arsula snuck another peek at Megan, who'd settled in with a couple of other ladies on the other side of the room. Megan was a good person. She cared about the town, even though she hadn't grown up there, and she'd uprooted her life for her boyfriend's family when they'd needed the help. She didn't deserve to be talked about just because she'd made a decision to move in a different direction with her life.

"Has Megan said anything?" she asked instead of answering their questions.

"About what?" Erica said. "The breakup?"

"That. And about Jaden staying at the office."

"Nothing, as far as I know. She's just acknowledged that the breakup did happen. She did call me about renting the apartment, though." Erica owned an apartment across from her house with Gabe that had been a fire hall in a previous life. She'd rented it when she'd first moved to town, and had fallen so in love with the place, she'd decided to buy it.

Arsula pulled her eyes back to Erica. "Are you going to rent it to her?"

"She's already moved in."

Ah. She hadn't been aware of that.

"Good for her," she said, and this time, her approval of Megan's decision to leave the Wilde house had nothing to do with what might be best for Jaden and everything to do with Megan.

"Do you have any idea *why* she broke up with him?" Maggie questioned before cramming a bite of fajita into her mouth.

"I do."

"Why?" they asked at the same time.

"And when?" Erica added. "They came to the wedding *together*."

"But they weren't speaking to each other *at* the wedding," Maggie pointed out. "I noticed that. And it was her avoiding him. *And* she left early."

"Exactly." Arsula lowered her voice. "Because she ended things before the wedding. In the church parking lot."

"Ouch." Maggie grimaced.

"I know."

"So that's why they sat in his car for so long?" Understanding dawned on Erica's face. "Gabe knew they'd broken up, but even he didn't know exactly when."

Arsula didn't fill them in on the fact that a proposal had led to the breakup. Jaden could share that nugget if he chose to.

"But why did she break up with him?" Maggie asked. "They've been together for several years, and weren't they planning on moving here after he finishes his degree? I expected them to eventually get married."

"He did, too," Arsula answered honestly, and she tried to figure out how best to explain Megan's decision without revealing too much. She'd never taken any sort of oath of secrecy, but sharing one-on-one conversations felt like a mistrust of privacy.

It turned out she didn't have to explain, though, because Maggie guessed it.

"She had a dream," Maggie stated, and Arsula nodded.

"About Jaden?"

"About her comfort level *within* their relationship."

Erica glanced at Megan. "And you think she'll stick to it?"

"I do." Arsula didn't let herself look at the other woman again. She suspected Megan already felt uncomfortable enough. "I know she still cares for him, though. She was clear about that. They were friends first. And they didn't have a big fight or a major disagreement that led to the breakup. He just isn't the right person for her, and she realized that before it was too late."

"Poor Megan," Erica murmured.

Arsula and Maggie agreed. Any breakup was hard.

"She'll rebound." Arsula didn't doubt that fact. Megan was a sharp, capable woman. And she *would* find the correct person for her. Whenever the timing was right.

The three of them fell silent for several minutes as they ate, before Maggie pushed her plate away and crossed her arms on the table. She leaned in, her gaze locking on Arsula. "Time's up," she announced. "No more avoiding. How did Jaden end up falling down your stairs?"

"And don't feed us any the-steps-were-icy bullcrap."

Arsula hid her grin as she took a sip of her margarita. "But the steps *were* icy."

"Uh-huh." Erica nodded. "And the man apparently showed up at the hospital not fully dressed."

"That's not true at all," Arsula argued. "And anyway, who told you that? None of his family was even there when he first arrived."

She supposed one of the emergency personnel could have said something. Embellished the story.

"Then why were you pulling his socks out of your coat pocket?" Erica asked, and Arsula froze at the words.

"Caught red-handed," Maggie murmured. "Can we assume he was leaving in a hurry for some reason?"

"You mean, as if he'd woken up and been horrified to find himself in bed with me?"

Maggie gave a tilt of her head. "That's one option."

"And what was *your* thought?"

Maggie and Erica exchanged glances, but they didn't say anything else, and Arsula understood that to mean they were through talking. She had to finish the story.

"Fine. Yes," she groaned out. "He didn't handle waking up with me well, okay? In fact, he might have handled the situation so poorly that I could have possibly . . . maybe . . . *helped* him to leave a little faster than he'd intended."

They both grinned. They'd each witnessed her flare-ups before, though her anger had never been directed at them.

"What did you do?" Erica asked, and Arsula wouldn't have been surprised to see her rub her hands together as any good cartoon villain might. She sounded downright greedy for the answer.

Arsula sighed. "I threw a vase at him. Then I threw a book." She puckered her mouth in disgust. "And possibly I threw a lamp after that—just as his foot reached for the first step."

Her friends cackled with laughter when she finished, and this time every diner surrounding their table turned their way.

Then Erica pulled a twenty from *her* purse. "I lose," she declared.

Arsula stared in shock. "Are you kidding me? You bet on whether I threw something at him or not?"

"No." Maggie passed the money in front of her nose and smelled it. "We bet on whether you pushed him down the stairs or not. And then took him in out of guilt."

Arsula reached across the table and snatched the second twenty. "I was fifteen feet away when he fell. I didn't *push*. And guilt isn't the reason, either." She checked her voice again, realizing she'd gotten too loud, then she leaned in close. "*He's* the reason I'm here," she whispered. They both knew how she'd ended up in Birch Bay. "He's the one," she repeated, her excitement now palpable. "He's the person I was meant to help."

Chapter Ten

The tension in the office had remained throughout the weekend and into the middle of the week, and at this point, Arsula was almost ready to beg for forgiveness. She was tired of walking on eggshells.

Jaden had continued being his grumpy self. However, since she'd called him out for staring at her behind the week before, she'd now swear that whenever she stood from her seat, he did it even more. She hadn't made a production of catching him in the act like she had the first time, but she had noticed that whenever she either pulled the shades she'd had Tim install on Jaden's doors, or closed the doors altogether, the second she stepped out of the room and came back, Jaden's view was always unobstructed.

She was pretty sure everything he did at this point was to push her buttons. She'd been around enough brothers and past boyfriends to know when a man was being a pain in the rear simply for the fun of it. But given that she'd still barely said more to him than "are you ready for food" and "do you need anything," she didn't know him well enough to say for sure.

And wasn't that proving herself worthy? She'd declared she'd come here because he needed her, yet she'd done her level best not to speak to him since then. Aunt Sul would *not* be proud.

"That's all I can manage today," Dani announced as she exited her office. "I have a baby at home who needs her mama to come feed her. Not to mention I'm exhausted after taking almost four months off."

Dani's first day back had been today, and she'd made it until noon.

Arsula winked. "I'd say you did good. Four full hours."

Dani shot her a teasing smile as she gathered her coat. "There are benefits to being the owner of the business." She shrugged into her jacket and slung a tote over her shoulder. "I am available the rest of the day, though. I'm officially back on the job. So if anything pops up, let me know, and the moment Mia isn't crying, I'll get on the phone and play grown-up."

"You got it, boss."

Dani left, hunching her shoulders against the wind as she hurried to her car, and after she was out of sight, Arsula took a moment to stare at the reflection in the front window. She could see Jaden's empty bed as clear as if she were turned to face it, and a pang of worry tapped against her breastbone. He'd talked Nate into taking him to Dr. Wangler's for his first observation session an hour ago. Arsula hadn't thought he was ready, but he'd insisted to everyone that he was fine. He'd just be watching from another room, and he could keep his foot propped up as he did so.

Still, she worried. He hadn't even had his first checkup with his surgeon yet.

His absence gave her a rare sense of freedom, though, as for the first time in a week and a half, she could focus her energy on something other than ignoring him. And her first order of business was to reach out to Megan.

Since seeing her Friday night, she'd been feeling more like they needed to have another chat. Only, this time to make sure the *two* of them were okay. Possibly to try to explain the night of the wedding—though she wasn't sure doing so would be of any real benefit.

Things had happened between her and Jaden. *True.* And hate it as she might, she couldn't take it back. Nor would she deny the facts if questioned. The reality was, though, that Megan and Jaden *had* been broken up. And if a conversation *was* needed, her instinct said it should happen between Megan and Jaden.

Still . . . she could check in with Megan. It would be the right thing to do.

She pulled her cell out from under a pile of papers and punched in a text.

> Hey. So . . . the night of the wedding . . . I feel like we might need to meet up and talk.

No reply came within a couple of minutes, so she decided she would definitely seek her out.

Her second order of business was to call her mother.

Propping her tablet on her desk, she scrolled through the contacts until she found her mother and tapped the button to make a video call. When she'd looked at the calendar that morning, she'd realized she hadn't spoken with her family since before Jaden's accident. And she usually called home at least once a week.

While waiting for the call to connect, she loaded her email on her phone and pulled up her consultant account. Until Jaden had become her priority, she'd regularly used lunch hours to handle personal business. And now that she'd been in town for several months, along with requests for individual dream interpretation, she also got invites to be the entertainment at events. People would often seek her out, wanting her to attend a bridal shower or a girls' night out, and if her schedule allowed, she always agreed. Social events were how she met a lot of the people she knew, and oftentimes, a true client would arise from the lighthearted fun.

"It's about time you called."

She glanced away from the list of emails that had come in over the last nine days and smiled at the sight of her mother's rounded face. "Hi, Mom. Sorry for missing last week. I've been extra busy lately."

"I suspected as much. I don't suppose it's been baby-making kind of busy, has it?"

Arsula scowled. Her mother was often as off-kilter as she was. "I swear, Mother. One of these days I'm going to answer that question with a yes. And *then* what are you going to do?"

"Well, I'm going to tell your dad, is what. And he'll dance with joy, just like I will."

Arsula shot her mom a look. Her parents were very much enjoying their three grandkids—soon to be four—and though her mom might like to tease her that it was time she did her part by adding to the herd, she and her mother both knew her father would have a stroke if his single baby girl turned up pregnant.

"Neither of you would dance with joy if I answered with yes, so don't even pretend otherwise."

Her mother's smile turned gentle. "If the yes came with the love of your life, I would."

"Yeah, well"—she glanced at the reflection in the glass again—"I'm not sure the love of my life lives in Montana. At least, not in Birch Bay. But I'll keep looking."

The view on the screen bounced as her mother moved, and Arsula could tell from the glimpses of the background that her mom was at work. At the same time, Arsula's cell buzzed with an incoming text.

"Are you busy, Mom?" The text was from Megan. "Do I need to call you back?"

"Of course you don't. I'm just taking you into the break room to refill my coffee."

Arsula tapped to open the text window.

No need to meet up. We're good.

The words didn't exactly settle her.

"Refilling coffee is definitely better than one of the many times you've taken me into the bathroom with you to get *rid* of coffee," she pointed out to her mom as she quickly typed out another message.

There are also rumors about what's going on while he's staying here, but nothing is going on. He didn't want to stay at the house, and I'm just trying to help. I feel somewhat responsible since it was my stairs.

She held back on mentioning that it had also been *her* lamp meeting the back of *his* head.

I broke up with *him*, Arsula. Not the other way. And I'm good with that. And YOU know that.

She nodded. She did know that. Another message came in.

Also . . . concerning that night . . . I will admit that it *was* shocking to discover he'd been at your place. And I'm not asking what did or didn't happen because again, we *were* broken up. Any lingering issues with that are between him and me. But I do want to say that . . . well . . . if you *did* decide you wanted to go out with him . . .

Arsula reread the message in confusion.

If I *did* decide I wanted to go out with him . . . what?

I'm just saying . . . my current irritation with him notwithstanding, he is a good guy. And you're a good person . . . And I'd love to see you both happy.

Arsula stared at the follow-up message. Was Megan saying that she'd be okay with it if *she* wanted to go out with Jaden?

But she didn't want to go out with Jaden. Why would Megan even think that?

"So what is it that's keeping you so busy lately?" Her mother's voice sounded from the tablet's position on her desk, and Arsula's attention flew back to the conversation she was supposed to be having.

Her mom took a casual sip of coffee, her eyes slightly narrowed as if trying to figure something out.

"Mostly just working." Arsula set down the phone, then she readjusted the angle of the tablet when she realized Jaden's unmade bed could be seen in the background. "How's Dad?"

"As busy as ever. He flew down to New Mexico over the weekend for a coin show that had a rare dealer attending."

She picked up her phone again. "He's passionate about his coins." She used to go to coin shows with him when she was a kid. "How about Whitney?" She began typing another message. "She and baby still doing okay?"

Whitney was Boyd's very pregnant wife.

"Doing fine. The doctor remains firm on the end of March. Are you still planning to come down?"

She finished tapping out the message and looked back at the tablet. "Am I coming in for the birth of what could potentially be the first girl born into the family? *Absolutely.*" Tradition was that the first girl born per generation was to be named Arsula. Her brother had yet to commit to whether he'd follow tradition if they had a girl, however. "I *would* prefer if Whitney could hold off a few weeks, though. I think my namesake should be born on my birthday."

Her mother laughed, her tone more "yeah, right" than filled with humor. "I'll let Whitney know of your request."

Arsula smiled. "Please do."

She pushed "Send."

I don't know about *dating* . . . but thanks??? And back to the subject at hand. Any chance you'd consider talking to him? I think he's still "confused."

She wasn't sure how much Jaden talking to Megan would actually help, but between him still wanting her back and him now being upset at the role he felt Arsula had played in the breakup, possibly a follow-up with his ex would allow him to chill long enough to be civil with *her*.

"If Whitney could hold out"—she went back to the conversation with her mom—"then I'd be able to see you all on my birthday." The Morettis were excellent at celebrating birthdays. There was always an event of some sort, with tons of friends and family showing up. That was one of the few things Arsula hated about not living in Cheyenne. She feared her birthday wouldn't feel special this year.

Buzz.

I don't really have anything to say to him. I am fine. Truly. I was just . . .

Arsula nodded. She got it. She thumbed out a one-word message.

Embarrassed.

Yeah.

Megan, I'm so sorry for my part in that.

Maybe she *should* go into detail about that night.

Megan replied. Don't worry about it. YOU are forgiven. You and I aren't the ones who dated for three years.

Arsula appreciated the words, as well as the unspoken ones. She also wasn't the one Megan had broken up with only hours before.

Her phone buzzed again.

But if you *really* wanted to make me feel better . . . I will take
you up on your original offer to meet up. Let's get together so
I can show you your website. I'm loving what I've done with it
so far.

Arsula dropped the phone to her desk. She'd only talked about a
potential website on a whim. She hadn't really thought Megan would
go off and build it.

That didn't mean the idea didn't excite her, though. Forming a true
business. Shaping her future in a way that would not only make her
accessible to those around her, but to anyone—*anywhere*—with a need.
Taking dream interpretation to the next level.

She swallowed against her nerves. There were people worldwide
striving daily to find a sense of wholeness. People unable to see their
paths only because they didn't possess the skills to center themselves.
To look at fulfilling from within before attempting to "have it all." And
she could help those people. She *wanted* to help them.

Yet at the same time . . .

"You still with me, Lula-bell?"

Arsula jerked her attention back to her mom once again, her heart
pounding as if she'd just stood up to her father in front of a room of his
own colleagues. "I really am sorry, Mom. I just—"

"Do *I* need to let *you* go?"

"*No.* Definitely not." She stared into her mother's curious face. And
she thought about her dad's disappointed one. She held up her cell.
"Just a friend reaching out. Something I didn't expect. Can you give me
one more minute to finish this? But don't hang up, please. I miss you.
I want to talk to you some more."

"Of course, baby." Her mother took another sip of coffee, and
Arsula offered an apologetic smile.

Then she went back to her phone.
Lunch sometime? Megan had said.

I don't . . .

She closed her eyes briefly, then opened them and erased the message she'd started.

I'm still not sure I want to go down that path. I've been thinking . . . I might decide to do something entirely different with my life.

Why in the world would you do that?!?! This is who you are.

She nodded. She knew that. Or, it's who she *could* be.
Another message came in.

What are you scared of, Arsula?

Losing my dad's love forever?
She shook her head. She definitely wasn't about to say that. And when her mother made a slight *hmmm* sound, she remembered that her mom was also still watching. She masked the concern on her face and thumbed a quick reply.

I'm not scared. Just not sure.

There was a delay before her phone buzzed again, and Arsula felt as if Megan knew she was lying. Because she was *terrified*.

Fine. But I'm going to keep working on it whether you help me or not. For when you *do* decide you're ready. I also have an idea for the book cover I want to work up. In case you want to see that, too.

Arsula didn't reply. She knew she should, but her thumbs no longer seemed to work. Megan had created a book cover.

For the book Arsula hadn't worked on since going home for Christmas.

She carefully put the phone down, turning it over as if not wanting to risk seeing the last message again, and then she went back to her mom for good. She'd tell anyone who asked to trust in their gut. To go for what they believe in their heart to be true. And for the first time, she was disappointed in herself for *not* going with her gut. For *not* knowing what she needed to do.

Her mother gave her a gentle smile. "Are you okay, Lula?"

"I am." She put on a brave face, for some reason expecting her mother to mention that her father still wanted to know when she'd be returning for good, but her mom didn't bring the subject up.

Instead, she said, "So tell me about this new man in your life."

Arsula choked on the water she'd just taken a sip of. "What makes you think there's a new man in my life?"

"Because you didn't call last week. You only forget to call when a new man enters your life."

She gaped at her mother. "That's not true at all. Sometimes I just forget."

"Yes, but then you remember at some ungodly hour and leave me a voice mail." What her mother said made sense. She had done that. But she wasn't about to validate it.

Instead, she argued. "If you knew I'd forgotten, then why didn't *you* call me? The line goes both ways, you know."

Her mother sighed. "Lula, honey. I *couldn't* call you because I had to wait in order to see if there *was* a new man in your life."

Talking to her mother could be like running in circles.

She caught sight of Nate's truck as he pulled onto Main Street, and she quickly scanned the parking spots in front of the building. The downtown area was busy today, and there weren't any empty slots outside the office. Nor in the handicapped area just around the corner.

"No new man, Mom. Just some friends." The truck disappeared.

"You're still fitting in well, then? How's the job?"

Nate made a second pass in front of the building, and she could see Jaden sitting in the passenger seat. His back seemed to be a little too straight. "I love Birch Bay. You should come visit. And the job's a job. Dani's a great boss."

"I don't mean the *PR* business," her mother said, her tone serious, and Arsula looked back down. Her dad might never understand her sudden whim to move away from all she'd ever known, but her mom got her perfectly. "The real job," she continued. "The one of your heart. How is that going?"

Her mom touched a fist to her chest, and a knot lodged in Arsula's throat. The women in her family were taught that the heart was the most precious gift and that it should always beat the loudest.

"That's going well, too, Mom." She opened her mouth to share that she'd found the person she'd moved to Birch Bay to help, but Nate suddenly appeared from the left side of the building, and a half second later, Jaden came into view. He was moving on his own, but Nate had an arm lifted, ready to catch him if he fell.

She rose. "I've got to go, Mom. Someone's coming that I need to speak with."

"Okay. I'll tell your father you said hello, and you tell that gentleman of yours that I did."

Arsula glanced back down, twisting her mouth into a frown. "There is no man, Mom."

"Okay, baby. You keep telling yourself that."

Arsula pushed the button to disconnect, then she hurried to open the door. A blast of frigid air hit her in the face, but she didn't let it slow her. She hurried out, getting on Jaden's other side, ready to help carry him as well.

"I'm fine," Jaden gritted out, white as a ghost.

"Yeah." Her sarcasm barely hid her concern. "You look fine. I'm just out here because I like being cold."

They made it to the door, and she held it open. Nate helped him inside, and for the first time since she'd met him, Nate Wilde didn't scowl at her. "I shouldn't have let him talk me into taking him today," he admitted.

"I told you it was too soon." She frowned at Jaden when he opened his mouth to argue, then she hurried to smooth the covers back on his bed.

"Do you need to take a leak?" Nate asked.

"Just get me horizontal," Jaden pleaded, and as his face turned into a maze of lines and grooves, Nate eased him onto the mattress.

Arsula had a pain pill in hand before he could claim that he didn't need one, and shoved it into his mouth. He swallowed it, even before she handed over the water, then Arsula met Nate's gaze in matching concern.

"The dumbass apparently tripped going into the building, yet he sat there for the entire session anyway." He nodded toward Jaden's foot. "It's swelled more than it has in a week."

Arsula uncovered his foot and loosened his splint.

Jaden groaned.

"Should we call his doctor?" she asked.

"I'm fine," Jaden grunted out. "Maybe just some ice."

"I'll get the ice." Nate disappeared into the kitchen, and Arsula rushed to the bathroom to wet a cloth.

She came back, pressing it against the sweat lining Jaden's brow at the same time that Nate returned with the ice. The two of them worked silently together, both forgetting any irritations with each other and focusing solely on Jaden, and once they'd done all they could, they stood back and watched.

"Quit eyeing me like I'm a piece of meat," Jaden grumbled. "Stretched out here like I'm a smorgasbord for your pleasure."

One corner of Nate's mouth lifted. "Those damned pills sure do work fast."

"Don't say damn," Jaden added, his eyes now closed and his breathing beginning to return to normal. "Jesus doesn't like it."

Nate turned to her in confusion, and she lifted a shoulder as if she didn't have a clue what Jaden might be talking about. He must remember her shouting that at him right before he'd fallen down her stairs, though. And that knowledge loosened something she typically kept locked tight inside.

"Go away," Jaden added. His eyes remained closed. "Let me die alone."

Nate shook his head and passed over a bag of fast food. "He's all yours. If he isn't being as pissy as he"—he shot her a look—"*heck*, then he's loopy off these blasted meds. And I'm tired of both personalities."

Before leaving, Nate moved closer to his brother and peered down, and Arsula watched as the concern eased from his face. Jaden was already asleep.

He stepped from the room, and she followed.

"Let me know if the swelling goes down tonight. If it doesn't, I'll be over in the morning to get him to the doctor."

Arsula agreed, and Nate left. She then returned to Jaden's side, having heard him whisper her name.

"What can I get for you?" She dotted away a few more beads of sweat.

"Sit with me."

"Okay." She turned for the chair she kept in the corner, but he latched on to her hand.

"No." The blue of his eyes was barely visible between his lashes. "Sit on the *bed* with me."

She nodded, and she sat on the bed. They hadn't been this close since the morning after his surgery, but she'd do whatever it took to calm him so he could sleep through his pain. But then his hand landed on her thigh.

"Quit being mad at me, Arsula," he slurred out. "I don't like it when you're mad at me."

"You're the one who's mad at me," she reminded him. She also fought a smile. She did like this man when he was drugged.

"I'm not anymore." He patted her leg. "I don't want to fight anymore."

She covered his hand with hers. "Then we won't fight anymore."

"*Good.*"

They sat there like that for a while longer, his breathing evening out almost immediately, and just as she decided it was time to return to her desk, Jaden opened his eyes.

"You know you're not a real counselor. You don't have the right education."

And there went the warm fuzzies the prior moment had created. "I've never claimed to be a counselor."

"Yet that's what you do." He pointed toward her desk. "I've watched you. You offer everyone advice. You listen to them."

"I told you before. I'm good with people."

He shook his head. "It's not real. You don't have a gift, and you're not a real counselor."

"It is real," she said softly. And she thought about what Erica had told her after they'd left the restaurant Friday night. Carol Wilde had been a narcissist, leaving a path of destruction both before and after her death. She'd played with her kids' emotions and pitted her children against each other. And Arsula could only imagine the list of grievances Erica *didn't* know about. "And I'm going to prove it to you."

She held Jaden's hand in hers, and that seemed to keep him from slipping into sleep.

"Don't prove it. Just help me get Megan back."

His plea hurt her heart. "Why do you want her back, Jaden? What makes you think she's got to be the one?"

His eyelids drooped. "Because I need her to love me."

Chapter Eleven

S uck it! I win!” Nick rose from his seat in Dani and Ben’s rec room, hands in the air, and strutted around the room as if he’d just taken down a moose. In actuality, he’d won a game of Clue.

“Impressive win, honey.” Harper infused her congratulations with a heavy dose of irony.

“I remain the champ.” Nick pointed out the reason for his over-abundance of joy. “That’s all I’m saying. No one can touch me.”

“No one wants to touch you,” Jaden added with a smirk. He reached behind him for the game box and began helping Dani put the pieces away as everyone else gathered up empty glasses and plates. It was family night for the Wildes, and Dani and Ben had offered to host. The family got together one Saturday night every couple of months to either have dinner or play games, and whoever could be in town showed up.

Cord wasn’t there this time. Having driven over only two weeks prior for the wedding, he hadn’t had the extra time to make it. But Nate wasn’t there, either. And he was definitely still in town. It was anybody’s guess where he’d disappeared to.

"I'm going to run your dad and Gloria home," Ben told Dani. He rose with the game in his hands. "I'll put this away and check on Mia before I go."

"Can I go with you, Dad?" Haley asked.

"Of course you can." Ben and Haley disappeared from the room, and a few seconds later, Ben could be heard through the baby monitor, checking on the baby.

"You and Ben have created a good life here." Jaden spoke quietly, not wanting to be overheard as the others were still milling about the house.

"It's turned out really well," Dani agreed. Ben had purchased a lake house just up the road from where Jaden and his siblings grew up, and though it kept Dani separated so she and her new family could do their own thing, it also allowed her to be close enough to check in on their dad if the need arose.

Everyone except Ben and Haley came back through with their coats on and leftovers in hand, and Gabe and Erica offered to drop Jaden off on their way through town. "We'll get him back," Dani told them. Then she reached over and patted Jaden's outstretched leg. "You've all spent a lot of time with our baby brother lately. It's my turn now."

In understanding, the group left. Ben and Haley followed seconds later, and suddenly, the house that had been nothing but chaos for the last several hours was as close to silent as it would ever be.

A clock ticked from the mantel in the office across the hall, and Mia made a cooing noise through the monitor. Dani moved to the couch and smiled as she relaxed back into the cushions, and Jaden followed her across the room. He stretched out in the recliner.

"I'm happy for you, sis." He closed his eyes and felt himself relax. "You deserve everything good in the world."

"Thank you." With Dani being eleven years older than him, most people might not think they'd be as close as they were. But Dani had practically raised him.

"I was glad Dad and Gloria made it tonight," he added. Earlier in the day, he'd been told their dad wasn't feeling well and planned to stay home.

"Me too. He's been feeling 'under the weather' a little too often lately."

Jaden opened his eyes. "What do you mean?" He hadn't noticed anything.

But then, he hadn't been around his dad because he'd refused to stay at the house.

Dani glanced over. "I think something might be wrong with him, Jay. Gabe had concerns a few months ago, and Cord did some questioning at the time, but nothing ever came of it. Only, Doc Hamm has been out to the house a couple of instances that we know of, and I've heard that his car has been seen pulling away from there another time or two."

"Doc Hamm is still practicing?" Doc Hamm had been their family doctor when Jaden had been young.

"And apparently making house calls."

Jaden readjusted the chair so that he sat up. "What do you mean *wrong*? Is he *sick*?"

"I don't know." Her look of concern only increased. "But haven't you noticed that sometimes he seems to be . . . somewhere *else*? Sort of like he just spaces out?"

Jaden thought back over the night, but he honestly hadn't picked up on anything.

He did remember a phone conversation with Megan about a month ago, though. She'd run over to the store to meet with the maintenance man late one night, and when she'd returned, her headlights had highlighted his dad out on the front porch. He'd been brandishing a broom. She hadn't been able to see whatever he'd been swatting at, and when asked, his dad had mumbled something about bees and gone back in.

Jaden hadn't thought anything else of it. But now he had to wonder. "Do you think his mind is going?"

"Possibly. But I also caught him using a cane one day. I stopped by unannounced, and when I came in, he was in the kitchen with Gloria, and I'd swear he needed the cane just to stand. He explained that he and Gloria had found it while browsing in a local consignment shop and that she'd fallen in love with the design on the shaft. She then took it from him, and he sat down at the table."

Jaden studied her. "And have you seen *Gloria* using it?"

"Not once. Nor have I seen Dad with it again. But it is still in the house. It's propped by the fireplace. As if it's a decorative piece."

"And you don't think that's all it is?"

She shook her head. "My gut tells me that he *needs* it."

Jaden frowned at her phrasing. He wasn't in the mood to hear about listening to one's gut. "So he's got arthritis," he said, explaining it away. "And he doesn't want us to know it's affected his mobility."

"I considered that, too."

"But that's not what you think now?" Worry gnawed at him.

"I don't know what I think. Something about it worries me, though."

Jaden glanced away. His sister's look was becoming too intense, and it was hard to think with that kind of pressure directed at him. And then he realized who *should* know about their dad. "Has Nate said anything?" Nate had been staying at the house while he'd been in town.

"I don't think Nate's spending a lot of time there," she offered.

"Then what *is* he doing?" At first Nate had stopped by the office most days, but that had slowed. He still showed up when Jaden needed to be taken somewhere. But other than that, he'd been scarce.

"I don't know," Dani admitted. "But I think something might be off with him, too."

He shot her an incredulous look. "You think he's sick, too?"

"No." She shook her head. "Sorry. Poor word choice. I just meant like he's walking around unsure of what he's supposed to be doing."

A whimper sounded from the baby monitor, then the sounds of Mia fidgeting in her sleep. Both of them paused in their conversation, Dani having pushed up on the couch cushions, ready to go the second her daughter indicated she needed her. The noises soon subsided, and Jaden picked up where they'd left off.

"Why is Nate even still here? Do you know?" Nate hadn't stuck around this long since he'd left at eighteen.

"You mean, other than trying to take care of you?"

"Yeah." He smirked. "Other than trying to take care of me."

"Beats me." She returned to her slouched position on the couch. "I asked him last week if he was thinking about moving back home, and he changed the subject."

"I'll talk to him." Jaden began forming the conversation in his head. Nate would be picking him up for his surgical follow-up appointment Monday afternoon, so Jaden could use the time to feel him out. He just had to try not to make it come across as if he were doing exactly that.

"Good luck," Dani said wryly. Then, as if understanding that his thoughts had gone to his counseling skills, she turned her head to look at him. "Are you going to be able to finish everything with school okay? Do you need me to do anything?"

"You're assuming I won't be going back?"

She eyed his splint. "I don't see you up and running anytime soon."

"Maybe not," he admitted. And maybe it wouldn't be so bad to stick around there, either. He liked that he'd been able to spend time with his family tonight. They'd rarely had those kinds of relaxing evenings when he'd been growing up.

And what would be the point of returning for one month when he planned to turn around and come back, anyway? Which was likely all it would be if he wasn't able to put weight on his ankle for another four weeks.

"I'm good," he said instead of arguing the point further. He'd figure things out when the time came. Right now, he just had to make it through the next counseling session without needing to be helped back into bed.

His next appointment to work with Dr. Wangler would be the following Tuesday, and assuming he didn't slam his foot into anything, he should be fine.

"Your friend is good," he said. He was glad he'd taken his sister's recommendation and would be studying under her for the upcoming year.

"She is. She worked with Ben and Haley when Ben first got custody."

He wasn't sure why he hadn't realized that. "No wonder they're doing so well."

Janette Wangler had a natural ease with patients that he knew he hadn't fully developed yet. She had a way of simply . . . *connecting* with them. Sort of how Arsula seemed to do with every person who came into the office.

He frowned at his own thoughts. He'd told himself he wouldn't think about Arsula tonight. Mostly because he'd done nothing but think about her for the last couple of days. Since he'd told her—while in a drugged state—that he didn't want her to be mad at him anymore.

He'd also basically begged her to make Megan love him again.

What a sap. Stupid painkillers. They made him run his mouth like an overflowing dam. He refused to take any more of them.

But really, Arsula had been the one to mess things up between him and Megan. Why *shouldn't* she be the one to fix it? And after what he'd witnessed over the last two weeks, he'd bet his right hand that if anyone *could* talk some sense back into his ex, it would be Arsula. The woman seemed able to get everyone to open up. To *see* things her way. Not that he'd been eavesdropping or anything.

"Are you aware that your office feels like a counseling session most of the time?" Jaden complained, and his sister peeked out from under drooping lashes.

"So we're finally going to talk about Arsula?"

He held back his smirk. He'd skirted the subject when Dani had picked him up earlier, only to bring it right back there now. "I'm just pointing out . . . does the woman ever actually do any work for you? Best I can tell, all she does is talk to people. About everything. And I swear, I think they make appointments to come in and see her."

"No." Dani chuckled lightly, her eyes once again closed. "She keeps her appointments outside of office hours. They just stop in with updates. But I don't see any harm in it. It gives them a chance to take in the ad work I have hanging on the walls, to see some of the projects we've done. You never know when a friendly visit might turn into a new client."

Jaden had missed half of what his sister said, because his head had almost exploded after her first sentence. "Are you saying that she *does* meet with people? As in, she counsels them in some fashion?"

He'd *known* that was how she saw herself.

"Not counseling so much. She just helps them to see *themselves* better."

"That sounds like counseling."

She eyed him as if bored. "It's not the same thing at all. She's helping them to *hear* themselves as opposed to analyze themselves."

"As in, *hearing* your subconscious telling you to break up with someone?" he muttered, not meaning to say that out loud, but at Dani's instant cringe, a question he'd been asking himself got answered. His sister knew the reason Megan had broken up with him.

He hadn't told anyone that part of the story.

"Something like that," Dani finally replied, her tone heavy with sympathy.

"And you don't think Arsula's a nutjob?"

Dani smiled with fondness. "I think she's fantastic. She can be whimsical, but also freaking brilliant. So no, I do not think she's a nutjob. Granted, I'm also not positive everything that comes out of her mouth is one hundred percent spot-on, but she's not stupid, Jaden."

She peered at him with seriousness. "Look closely at her. Have you bothered to do that yet? You'll see something way more than what she presents on the surface."

"Why wouldn't she just present reality? What's she hiding?"

"I'm not saying that she's hiding *anything*. Just that she doesn't wave all her greatest attributes around for the world to see. She can be subtle."

He thought about her looks. About her constant talking. And about her losing her shit and throwing things over one little disagreement.

Or threatening to flush his drugs and steal his crutches.

"We'll have to agree to disagree on that one," he told her. "I don't believe there's a subtle bone in her body."

Something akin to disappointment flashed across his sister's face. "She's been helping you out for almost two weeks, Jay. You're living under the same roof. Am I guessing right that you haven't had even one real conversation with her? Gotten to know her at all?"

Mia cried through the monitor, a sound that said she meant it this time, and Dani pushed herself up without waiting for his reply. But the second she returned, with Mia bundled in a blanket covered with pink monkeys, she settled into a wooden rocker—then she angled an answer-the-question-before-I-have-to-*make*-you look his way.

He grudgingly confessed, "I've not exactly been the best patient."

"So you're saying you've been a pain in the butt like you were as a kid?" She chuckled. "Anytime you didn't feel well, you'd stomp around the house, making sure everyone knew it."

That had only started after their mom died, but he didn't point that out.

Before that he'd stayed silently in his room. Being ignored.

Mia made a slurping noise as she fed, and Dani turned wondrous eyes on her daughter. He liked seeing his sister like this. So loving. So . . . *nurturing*.

So the opposite of their mother.

"She's a miracle, Jay," she murmured. "I never thought I'd have kids after coming home to help with you guys."

"You seem to be adapting well." He watched as she stroked a hand over Mia's dark hair. "You and she are bonding okay? No issues with new motherhood?" He knew issues could arise, even for people who *hadn't* grown up with a mother incapable of love, but for people like Dani . . .

She lifted a knowing gaze. "Don't try to psychoanalyze me, baby brother. I pay good money for that already."

"And it's done wonders. You've come so far. You and *Dad* have come so far."

She kept her gaze on his. "And how about *you* and Dad?"

"What do you mean?"

Dani rolled her eyes. "Why wouldn't you stay at the house after your accident, Jay? You know Dad would have been fine with it. Plus, it's not even his house anymore. It's ours."

When their dad had originally retired from managing the orchard, he'd deeded the house and orchard over to the six kids. Dani had opened the retail store after that, but it had been done as a subset of the business.

"I'm aware of that." Jaden didn't offer an answer to her question.

"Then what's the issue? The house isn't even the same one we grew up in. Gloria has brought a whole new life to the place. Every room is different."

"I know that, too."

She growled with frustration. "*Jaden.* Talk to me. I just want to help."

And he didn't *want* her help. "Don't try to psychoanalyze me, big sister."

For a moment she looked as if she didn't intend to stop her line of questioning, but finally she acquiesced. "Fair enough. We each have to work through our own crap. I get that. But as an outsider looking in, let me just tell you that unless there was a lot more going on the night of the wedding than either you or Arsula admitted to, then your staying with her doesn't make a lot of sense."

"I had to stay somewhere," he argued. "And Megan was at the house. *And* she'd just broken up with me."

"And you know she could have stayed with me until she moved out. Heck, *you* could have stayed with me. For as long as you wanted!"

He took in his niece. Dani's first biological child. "You're a new mom, Dani. With a history that could make *being* a mom a struggle if you aren't on top of things."

"But I am on top of things."

"True. But you don't need the added stress of having me underfoot."

"I'm also your sister." Her voice lowered, and she pleaded with her eyes. "I'm your *big* sister. I'm supposed to help out when you need it."

"You helped out plenty years ago."

Hell, the woman had practically been his mom. Even before their mom had died.

"You know I was happy to do that, right? To come home and be here for you guys." She lifted Mia to her shoulder. "I wouldn't change those years for the world."

Jaden didn't reply to her statement. Because that wasn't exactly the truth, he knew. But he also knew that she didn't regret being there when they'd needed her. Without her, he, Nick, and Nate would have ended up a mess. And the verdict was still out on Nate.

He wondered again where Nate had been tonight. Then he wondered how Megan had spent her evening. Normally she'd have been at his family's get-togethers, too.

He decided to change the subject. Enough talking about him and what might or might not be driving his need to *not* be living in his childhood home. Plus, he was desperate to know *something* about Megan, and at this point, pretty much anything would do.

"How's the manager search going?" He then came right out with what he really wanted to know. "How's *Megan* doing?"

He meant how was she doing both as manager and just *doing*, and he hoped his sister would key in to that without him having to spell it out for her.

"It's going . . ." She quit talking as she readjusted Mia to her other side, and then she offered him a tight smile. "Megan seems good. She fits in well around town, and I know she's getting out occasionally. She's living in Erica's old place now. Also . . ." She let out a little sigh. "She's thrown out the idea of offering her the job, Jay. Permanently."

His expression fell. "As in, her staying here in Birch Bay forever?" He'd been worried she'd leave without him getting a chance to talk to her.

"At least for a while," Dani confirmed, and Jaden's next thought was to wonder if Megan's consideration of staying meant that she was changing her mind. Was she thinking she'd been rash in breaking up with him?

"Are you going to offer it to her?" He tried not to let too much hope creep in.

"I don't know. She's good. Really good. And she has big ideas. The website has been revamped already. She did the coding herself, but she also researched a better back-end solution for us. And I've already told you how our online sales have soared since she's been here. That's just in two months, Jay. Think of what else she could do."

He could imagine. "How's she handling everything so well when she has a second job?"

"She quit her other job."

She'd given up the six-figure income she'd gone to school for? That was mind-boggling. But it must mean that she really did intend to stay.

And there had to be a reason for that.

He studied his sister, wondering how much Megan had shared with her, and then he found himself wanting to share something of his own.

He might not want his big sister trying to play mom anymore . . . but she *could* play big sister.

"Did she tell you that I asked her to marry me that night?"

Her face crumpled. "Oh, Jay. No, she didn't mention it. I'm so sorry."

"It's okay. I haven't given up on her yet. I think she just needs some time."

At least, he hoped that's all she needed. Because he didn't know what else to offer.

"What does Megan think about you staying with Arsula?"

He pushed the recliner into a horizontal position. "I'm not actually staying with *her*, you know? I'm staying in your office."

"Semantics," Dani muttered. "But okay. What does Megan think of you staying in the office? So Arsula can take care of you?"

He stared at the ceiling, considered pointing out that he didn't actually need taking care of, but then had to admit to himself that Arsula had done a lot of that very thing during those first few days. Even though he'd been a total jerk. And even though she'd barely spoken to him while doing it.

Things had been slightly better over the last few days. They hadn't spent all that much more time in each other's company, but their conversations *had* consisted of a bit more than "what can I get for you" and "are you hungry." He'd also noticed a slight warmth in her attitude toward him. Just as he knew his had thawed toward her.

"I don't know what Meg thinks," he finally admitted. And oddly, he was finding that he no longer cared as much. "I still can't get her to talk to me."

Granted, he hadn't actually tried in days. Even though he'd asked Arsula for help Wednesday night, he hadn't reached out to Megan since a couple of days before that.

"Are you okay with the idea of offering her the job?"

They'd be stupid not to keep her around if she wanted to stay. And not only because sales had risen significantly. Since the first time she'd seen the place, Megan had fallen in love with all things cherry. She was a perfect representative for the business. "You do whatever is best for the store. I'll make it work."

And possibly, he could still make *them* work.

Maybe.

"If she really wants the job," Dani went on, "I'm going to insist she reach out to you. You're both adults, I know, but the store is yours, too. I don't want to enter into a contract with a possible issue hanging over our heads."

"That makes sense." And if Megan did finally reach out to him . . .

A door opened in the back of the house, and Ben and Haley came in. At the same time, Jaden caught his sister hiding a yawn. He pushed out of the chair before his brother-in-law made it to the room. "Don't take off your coat," he called out. Ben poked his head through the door, and Jaden said, "You okay running me back?"

Haley's hand was still clasped in her dad's. "Can I go, too?"

Jaden grinned at his niece, always happy to play super uncle to any of his nieces, but Dani spoke from her chair.

"It's past your bedtime," she said without looking up, and Jaden watched as the girl's shoulders sagged.

"But I promise I'll sleep late in the morning."

Ben chortled. "With Mia waking us all up before daylight, there's no way that'll happen."

"Then I'll take a nap," Haley announced. "And I won't even complain. *Please*," she wheedled. "I never get to see Uncle Jaden very much. And you know he's my favorite uncle."

Jaden grinned again, and all three of the adults laughed. Both Haley and Jenna regularly rotated between favorite uncles. They had for years.

"Go." Dani waved in a shooing motion. "But make your dad stop at the store and bring me back some ice cream. I need calories to keep up with this kid."

Ben crossed to his wife and bent down to kiss Mia on the top of her head. "Chocolate ice cream coming up." He pecked Dani on the lips.

"But no chips," she said softly. Dani ate ice cream and chips together when stressed.

"No chips." Ben kissed Dani again. "Be right back, beautiful."

Chapter Twelve

Most of the lights were off inside the building as they pulled up, and Jaden took in the quiet street in the middle of his hometown. He'd always loved Birch Bay. He'd planned to move back here since he'd first gone away to college. On the other end of the street was Flathead Lake, and the blocks surrounding the statue in the middle of the square contained storefronts of unique spaces. Even the building Dani had bought. It had been one of a handful of original houses that had been here since the beginning, and he thought she'd made a wise decision in purchasing it. It had strengthened her confidence in making her decision to remain in Birch Bay.

Ben shifted into park but didn't move to get out. Haley was asleep in the back seat. "Need any help getting in?"

"Nah." It hadn't snowed in days, so the sidewalks were clear. He gripped the crutches that sat beside him. "As long as I have my trusty sidekicks, I'm good."

Ben gave a nod. "I'll stay until you make it inside."

"Thanks." Jaden got out, but before walking away, he turned back. "Is she as good as she seems?" When their family had imploded a few years back and Dani had ended up moving to New York City, Jaden had worried about her a lot.

"She *is* good. The occasional bad day happens, but she stays on top of it. She's always working to be as good on the inside as she is on the out."

Relief filled Jaden. That's the feeling he got from her.

"I do think she's worried about *you*, though." Ben tossed a glance to the building behind Jaden. "She's fine with you staying here, but she is concerned about the reason for it."

"That's nothing. She just likes to worry. I'm good. *Better* than good. My only issue is a bum leg." He nodded toward his ankle, which he very much hoped would get its own personal cast come Monday.

"If you say so."

Jaden headed up the sidewalk after saying his goodbyes, and as he neared the door, he thought about another person Dani currently worried about. Their dad.

Which meant that *he* now worried, too.

Was the man hiding something? And if so, what? And why not just share it with all of them?

Reaching the door of the office, he unlocked it before tossing a wave at Ben, and as the other man drove off, Jaden stepped into the dimmed interior. There was soft music drifting through the room, and though he couldn't see the corner lamp beyond the open french doors, he could tell it had been left on. He glanced up the stairwell as he started past, assuming Arsula would be up there, tucked away in her apartment. However, when he shifted his gaze back, he found her sitting on the floor of his room. Peeking around the doors.

Stopping, he noted that she seemed frazzled. Her hair had been pulled up, but a good third of it now hung loose—all on one side of her head. She wore an old sweatshirt sporting the name of a medical school in Wyoming, and her brows were drawn together, as if angry at something *he'd* done. Only, he hadn't seen her all day.

145

"What are you doing in my room?" he asked carefully.

She brought one hand out from the other side of the door and held up a screwdriver. "About to chuck this desk you ordered out the front door."

His brows shot up. "You're putting my desk together?"

"Were you going to do it?"

"Of course I was. I . . ." He quit talking at the scowl she fired his way and finished hobbling to his room.

Peeking in, he found half the desk put together, more pieces remaining than he could possibly guess what to do with, and a small gash in the middle of the facing of one of the two drawers.

"Sorry about the drawer," she muttered. She shoved at a hammer, sliding it under the desk.

"And I'm sorry I wasn't here to see you bust it," he replied.

The hospital bed he'd been sleeping in had also been replaced. In its place was a twin frame and mattress, as well as a large triangular-shaped foam pillow that appeared to be for propping up in bed.

"You've been a busy woman." He slowly lowered himself to the floor, putting his back to the bed and stretching his feet out before him.

"I got home and you weren't here, so . . ." She trailed off and went back to working on the desk. She'd had an appointment scheduled for that afternoon, he knew. A gathering where she'd apparently been the main attraction.

"What did you do with the other bed?"

She glanced at him. "Dani was renting it, and you don't need that kind of assistance anymore, so I borrowed a bed from one of my friends."

He took in the room again, with fresh bedding piled on one end of the mattress and cardboard and desk parts scattered across the majority of the floor. It was a mess. "You seem to have a lot of friends."

"That's because I like a lot of people."

"You're also very good at talking to them."

She shot him another look but didn't comment before returning her focus to the desk.

"I would have gotten it together somehow, you know?" He eyed the virtually worthless appendage protruding before him. "Just as soon as I get out of this splint and into something that protects me a little better."

"I don't mind doing it."

"Then why is one of the drawers busted?"

When she ignored his question, he followed with, "Didn't you once tell me that you didn't normally lose your temper like that?"

The screwdriver dropped from her hand, and she turned to face him, her features twisted in annoyance. "Did you *have* to order a desk with fifteen thousand different parts?"

He might have done that on purpose.

"How was I to know it would be so time-consuming?" He smiled in all innocence. He *had* wanted an excuse to get her to spend more time with him.

"Then I guess you're more of an idiot than I've given you credit for." Her grumbled words had him laughing out loud, and he realized how good it felt. He wasn't sure he'd laughed like that since the night they'd met. He scooted a couple of feet closer.

"Surely it's not all that bad." Picking up the instruction sheet she'd tossed to the side, he scanned over it. "How long have you been at it?"

She went back to work. "What time did you leave here with Dani?"

"About five." He glanced at the clock. It was almost ten now.

"Then about that long." Her voice was muffled as she peered up under the main area of the desk. "I saw you pulling away as I was coming home."

He'd been watching for her, hoping she'd make it back before he left. "Did the party go well?"

He eyed her, trying to picture her in the middle of a crowd of women, reading dreams as if she should be sitting inside a dark tent with a crystal ball between her hands. He didn't understand that at all.

"Everyone seemed to enjoy it."

"And that's good enough for you?"

Her head disappeared ever farther under the desk. "Is what good enough for me?"

"Whatever that was you did today."

Two seconds later, she peeked back out. "What do you *think* I did today?"

He could tell from her chilly tone that he should tread carefully. However, he'd never been one to follow all the rules. So he jumped into the deep end. "Being a circus attraction?"

Chilly no longer came close to defining her look. "Excuse me?"

"I just mean—"

She let the screwdriver drop to the floor again . . . only this time, she threw it. It nicked off a sliver of wood.

"What you *meant*," she started, her eyes now flaming with fight, "was to insult me. Which you did. So thanks for that. *Great job.* But here's the thing, Jaden." Her look became deadly. "You don't have the right to make judgments about me. You may think I'm a joke, but I couldn't care less."

She was right. About all of it.

He thought she was a joke, and he'd intended to insult her.

Although insulting her *hadn't* been what he'd wanted when he'd first seen her. He'd been happy to find her in his room. And he'd had the thought that it would be nice to spend the rest of the evening talking to her. Maybe laughing. Like they'd done that first night.

But he couldn't seem to help himself. He found the entire dream-reading thing beyond silly.

"I know I shouldn't have—"

"No." She wrapped her arms around her knees. "You *shouldn't* have. And I'm beyond tired of it. Have a little respect for others, can't you? Did your mother teach you nothing?"

The second the words left her mouth, her gaze widened and her mouth slammed shut.

"Correct," he answered flatly. "My mother taught me nothing."

He hadn't meant to insult Arsula tonight, but neither did he want to talk about his mother.

"Jaden. I'm sorry." Her voice wavered, and she lowered her hands. "I know you were young when she died."

"Being young had nothing to do with it."

He stared into her expressive eyes. Even being a dark brown, they contained more color than his own blue. And in them tonight . . . he saw that she knew. Dammit, someone *had* been talking. He forced in a breath, telling himself to look away. To not be lured in by whatever power she held. She had the most amazing ability to get people to want to spill their guts. And he, it seemed, was no exception.

Because he suddenly found himself *wanting* to talk. And wanting to talk about his mom.

Which was a totally foreign concept.

He reached for the screwdriver she'd discarded and flipped it from grip to flat-head in the palm of one hand. And then, to the only person other than his past counselor and Megan, he began to share.

"She had narcissistic personality disorder." He kept his voice unemotional and started off slow. As if feeling his way along a freshly snow-covered road. "But I suspect you already know that. She didn't care about any of us kids. She barely got out of bed during my first years of life because she always had 'headaches.'" He air-quoted the word and kept on going. "And we were extremely fortunate that she did us the favor of dying so young. Otherwise, she might have destroyed all of us."

Arsula had frozen as he'd begun to speak, and he could see that her anger had fled.

"Jaden." She said his name on a whisper, and he suddenly worried she might close the gap between them.

"Don't." He held his hands up. "I don't want your sympathy or your sad, poor-Jaden eyes. I'm fine. I was the least affected of all of us, and I figured her issue out long before anyone else. I'm getting a counseling degree so I can help other kids from ever feeling like my siblings and I did. I know I can't help them all"—his voice cracked—"but by God, I can help some of them."

Arsula was beside him before he finished speaking, ignoring the hands he still held in front of him, and wrapped her arms around his neck. Her warm body pressed into his arm as she lifted to her knees and held tight, and he made sure not to return the gesture.

She held on, though, as if afraid turning him loose might cause him to vanish right in front of her.

"Arsula."

"Shhh." She shook her head, her nose buried in his neck. "Just accept my hug, will you? Sometimes even morons need hugs."

The line of his mouth softened, and he dropped his head to the bed.

She felt really good wrapped around him like that. Her hair brushed against the underside of his chin, and he wanted to bring his fingers up to see what it felt like.

"I'm sorry I insulted you," he said a few minutes later. He really hadn't wanted to hurt her feelings. "It's none of my business what you do with your life."

"And I'm sorry your mom didn't love you."

He squeezed his eyes shut. This was why he didn't talk about his mother. He didn't like people being concerned that "his mommy hadn't loved him."

"I'm fine with it," he assured her. "I swear to you." He opened his eyes, and as he once again stared at the ceiling, he remembered that the ceiling above Arsula's bed had been painted a pale blue. "I've been over it for years."

She kept her arms around his neck but, after another minute, lifted her face. And she was suddenly too close. All he could think about was the night he'd kissed her in the snow.

"How can a person ever be fine with their mother not loving them enough?" she asked, and Jaden looked at her mouth.

"She didn't love me at *all*," he corrected.

"Poor Jaden." She tucked her head back into his neck, and against his better judgment, he pulled his arm free and wrapped it around her. And suddenly, she was all warm curves and sweet smells, all of it hitting him in more places than where she touched, and he reminded himself that he wanted Megan.

"I promise you that I'm fine." He had to get his mind on something other than how good Arsula felt snuggled up against him. "But if you're hell-bent on worrying about someone . . ."

He stopped talking. She'd stiffened when he'd cursed, and he grimaced down at her.

"I'm sorry," he offered. "I know you don't like cursing."

"Thank you. And it's not me who doesn't like it so much as it was Aunt Sul." She chuckled lightly and dropped her forehead to his shoulder. "And I guess she's still in my head."

"I can understand that. Will you tell me about her?"

She looked back up. "Do you really want to know?"

The way she looked at him, as if someone had asked what she really wanted for her birthday for the first time in her life, made him want to know even more.

"I do." He nodded. He wanted to do anything that would give her that happy glow. "Start with her dislike of cursing." He winked, and her body relaxed against his. "Maybe understanding her will stop me from doing it so much."

She laughed, and then her smile turned nostalgic. "Aunt Sul was the best," she said on a sigh, and her body softened against his even more. "After I turned seven, I started getting to stay with her for a week

151

every summer. Just *me*. Not my brothers. And that first year a boy from school had taught me quite a few words I knew I shouldn't be using." She grinned. "I tried them out while at Aunt Sul's, thinking she was the 'cool' aunt and would find it endearing. She literally washed my mouth out with soap, instead. And then she did it again . . . once a day for the entire week. After that, she decided that what I needed was more Jesus in my life, so she began picking me up every Sunday." Her eyes filled with tears, and she gave a little shrug. "And she did that until the day she died."

His chest tightened for her loss.

"When did she die?" He wiped away an escaping tear.

"The year I turned fifteen. She'd gotten sick and tried to hide it from us. Cancer," she told him. "I dreamed about it one morning before she picked me up for church, and when I confronted her, she admitted that she'd messed up. She hadn't gone to the doctor soon enough, and it was too late for treatment."

Jaden brought his other arm around her. "I'm so sorry," he whispered into her hair. "I know you loved her."

"Yeah." Her head moved, nodding against him, and he tightened his arms even more.

Not ready for her to extricate herself, he dropped his head to the bed again and tucked hers against his shoulder. His position on the floor had him sitting eye-level with the stack of books that had been on the corner of the mini fridge since he'd moved in, and for the first time, he read the titles.

Then surprise had him squinting at the spines.

A couple of the books had been used in his junior- and senior-level psychology courses. Another two sounded interesting enough; they were about the brain and how it worked. There was also one about dreams, one about balancing chakras, a horror novel, and then a final book that he thought he recognized as being written by a romance author.

He stroked his palm over her hair. "You didn't go to college, right?"

Her body stiffened against him. "Are you about to insult me about that again now, too?"

"No." He tucked in his chin and looked down at her. "I'm not. And I'm sorry I did to begin with. I shouldn't have, and the only excuse I have is that I was hurting . . . and angry . . ."

"And childish," she grumbled, and he smiled.

"Yeah. That too. I apologize for that as well. Dani always said I could be a horrible patient."

He waited to see if she would reply, and when she didn't, he went back to staring at the stack of books.

"So your three brothers," he began a few minutes later, "they all went to medical school?"

"My dad, too."

"They must be a smart bunch." He didn't comment on *her* intelligence, but for the first time since meeting her, he began to wonder about it in a positive light.

Was she anywhere near as capable as her brothers?

"They're super scholars," she informed him in a bored tone.

"And your mom is a teacher?"

"*Was* a teacher." She pushed against his chest and sat up—though her thigh remained pressed to his. "She also told me to tell you hello, by the way. For some reason, she thinks you're 'a new man' in my life."

He knew he wore a look of surprise. "Your mother thinks *I'm* a new man in your life?"

"Yes."

"And how does your mother even know I exist?" He narrowed his eyes, wondering what had been said. "You've been talking about me?"

"No, actually. I didn't mention you at all."

"So what are you saying? That your mother knew about me because she's also a little"—he decided to rephrase his question due to the glare Arsula leveled on him—"because she has a 'gift' as well?"

Arsula chuckled at his save. "Actually, she *doesn't* have a gift."

"Then I don't understand. How would she have known I exist?"

And why did he sound as if he might think someone could just *know* about another person?

Sheesh. Arsula was making *him* loony.

"Get this." She scooted around until she faced him, crossing her legs in front of her, and leaned her elbows on her knees. "She came to this conclusion because I apparently only forget to call home when there's a new man in my life."

"Ah." That made much more sense. "And there are a lot of new men in your life, I take it?"

"No," she stressed. "That's the thing. It's why her comment was so odd."

Jaden thought this entire conversation was odd, but he refrained from pointing that out. He did add to it, though. "You told me before that the women in your family are born with a gift."

The happiness that suddenly shone back at him had him forgetting whatever else he'd intended to say. Arsula hadn't smiled at him like that since the night of the wedding.

"Why are you so happy?" he asked.

"Because you not only remembered what I told you about the women in my family, but for the first time, you just asked about it without looking like you were sucking on a lemon."

He supposed he had. So he smiled along with her. "Why doesn't your mother have a gift?"

"I don't know. She's the only one it seems to have missed."

"Interesting."

"Right?" Again, she smiled, and Jaden decided that he could get used to that. "I've always felt bad for her. I'd share mine if I could."

He touched the back of his fingers to her cheek, and he knew he didn't want the evening to end. "Let's forget the desk tonight, Arsula. Do something else instead."

"What did you have in mind?"

He glanced over to where the TV hung on the wall. It was currently tuned to a music station. "Watch a movie with me?"

She hesitated only long enough to look at the TV and then at the hard-back chair she often used. "I suppose I could do that."

"Good." He nodded toward where they sat. "Help me get off the floor first?"

Smile three was directed his way, and he decided he was a little bit in love with the curve of her lips. "I can do that, too," she confirmed.

She rose, and when she held a hand down to him, he wrapped his fingers around hers. But as he stood, he didn't let her go. Not until she looked up in question.

"Truce?" he said. They'd pretty much been living with one since Wednesday afternoon. But he wanted it official.

"Truce," she agreed.

Chapter Thirteen

Arsula opened her eyes to the sound of an infomercial and to the feeling of utter contentment. And then she stared at the profile of the man sleeping next to her. She was in bed with Jaden. Again.

Dang it!

But at least this time they weren't naked.

She glanced down the length of their bodies, as if to make sure, before rolling from her side to her back. Reinstituting the separation she'd insisted upon when she'd first moved from chair to mattress—and then adding to it by cramming her pillow into the space—she then asked herself what in the heck she thought she was doing.

Sure, the couch was shoved under the television and the chair didn't come close to being comfortable. But really? Letting herself be talked into his bed? Was she that gullible?

She was not. Nor was she pleased about the feelings she'd awakened from.

She glanced back over at Jaden. Dreams that left a person with such a sense of peace and fulfillment could be a good thing. They could signify a relationship worth exploring—or even one worth hanging on to. But waking with those feelings while curled next to a man who was still hung up on another woman?

Bad thing.

Especially when the idea of being with that man was the furthest thing from her mind.

Almost the furthest thing.

Her breath hitched at the thought, because she had to face up to the fact that the idea of being with Jaden *had* passed through her awareness a time or two. But only since Megan had offered "permission" to date him. Her thoughts hadn't ventured into *wanting* to date him, though. More like . . . what would dating him actually be like? The last few days had been far easier. They'd gotten along better, and there'd been little to no stress. Therefore, against her better judgment, her subconscious had insisted on pulling the idea out at odd hours of the day.

Arsula turned back to the ceiling. She didn't want to date Jaden. And she wouldn't even if he *had* moved on from Megan. He was her "charge," not a potential boyfriend. Not to mention, his attitude thoroughly reeked of superiority.

His head jerked suddenly, pulling Arsula's attention back to him, and she watched as his eyes twitched behind his lids. He was having a dream.

"Dad." The single word came out sharp and loud. *"Daaaaad!"*

She felt like an interloper as she lay there, but her need to help wouldn't let her look away.

"Where are you?" he whispered now, and heartbreak pulled at his features. Then he jerked again, and this time the move dragged him from the dream.

He seemed dazed as his eyes opened, and as he lay there, eyes blinking and his breathing coming back under control, Arsula held her breath. She waited for him to see her. To remember that halfway through the movie she'd climbed into bed beside him. And she wondered what he'd think about it this time.

Finally, he seemed to focus, and his gaze went to the TV. Then to the ceiling.

He lay there silently for another moment, his attention not straying from what was essentially the floor of her bedroom, before he slowly turned his head and looked at her. He took in her face . . . and then the pillow wedged between them.

Then he sank back into his own pillow.

"Christ," he muttered.

She had to agree.

A few seconds passed before he turned back. "Morning." His voice came out as a rough rumble.

"Good morning." She studied him quietly. He didn't seem upset to find her there—exactly. More like resigned. "You were dreaming about your dad just now?"

As she'd watched, the thought had whispered through her that his dad could also play a role in the pain Jaden carried. For what reason, she had no idea. As far as she knew, Max was great. But she was also aware that she didn't know everything.

"I . . ." Jaden closed his eyes, his brow wrinkling as if trying to recall, before he finally nodded. "I guess I was."

"Do you want to talk about it?"

His lips instantly flattened. "No, Arsula. I don't want to tell you about my dream so you can then try to tell me what it means."

"Can't blame a girl for trying."

His tone had annoyed her, but she ignored the insult implied within. She didn't need him to believe in her gift for it to be true. She didn't even need him to open up to her in order to narrow in on the root of what might be causing him pain. Not completely. All she had to do was listen and hear.

And what she'd just "heard" was a replay of the conversation at the hospital the morning she'd offered to let Jaden stay with her. His family had tossed out several ideas of where Jaden could stay, but in them—she'd realized—their dad had never once been mentioned. *Gloria* had. In the vein of Jaden not wanting to be a bother to her. But neither Jaden nor his siblings had said a word about their father. And that was something worth bringing back out to explore later.

Jaden scrubbed his hands over his face, the act seeming to awaken him further, and his jaws stretched wide with a yawn. "Waking up with you seems to be becoming a habit," he mumbled.

"Two times doesn't necessarily make a habit."

He cast her a look. "It also doesn't make it right."

True, she thought. But neither of them made a move to change things.

Instead, Jaden just kept sizing her up, and after several seconds his mouth quirked at the corners. "Right or not, I suppose I should at least be thankful you aren't throwing things this time."

"And right or not, I suppose the lack of flying objects might have something to do with you not looking at me as if I have the plague."

He blossomed into a full-on grin. "You probably *do* have the plague, don't you?"

"And you probably *did* deserve for me to knock you down my stairs."

His laugh caught her off guard. It was loud and booming, a sound she'd heard from him only once before, and her heart began to beat too fast. She rolled back to her side, keeping the pillow between them as she did, but lying there like that, just the two of them talking in the predawn light, was more intimate than she should be participating in.

Jaden yawned again . . . then he rolled to face her as well. And then all humor faded.

As he regarded her, the moment silent and suddenly too intense, Arsula lowered her gaze to the bed. She wasn't sure what was going on with them, nor whether she liked it. But she also knew she wasn't quite ready to get up.

Reaching for an excuse that would allow her to stay, she asked, "Who were you going to tell me to worry about last night?"

"When?" His tone came out too soft. Too personal.

Her pulsed raced faster. "Right before we started talking about your mom. You said, 'If you want to worry about someone . . .'"

"Oh." He gave a perturbed grunt and shifted in place. "I meant my dad."

"Max?" She pushed to her elbow, the memory of dancing with Jaden's dad resurfacing, as well as the sense that something hadn't been right with him. She should have dropped by and checked in on him already. "What's wrong with him?"

"Actually, I don't know that anything is."

The man was sidestepping. "Then why are you worried?"

"*I'm* not worried. It's Dani who is."

She stared back at him. Everything inside her had tightened with the mention of his dad's name, and it remained that way. "Why is Dani worried?"

And she didn't believe for a second that Jaden wasn't worried as well. Thin lines now bracketed his mouth.

He didn't answer immediately, seemingly attempting to get his thoughts in order before doing so, but finally offered up a response. "She mentioned last night that at times Dad seems 'off.' That's all. And she apparently caught him using a cane one day. All normal growing-old things."

"Yet your intuition is telling you there's a problem?"

He scowled. "I don't rely on my intuition, Arsula."

"But maybe you should."

"And maybe you should stop trying to 'fix' me."

They hadn't spoken about the reason she'd moved to Birch Bay since that first night, and at his words, the tension eased from her shoulders. "I don't want to 'fix' you, Jaden. That was never my intent. People don't need to be fixed." She touched her fingers to the center of his chest. "I just want to help you out in here. I can sense your turmoil. You reek of it."

"If I reek, it's because I haven't had a shower in a couple of days." He winked at her and covered her hand with his. She could feel the steady thump of his heart. "Don't worry. I'm fine in there, Lula-bell. I promise you."

Shock hit her like a bucket of ice water.

"What?" he questioned.

She tugged her hand from his. "Nothing. It's just that my mom calls me Lula-bell sometimes." "Lula" had come from her brother closest in age being unable to say Arsula, or even Sula, when she'd been born.

"Is that so?" Jaden pursed his lips as if considering something of great seriousness—though mischief danced in his eyes. "Then my *intuition* says that I should like your mom. Tell her I said hi in return, will you?"

She pulled a face. He was mocking her again. "I'll get right on that, jerk. That'll make her entire day."

He laughed, his smile radiating happiness, and he suddenly wrapped his arm around her waist. The pillow remained between them, but the warmth from his skin seeped through her cotton shirt.

"Can I ask you a question, Lula-bell?"

She maintained an unaffected gaze. "Sure. What do you want to know?"

His gaze flicked over her head before he spoke again, but came just as quickly back. "What's the deal with the cupcake?"

She bit down on her smile, but it still escaped. Two weeks it had taken, but the man had finally asked. She'd tossed the flowers the week before, when they'd turned brown and begun to crumble, but she'd left the cupcake—with its now sad-looking leaning candle—sitting exactly where she'd placed it that first day.

"I wouldn't recommend eating the cupcake at this point," she warned. His breath touched her face with every exhale. "If it's not already, it could be a science project any day now." Blue fuzz had begun to peek out from under the icing several days ago.

"I don't intend to eat it at this point."

"Good."

He stared at her, and she just looked back. They were far too close for two people unattached. "You didn't actually answer my question, though."

She licked her lips. "And what was your question again?"

She honestly couldn't remember. His eyes matched the unique color of the rest of his family, but none of them had ever been this close. She'd never had the opportunity to get lost in that particular shade of blue.

"What's with the cupcake?"

"Oh." She blinked, breaking the hold his gaze had on hers, and she gave a little shrug. "It was for your birthday."

Surprise softened his features. "You made me a cupcake for my birthday?"

"I did. I baked it while waiting on Nate to bring you from the hospital."

"But"—he glanced at the dilapidated dessert again—*"why?"*

The question should have been a simple one, yet it came across as if he truly had no clue. And she hated that he didn't get it. "Because it had been your birthday, Jaden." She smiled to soften the need for an explanation, but she didn't let herself reach out and touch his furrowed brow. "And because no one got you anything. I'm a firm believer that everyone deserves to feel special for their birthday."

He stared at her again, and she could see questions remaining. But also, comfort beginning to shroud him.

The tautness that had appeared in his shoulders eased, and he nodded his head. "I like that theory. Everyone *should* feel special for their birthday. And now I'm sorry I ignored it instead of eating it. I'll bet it was a really good cupcake."

His eyes danced back and forth between hers.

"It *was* a really good cupcake." Miniature cakes were one of the few things she'd mastered.

A hint of a smile returned to his mouth as he continued to lie there looking at her, and the color of his eyes deepened. "You make me smile, Lula-bell. Do you know that?" He removed his arm from her waist, but he reached for her hand. "And I like that you'd bake a cupcake for a person you'd just met, solely because he hadn't gotten anything for his birthday." He twined their fingers together. "Can I ask when your birthday is?"

She stared at their hands. "It's April 10."

"Soon, then?"

"Yes." She brought her gaze back to his. "Why do you want to know? Are you going to bake me a cupcake for my birthday?" She asked the question with a smile on her face, but unease had begun to seep through her. He was holding her hand.

And she was letting him.

And he still lay only inches from her.

"I might," he replied. "But what if I'm not a good cupcake maker?"

"Then I'd eat a bite of it, and I'd toss the rest when you weren't looking."

He laughed yet again, the sound vibrating through the pillow and into her stomach, and at the same time, the sun rose high enough in the sky that a beam of light slashed through the room and across his cheeks. And then he stopped laughing.

And then he put his mouth to hers.

Jaden's mouth closed over Arsula's before he fully realized what he'd done. He shouldn't be kissing her. He couldn't remember exactly why at the moment, but he knew that he *shouldn't* be kissing Arsula.

He couldn't seem to separate his lips from hers, though. Because for the second time in two weeks, he'd woken up next to her, all sleep-tousled and looking hot as hell, and all he'd been able to think about was the fact that a lack of erection would *not* be an issue this time.

When she didn't push him away, he angled his mouth and urged her to give him more. And damn, he got it. Her lips parted beneath his, a breathy little sound escaping from the back of her throat as her mouth reached forward, and with a moan, he slipped inside. Then he silently pleaded that kissing Arsula would never have to stop.

Lifting to his elbow, he brought his hand to her cheek, hoping to block the temptation of putting it elsewhere, but then she whimpered. And he completely lost his mind.

Lips heated as their tongues exchanged strokes, and the damned hand that was supposed to remain above her neck crept lower. It danced over the outline of her body, his fingers exploring at every point of connection, and she moaned with each touch. She was both hard and soft—in exactly the right places.

As his palm smoothed over her hips—and her leg lifted to slide sensuously over his—he cursed his memory for never retrieving the image of her with*out* her red bridesmaid dress. That was a vision he'd tried to conjure up way more than was likely healthy since the night of the wedding. But so far, nothing.

Maybe he could be lucky enough to get another chance, though.

Possibly this morning.

Arsula's body bowed as he continued to stroke over her, the pillow blocking full-body contact, so he reached to yank it out of their way. He'd just pulled it free when the sound of her voice hit his ears.

"Jaden." She breathed out his name, her chest heaving in sync with his. "This . . ."

"I know." Dropping the pillow behind her, he kissed her again. "It's freaking amazing." Their mouths brushed as he spoke. "Even better than I remember." And that part of his memory *wasn't* lacking.

He pressed a hand to the middle of her back, closing the remaining distance that separated them, and every inch of him sprang to life. The curves he'd previously traced now pressed flush to his body, her foot dropped to the back of his knee, locking him to her, and he returned his hand to her cheek. His intent was to kiss her again. *Hard.* To not waste a second without his lips being on hers. But instead he paused. And he simply feasted his eyes on her.

Black hair spilling out around her face, cheeks heated to pink, eyes glazed. Lips full and swollen from his touch.

She took his breath away.

And she was in *his* bed.

"Definitely better," she agreed. She then lifted her hand to cup his cheek, same as he was doing to her, and she pulled in several deep breaths. Her eyes never left his as they lay there, and he found himself desperate to know her thoughts.

Desperate to pick back up where they'd left off.

But then her lips curved . . . and her smile turned fond.

His brain stuttered on the thought. *Fond?* What the hell?

As if he were some long-forgotten pet.

Where was the heat that had been there only a moment before? Why was her leg still wrapped around his if all she had to offer was fondness?

And what had caused the change?

He covered her hand and slowly retracted it from his cheek. "Are you okay?" he asked.

She nodded, but she also removed her leg. "To tell you the truth, I haven't been this okay in a while." She pulled in another long breath, and her cheeks puffed as she blew it out. But she no longer made eye contact.

"Then what seems to be the problem?"

She rolled to her back, her previous chest heaving now a thing of the past, and she stared at the ceiling. "The problem is"—she shook her head back and forth—"that I can't do this."

"This?" He tried to keep the edge out of his voice, but he failed.

"Yes." She looked at him again, her eyes now showing regret layered in with the fondness. *"This."* She swept her hand in a circular swath that encapsulated both of them, along with the bed. "With *you.*"

"With . . . *me?*" He knew he sounded like an idiot by lying there, doing nothing but repeating her words, but he couldn't seem to come up with anything else to say. He still didn't get it. What had happened to change things?

Instead of replying, she was up and out of the bed, and her quick escape had him going from idiot to total fool. He glowered up at her.

"Why the hell can't you?" he barked out. "Because it certainly *felt* like you were doing it."

She snapped her hands to the sides of her waist, all previous fondness *and* regret disappearing. "Don't you dare 'why the hell' me, Jaden Wilde. No means no, no matter what I did."

That wasn't what he'd meant.

He pushed to a sitting position. "That's not—"

"And as for why . . ." Her mouth flattened into a straight line, and she jabbed a finger his way. "I won't do this with you because *you* are still hung up on another woman."

At her words, his thoughts turned to disbelief. *Shit.* He'd forgotten about Megan.

He'd been ready to make love to another woman—for the second time in two weeks—with no thought about the woman he was *supposed* to be in love with. What was wrong with him?

"And that's fine," Arsula went on. The edge of anger in her voice dulled, but only by a fraction. "I get it. The heart wants what the heart wants and all that. But I won't be that girl, Jaden." She shook her head. "I won't be the stand-in while you bide your time waiting for another woman."

The stand-in? He blinked. Then he shook his head. "I wasn't thinking you would be."

The problem was that he hadn't been thinking at all.

"Maybe you weren't. But *something* was." She scowled at his lap.

When she returned her eyes to his, her look said that he was scum of the lowest form. It also said that if a lamp were within arm's reach, she'd bash it over his head.

"No more kissing," she told him. "No more doing any of this. Because though I may not require a long-term commitment before sleeping with a man . . . I *do* require that man to actually be into me. And *only* me."

Chapter Fourteen

The splint was now a cast.

Hallelujah.

And though there was tremendous joy in knowing that the healing had progressed far enough to move him to the next state, Jaden's lower leg was already starting to itch inside the plaster.

Actually, it wasn't, and he knew it. *Logically.* It was all in his head. But he also knew that it eventually *would* itch, so the very idea of it bothered him. Just like the very idea of kissing Arsula bothered him.

But then again, it bothered him to *not* kiss her.

She just bothered him altogether. In both a good and a bad way.

He stared out the front window of his brother's truck, seeing nothing but passing colors, and thought about the fact that he'd just compared kissing Arsula to the itch of a cast. Which wasn't fair at all. Kissing Arsula was . . .

He sighed to himself. *Phenomenal.* Kissing her was a freaking joy.

Doing more would be heaven on earth.

But it also wasn't just kissing her. It was everything about her. She was kind of terrific. A little deranged in the head, but . . . terrific in a funny, quirky, sexy, caring, stiff-spine sort of way. Which confused the hell out of him. And "confused" was putting it mildly.

She'd spent Saturday night in his bed, then he'd been ready to shuck his clothes at the first touch of her lips. *Again.* What was it about that woman? And why was he even thinking about her when things with him and Megan remained unclear?

"What time is your appointment tomorrow?" Nate asked from the driver's seat.

"One o'clock." He had sessions set up with Dr. Wangler for each day the remainder of that week, and though he still couldn't put weight on his foot, he felt decidedly more mobile than during his last attempt.

"Want to grab a late lunch after?"

He glanced at his brother. "Works for me." If he didn't get lunch with Nate, he'd be left sitting in the kitchen, eating all alone. Since the morning before, Arsula had taken to leaving a plate of food warming in the oven for him instead of hanging out and talking while he ate. She'd been pleasant enough whenever they'd had to be around each other—but she'd also made it a point *not* to be around him.

He and Nate fell back into silence, and as the pines and birch trees whipped past the windows, Jaden turned his thoughts to Saturday's conversation with Dani. He needed to have a serious discussion with his brother. Was Nate still in town because he was hiding from something?

Running from something?

Or just what *was* going on with him?

The truck turned off the highway and a flash of lake glinted off to their right, and Jaden decided it was time to delve in. They would be back to Arsula's apartment soon, and he'd promised Dani he'd work on Nate today.

"Why are you still here?" Jaden tossed out. There was no need to beat around the bush.

Nate shot him a look. "Excuse me?"

"In Birch Bay," Jaden clarified. "What's keeping you around so long this time?"

"You, you dumb fuck." The look turned to a scowl. "What do you think?"

"I think you're avoiding something else right now as much as you've always avoided this place."

The hardening of his brother's jaw told Jaden that he'd ticked him off. It also said he was quite possibly on the right track. "You're wrong," Nate insisted, and went back to concentrating on the road. "Why are you bringing this up now, anyway? Do you *want* me to leave? Because I can. I don't need to stick around where I'm not wanted. But if I do go, who's going to take you to all your appointments?"

Jaden could walk to the counseling sessions if he had to. Dr. Wangler's office was only a few blocks away. But he *couldn't* walk to his doctor's office. Or to his physical therapy appointments when they started in a couple of weeks. And he still wouldn't be able to drive for a while longer.

But he also couldn't ask Nate to stick around if he wanted to go.

"Don't get me wrong," Jaden said. "I appreciate the help. It's huge."

"Yeah, you appreciate it by staying with Arsula."

"Don't start that again. I made my decision, you chose to help anyway. End of story."

"Excellent point. So then, why are you bringing it up?"

Good Lord. The man could be difficult. Jaden shifted on the seat so that he faced his brother's profile, then he tried another tactic. "I'm bringing it up because I'm worried about you. *Dani* is worried about you." Maybe bringing their sister into the conversation would help. "It isn't like you to hang around for so long, so we're just wondering . . . what's going on? Don't you have a job to get back to?"

The truck made another turn, and as they hit Main Street, Jaden glanced around, searching for Arsula's car. He found it where she normally parked, and he also caught a light burning in the living room of her apartment.

"I actually quit my job a year ago," Nate answered from the other side of the truck, bringing Jaden's shocked gaze back to him.

"You quit?"

And he hadn't told anyone?

Nate didn't look away from the road. "It's no big deal. I'd had enough. Being out on a boat for weeks at a time no longer appealed."

He pulled into a spot in front of the building and turned off the truck. It was after five, and most businesses on the street were already locked up tight, but they watched as the owner of the bookstore two doors down moved throughout the first floor, restocking her product.

"What have you been doing since then?" Jaden asked.

"Mostly nothing."

Jaden understood that he needed to tread carefully. Not only did Nate rarely stick around, he also made it a point not to share things. "Then what do you *want* to do?"

Finally turned his way, Nate seemed to have dropped his usual mask of protection as he answered more honestly than Jaden had ever heard. "I don't have a clue."

Jaden just stared at his brother for a moment, then he did a quick run-through of the changes that had been working their way through his family over the last few years. And as he thought through everything, a new sense of peace began to fill him. It seemed Nate wasn't immune to needing them as much as he'd like everyone to believe. Which meant, maybe they *could* eventually be the family they'd once pretended to be.

"It's okay if you want to come home, you know?" Jaden said, at the same time the light in Arsula's bedroom came on. He tossed a glance in that direction. "You don't need an excuse to be here."

"You're not an excuse." Nate didn't discredit the theory that he wanted to come home.

"Then why not just move back?"

His brother leaned forward in his seat, watching Arsula's window as well. "And do what?"

There was no other sign of the woman Jaden couldn't seem to quit thinking about. "College? Didn't you take some classes a few years back? Now could be a good time to finish up a degree."

"I'm not Nick, and I don't want to go back to school." A shadow moved through the room above them. "Nor do I need to prove myself like you," Nate added, and as his words registered, they pulled Jaden's attention off the apartment above them.

"What do you mean by that?"

Nate didn't look at him. "You'll end up going back for your PhD, won't you? Going as far in school as you can?"

"I'll do as much as needed to be an excellent counselor."

Nate nodded. "And you'll probably be okay at it."

Okay at it? Jaden's temper flared. "*Wrong.* I'll be *exceptional* at it."

Arsula appeared in the window then and looked down at them, and a strange silence filled the cab. She watched, making no bones about looking from one to the other, then as quickly as she'd appeared, she was gone.

The light went off in the room, and the quiet of the cab was once again filled with the sounds of their breathing.

"Maybe you should let her help you," Nate suggested quietly, and nodded toward the upstairs apartment. And Jaden's jaw once again dropped.

"Let her help me how?"

"She's good with people. I hear it all over town."

Jaden remained floored by his brother's words. "I thought you hated her."

"I never hated her." Nate's gaze scanned to the other room on the second floor, and Jaden got the impression he wasn't looking for Arsula so much as *not* looking at him.

"Then what *was* the deal? Because you sure as fuck *seemed* to hate her." Jaden quickly ran through a list of options and settled on the most obvious. "Was it more about jealousy?"

Nate's gaze flicked to his.

"Because you saw it as me choosing her over you?"

His brother didn't look away. Instead, a rare glint of vulnerability shone out from him. "That's possible. I mean, I was here. I wasn't doing anything else." He shrugged. "Why not let me help?"

"I *am* letting you help."

"Yet you're avoiding the house."

Jaden narrowed his focus on his brother. "You know what it was like growing up there."

"I know very well. I had more years with her than you. Yet you've never avoided staying there when you've come home before. So why now?"

Why not now, Jaden wanted to lob back. He didn't, though, because it would answer nothing. It would be no more than a childish taunt. Nate did make him think about the question, though. Really think about it for the first time. He'd assumed he was avoiding the house due to memories of their mother ignoring him when he was a kid. Of never being there for him. Never *being* a mother.

But Nate had a point. Why now? What was different now?

And how was it that this had turned into Nate trying to counsel *him?*

Jaden scowled at the thought. Arsula had brought this very subject up before, but suddenly, he found himself wondering if there was more to his reasoning than simply avoiding the house his mother had lived in. Had Arsula been clueing in to something he'd missed?

Nate turned back to the building sitting before them. "We've all got issues, Jay. Even you. You're staying here with her already—which is a giant red flag that you *do* have issues, by the way—so why not spend some of that time talking to her? Seeing if it helps?"

Because he didn't want to admit he needed help.

"I'm fine," he assured his brother. "You've got it all wrong. No issues for me. And also . . . there's nothing wrong with continuing my education."

He reached for the door.

"Except maybe it's your way of trying to best Cord."

Jaden's fingers stilled on the handle.

He took a couple of seconds to breathe, telling himself not to reach across the seat of the truck and beat the crap out of his brother, then he removed his hand from the door handle and once again faced Nate. "What did you say?"

Nate stared at him. "I'm just calling 'em as I see 'em."

"And you're seeing that *I* need to be better than *Cord*?"

"Don't you?"

Jaden didn't respond to the accusation, so Nate went on.

"You need to be the best," he explained. "You always have. I see it kind of like little-man syndrome."

"Are you fucking—"

"Hold up." Nate held a hand up between them. "Hear me out. I'm serious. You're the baby of the family, you're the only one of us men who didn't reach six feet."

"I'm going to kick your ass."

Nate made a face as if to indicate that was an absolute impossibility and went on. "And you basically didn't see our mother the first two years of your life." His tone softened as he continued. "Dani came home to help Dad with us, but Nick and I were twins. We had each other. Gabe and Cord were practically grown—and were gone within a couple of years—but you were the one who was alone. You were the one who had to wonder what *you'd* done wrong. You eventually picked up on what had been the issue with our mother, and now you're intent on saving all the sad little boys in the world whose mothers didn't love them, either."

Jaden could only stare at his brother.

"And what all of that says to me is that you're still holding on to something that hasn't healed. You still need everyone to know you're the best. That you're *not* the little boy who had no voice and that no one wanted." Nate shrugged. "Cord's a doctor. Therefore, I assume you'll earn your doctorate." He glanced back up at the apartment. "And I think talking to someone wouldn't hurt."

Jaden didn't move. Instead, he sat in utter bemusement. His brother had never strung this many words together in his life, yet when he did, he wanted to play counselor.

And he thought that Jaden should let Arsula play counselor, too.

Jaden took in the light still burning in the right half of the apartment. Had everyone around him gone crazy?

"How do you even know anything about her?" he finally made himself ask. He also purposefully ignored everything else Nate had said. "And why the sudden change of heart? Last I heard, you thought she was nuts."

A car pulled up beside them, and Nate nodded toward it. "Yeah. But then I talked to Meg."

Jaden stood in the street as his brother pulled away, trying not to glare at his ex. What in the hell had Nate and Meg been talking about? And why? Nate hadn't answered those questions before driving off, insisting instead that Jaden get out of the truck. And now Megan sat cautiously watching him from the front seat of her car.

If his ankle wasn't broken, he might go to her, open her door. As it was, he used his injury as an excuse, and he turned and walked into the building.

He should be thrilled. Clearly, she was here to talk. *Finally.* But instead, he found himself pissed. Because why had she been talking about anything with his brother when she couldn't even bring herself to talk to *him*?

Half a minute later, the door to the building opened, and Jaden called out from the couch to let her know where he was. When Megan appeared, he said, "Close the door."

He had to get his anger under control. This was the conversation he'd been waiting for.

Only, she looked as if she'd come prepared with the upper hand.

"How's the ankle?" she finally said.

He held the cast out in front of him. "It's healing. I can now knock chunks out of any wall I pass if I have the desire to."

She gave him a half smile, but there was no humor to it. "I figured it was time we talked."

"You figured, or did my sister make you?"

Or maybe it had been his brother's idea to come there tonight. They had *talked*, after all. The thought burned hot inside him as Megan stepped farther into the room.

"Does it matter why? I'm here. I'm ready to talk."

"Then let's talk." He motioned to the straight-backed chair now sitting at the fully completed desk. He'd called and asked Gabe to come over the day before, and Gabe had finished putting the desk together while Jaden and Jenna watched cartoons.

Megan didn't immediately sit. Instead, she paced the small amount of free space, and she seemed to take in every detail as she did. When she finally stilled, she stopped on the other side of the bed and touched her fingertips to the mattress.

"So this is where you've been staying?" she began.

"It's doing the job."

"And Arsula?" She glanced at the ceiling above them. "She's been taking good care of you?"

"I'm aware she's the one you talked to about your dream," he pointed out. He wanted to skip the pleasantries.

"She is."

"And no matter what Nate might have indicated, nothing's going on here." At least, there hadn't been before Sunday morning. Now he didn't know *what* was going on.

Or what he wanted to go on.

"I never thought there was," Meg countered.

"Are you sure about that?"

Her eyes danced over the bed in the middle of the room.

"Because I thought we walked away the night of the wedding on common ground," Jaden went on. "But then you refused to speak to me. You didn't even offer to help me out when I ended up in the hospital."

Damn. He hadn't meant to say that.

It seemed to get her attention, though.

She carefully lowered to the bed, and she jutted out her chin. "An ambulance had to pick you up at the bottom of her stairs, Jaden. The morning *after* the wedding. While you were still in your tux."

"Nothing—"

"Don't even. I'm not an idiot."

"But . . ."

He really wanted to tell her that nothing had been going on. That it had been as innocent as he'd like to believe himself. Because he didn't want the idea of him and Arsula to hurt her.

But this was Meg. And though he might not have always been as talkative as she'd wanted, he'd never told her any untruths.

"We didn't sleep together," he started again. "We didn't have *sex*. But there *was* sleep."

She nodded at that. "Okay."

Her seeming lack of concern confused him. "There was also kissing," he added.

She nodded again, and as she had when the conversation first started, she glanced toward the ceiling.

"And the fact was, I was drunk off my ass," he explained. "I know that's no excuse, but that was the situation. She and I were hanging out, I was trying to prove myself a man, apparently, by drinking all the booze I could get my hands on, and the next thing I knew, we were standing in the freezing snow and I didn't have on a coat. And then I kissed her."

She brought her gaze back to his. "And then you came here."

"And then we came here."

She waited for him to continue, so he added, "And karma is a bitch, apparently."

At her questioning expression, he stood from the couch. But since he couldn't pace, he merely hung over his crutches.

"I couldn't . . . perform, okay?" Humiliation heated his face, but he figured he deserved the punishment. "I don't even remember it, but apparently, if you drink too much whiskey . . ."

The smile he'd once fallen in love with suddenly glowed back. "You couldn't get it up?"

"Stop."

"Well, that's a first."

He smirked at that, but they also shared a moment as they silently looked at each other. Because early on in their relationship, they'd gone at it like rabbits.

"So"—she spoke again—"you did intend to sleep with her?"

"Yes. But don't blame Arsula. She's not at fault for any of it." Now it was his turn to look up. "In fact, I wouldn't be surprised to find out that I'd personally poured half her drinks down her throat. I was a man on a mission that night, Meg. One of destruction. *I* shouldn't have kissed her. *I* shouldn't have come here."

She nodded, but he wasn't sure if it was in agreement or understanding.

"And *I'm* the one you should be mad at."

She remained quiet for another moment before smoothing her hand over the comforter covering his bed. Then she gave him a tight smile. "I'm not actually mad about that. Not really, and not at either of you. You and I *were* broken up at that point. And yeah, maybe it had only been for a few hours, but in my head, it had already been a few weeks."

The confession stung, even though she'd said as much that first night. "Then why have you refused to speak to me?"

"Because I was *mortified*, Jay. Don't you get that? No one knew we'd broken up, yet here I come to the hospital, worried about what might have happened to you, and I'm faced with having to take your clothes from another woman."

He cringed. "I am *incredibly* sorry that happened." He probably hated that the most.

"Yeah. Me too. But the thing is," she went on, "even standing there accepting the clothes, I'm not sure I could be mad at her if I wanted to. I *like* her, Jaden. She's genuine. And *sweet*."

"You like who? Arsula?"

She nodded, and as they stared at each other again, each struggling with their own thoughts, Jaden pushed the woman who lived above him from his mind and returned to the moment just before he'd stepped out of Nate's truck. To the incredibly inappropriate thought that had crossed his mind.

"And how do you feel about Nate?" He had to ask, even if it didn't matter at this point. "Do you like him, too?"

Confusion colored her features again. "What?"

"Nate said you two have been spending some time together." He'd actually said "talking," but Jaden had wondered if that hadn't also meant "together."

She picked at one of her fingernails. "We've talked a few times."

"Right." Jaden smirked. "At which point, you apparently offered your opinion that I should share my 'troubles' with Arsula."

"I never said that." Her head tilted as she studied him. "But now that you mention it . . ."

Now that he'd mentioned it, he wished he hadn't. "Forget it. What else have you talked to Nate about?"

"Just . . . *things*." Guilt suddenly crossed her face, and any other words Jaden might have uttered sat lodged in his throat.

Really?

With his own brother?

"Oh, good grief," Megan said, clueing in to his silence. "I am not seeing your brother, Jay, if that's what you're thinking. Not that you'd have a say in the matter if I were."

True, he wouldn't. But he would have an excuse to kick Nate's ass. "Then what are you doing?"

She glanced away now, staring through the glass panes, out to the desk where Arsula spent so much of her time, and when she turned back, all traces of guilt and hesitancy were gone. "I'm staying in Birch Bay," she told him. "That's what I'm doing. I'm going to take the job at the store. And I'm going to *move* the store to a better location. I've spoken to Nate about this idea—as well as to Dani—and they're both on board."

Jaden blinked at her announcement. "You're going to move the store?" He hadn't seen that coming.

"Yes."

"*Away* from the orchard?"

"I want to find a location here in the downtown area. Where the majority of the businesses are. It'll be better for sales, better for visibility."

"And you had this idea . . . *when*?" Shouldn't that be a decision the whole family was a part of? But then, when had he ever shown real interest in the business? In anything other than helping with the harvest?

But then . . . when had *Nate*?

"I've been thinking about it for a while now," Megan answered, and the hint of guilt that reappeared on her features altered Jaden's train of thought.

She'd been thinking it for a while? Meaning . . . *what?*

And then he got it. He straightened on his crutches. She'd been thinking about moving the store for *longer* than two weeks. For longer than the two of them had been broken up. She'd been making plans for her life, both personally and career-wise, and she hadn't included him in any of it.

Clearly, he wasn't the only one who hadn't been sharing things during their recent calls.

"So that's it, then?" His chest began to ache as badly as his ankle once had. "You've made up your mind, and I get no say in the matter whatsoever? You're out of the technology field, you're going to run my family's store, and you've been discussing all of this with everyone but me? Oh, and by the way . . . *we're done.*"

"Come on, Jay. Don't be like that."

"Don't be like that?" Using his crutches, he did finally try to pace. He didn't get far, though. "Then what am I supposed to be like, Meg? Tell me, because I still don't get it. I come home, offering you a ring, only to find out that you've already moved on without me. To find out—*out of the blue*—that we're done. Just like that."

"Out of the blue?" She rose to face him. "Are you kidding me? We'd been nitpicking at each other for months. We *never* talked."

"Apparently." He scowled down at her. "And I explained before that my issue was that I'd been busy. What's your excuse?"

"My excuse is that you *never* talked. So why should I?"

Her accusation came at him like a slap in the face, and he took a step back. "What do you mean? I talked all the time. *We* talked. We always have. Even before we started dating. Do you not remember what good friends we were before I ever asked you out?"

"Yes, we were friends. And yes, we talked. *Intellectually.*"

He didn't understand her point. "We're both smart people. How else *would* we talk?"

She groaned and gripped her fists in the air. "You can be so frustrating sometimes, Jaden. My *point* is that we rarely shared much emotionally. At least *you* didn't."

He almost laughed at that. "You're wrong. I told you I loved you all the time."

"Jay." She began to pace. "There's so much more to love than saying the words. Don't you know that?"

"But I did love you. So why weren't the words good enough?" As he waited for her answer, he realized he'd said *did* and not *do*. And he wondered if that was true.

"And I loved you," she replied quietly. She stopped in front of him again, and she touched a hand to her chest. "But I need more than that. I need you to be able to share more with me. To let me hurt when you do."

To hurt when he did? Was she out of her mind?

Why would he want to hurt someone he cared about?

"I had a counselor," he reminded her. "For years. *Her* job was to listen to my issues. To hear my hurts." He shook his head. His ex might be brilliant, but she was simply delusional on this one. "It would have helped nothing to come home and rehash the same things with you."

"It would have helped *us*, Jay." Her softly spoken words hinted at a hurt he never would have guessed at. "It would have bound *us* in the way we should both want to strive for. In a way that connects two people long term." She tilted her face to the ceiling as a noise came from overhead. "But you guard your heart too well. You always have. And your *heart*," she went on in a whisper, his eyes still focused above them, "is what I needed the most."

A tear slipped down her cheek.

"Meg." He spoke as softly as she had, and she brought her gaze back to his.

"Nate might be onto something." She pointed to the ceiling, ignoring his silent plea to understand that he'd done his best. "I don't want you to be alone forever, Jay. I really don't. I want nothing but happiness for you. Talk to Arsula. Open up to her. She really is good at helping people do that."

His soft plea turned to an irritated glare. What the hell was wrong with everyone tonight? He didn't need to talk to *anyone*. He didn't have anything to open up *about*! But if he did decide he wanted to talk, he'd find a certified psychologist to do it with. *Not* someone who wanted him to share his dreams so she could guess at his deepest, darkest secrets.

Megan moved to the doors, and panic suddenly gripped him. She couldn't just walk away again. Not like this.

"What if I help you find a location for the store?"

She looked back at his question. "I don't think—"

"As a friend. That's all. I get it, Meg. We're done." And surprisingly, he did get it. And he *had* loved her, instead of still *did*.

Well, wasn't this a big night for revelations?

"Why should our friendship have to change because our relationship does?" he went on. "But also, I want to help out as part owner of the business." As he said the words, he realized the truth they contained. This was *his* company, too. Wasn't it time he finally acted like it? "The orchard, the store, they're a part of me as well, you know? I own a portion."

"I am aware of that."

"And that's something you're going to miss out on by not marrying me," he teased, reaching deep for a smile when a smile was the last thing he felt like offering. A relationship was dying tonight, and no matter how long it had already been over, it still hurt to see it happen. "You could've been half owner of my sixth of the business."

She gave him a rueful smile of her own. "I'm also aware of what I'm losing."

He moved across the room then and took her hand in his. "I'm sorry I wasn't what you needed, Meg. I wish I could have been."

She cupped his cheek. "I wish you could have been, too. And I'm sorry *I* wasn't the one able to help you to be your best you. I do agree with your suggestion, though. I'd like it if our friendship didn't change. So yes, you can help me find a place. I'd appreciate the help, actually. You know the town better than me, you know what's likely to be a better location, better landlord."

"Maybe we can build instead of rent?"

She shook her head. "No. I want the new location operational before cherry season. It's already the first of March, and tourists will start coming in well before the cherries are harvested. I want to be up and running soon, so the kinks are worked out long before the masses flood in."

He took in the woman he was supposed to love. Who was supposed to love him. Who'd ditched years of schooling because she'd found a passion to improve upon his family's business.

"You're going be fantastic at this job, you know?"

"I'm already fantastic." She winked and wrapped her hand around the doorknob. "Mess with me, though, and I'll weasel my way in to part-owner."

"Not without me you won't."

She chuckled, and then she released the door and wrapped her arms around him. As she did, she gave him a kiss on the cheek. "I'm still your friend, Jaden, and I always will be. You can always give me a yell if you need anything."

As they separated, he had the thought that he'd needed her two weeks ago. Only, she hadn't been there.

Then it occurred to him who *had* been.

Chapter Fifteen

Y̶ou look like a pretzel folded up in my car like that." Arsula stared down at Jaden sitting in the passenger seat of her hybrid, his knees practically at his neck. It wasn't that he was that large of a man, but her compact combined with his need for extra space due to his cast almost made the idea of her lunchtime outing undoable.

"I feel like a pretzel." He shoved at his left knee, as if his healthy leg needed the extra push just to fit into the allotted space. "Or maybe more like a jack-in-the-box. Once you park and I open the door, I'll just spring out."

"A Jaden-in-the-box," she muttered. He painted a cute picture. "Just what I always wanted."

Closing the door before he could say anything else—and hopefully before he would read anything into her "want" comment—she headed for the driver's side. They hadn't talked about what had happened between them yet, but that was on her. First, she'd avoided him the remainder of Sunday. Then yesterday, she'd been too busy working. Mondays tended to be more rushed around the office anyway, but it was possible she'd completed a handful of tasks twice—for the sole purpose of *appearing* busier.

But then last night . . . he'd rung the bell. And she'd flat out ignored it. She'd been unwilling to go downstairs and risk a personal conversation she wasn't yet ready to have.

The ringing had started within seconds of Megan pulling away from the building, and Arsula had doubted Jaden really needed anything. She *had* listened at the door, though. To make sure he didn't legitimately need any help. But as soon as she'd heard him moving around, she'd returned to what she'd been doing since Megan had shown up. What she'd been doing the majority of the prior thirty-six hours. Which had been lying on her bed and staring at the ceiling.

She and Jaden had kissed. Again.

They'd come darn close to doing more. Again.

And just like the first time, all of it had pretty much knocked her socks off.

She blew a shaky breath out now, before opening the door and climbing behind the wheel, and mentally psyched herself up to talk about it. Because she knew she couldn't avoid it forever, but also because she had no doubt the subject would come up. Jaden had been loitering in the main area of the office all morning, as if intent on finding a moment to say whatever it was he had on his mind. Yet with Dani and Tim both in the office today, a private conversation had been impossible.

"So where are we going?" Jaden asked as she pulled away from the curb.

She tossed him a quick peek. He smelled like cologne and soap today. "I'm not saying." She wasn't saying because chances were good if he knew their destination was Wilde Orchard, he might open his door and spring out like the jack-in-the-box he'd mentioned.

He studied her for a moment before settling back into the seat as much as possible. "As long as it's not the inside of a doctor's office, I'm game."

Arsula had been vague about her plans, only saying that she needed to get out of the office and asking if he wanted to tag along. However, she'd known from the moment she'd opened her eyes that morning what she needed to do. And not just because she wanted to see if there was merit to her theory that Jaden had unresolved issues with his father. She also just wanted to *see* Max. He'd shown up in her dreams last night. Nothing concrete had come from it, but enough concern filled her to get her out there.

"You're not going to take me to a cliff and drop me off, are you?"

A hint of humor threaded through Jaden's words, and with her silence of the last two days and the way she'd stomped away from him Sunday morning, she could see why he might ask the question. The fact was, though, that her anger had been directed more at herself than at him. She'd just used the excuse of his poor choice of wording to fuel the flame.

"I hear the views are good just before jumping off." She hadn't intended to kiss him again, but she certainly hadn't imagined herself two seconds from helping him out of his clothes, either.

"And what have you heard about the views just before someone *pushes* you off?"

Her laugh slipped out involuntarily. There seemed to be no anger running through him today, and the more positive vibrations had been an assault on her senses since the moment she'd come downstairs.

"Don't be funny," she scolded him. "I'm still busy being mad at you."

"I know. But I don't like it when you're mad at me."

That one statement finished her off. Dang it. How could she hold on to a good fake anger when the man wanted to be cute? She made a turn and headed north. "Fine," she admitted reluctantly. "I'm not mad at you. Does that make you happy?"

"Ecstatic. And for the record, I'm not mad at you, either."

That had her whipping her gaze to his. "Why would you be mad at *me*? I didn't do anything."

"Au contraire, Lula-bell. Aren't you the one who's supposed to be taking care of me?"

"I *am* taking care of you!"

"Then why didn't you come when I rang the bell last night?"

She growled under her breath at his pointed question and went back to focusing only on the road. "You didn't really need my help, so there was no reason for me to respond."

"But I did really need to talk to you." His voice changed, and she steeled herself for the conversation ahead. The issue was, she still didn't know what she wanted to say. Or how to react when he brought it up.

Or how to make sure she didn't end up kissing him again.

Because if Megan's presence at the office the night before had only been to clear things up . . .

"So talk," she said now. She swallowed and wet her lips. "You have ten minutes to get whatever you want off your chest."

"Ten minutes until you arrive at my dad's house?"

Again, she looked at him. How did he know that?

He twisted his mouth into a smirk. "Seems I can read you better than you thought. So why are you taking me to see my dad, Arsula? What are you up to?"

"I'm not up to anything." She couldn't make eye contact when she lied. "You're the one who said you're worried about him, don't you remember? I'm just being nice. I figured you'd like to check in on him."

"Dani's the one who's worried about him."

"And you're saying that you're not worried at all?" She split her attention between Jaden and the road. She wasn't sure why it was so hard for men to admit to a fear, but it seemed Jaden suffered from the same affliction. Finally, after an obstinate stare, he shrugged his shoulders in a couldn't-care-less manner, and she was left to wonder if it wasn't resistance to admitting his concern so much as it was a fear of the concern being valid.

"I'm worried about him, too, Jaden." Her words were little more than a scratch from the back of her throat. "That's the thing. I have been since the night I danced with him at your brother's wedding."

"Intuition again?" he asked.

"Intuition gets me through a lot."

She expected him to give her the mighty brow lift—as usual—but he surprised her with an agreeing nod. "Fine. Then we go check on him." He motioned toward the side of the road. "But can we pull over and talk first?"

"We can." She could even do him one better. There was a pull-off up ahead. One that wasn't situated at a cliff, but that looked out over the lake nonetheless. She kept driving until she got to it, then veered off the road into the empty lot. After easing into a parking spot and shifting into park, she didn't let herself get sucked into the view of the crystal-clear lake spread before her. Instead, she turned to face Jaden.

He did the same.

"You would never be a stand-in," he started, and Arsula's fingers clenched involuntarily. For some reason, she'd assumed he'd lead with Megan.

"Maybe stand-in wasn't the right word. But the reality is, I *was* convenient."

"No." The word had strength behind it, and he shook his head before trying it again. "No," he said more calmly. "Yes, okay. You *were* in my bed."

"Which *was* pretty convenient."

"True. But that's not why I kissed you, Arsula." His voice softened even more. "That's not why I wanted to do more."

She didn't let herself say anything. This was his moment, so she'd give him free rein.

Plus, she wasn't sure she could speak if she wanted to.

"You would never be a stand-in because you're *you*. Don't you get that? And *you* . . ."

He trailed off as if searching for the right way to explain it to her and ended up letting out a sad chuckle.

"How can I even ask if *you* get it when *I* don't?" he finally admitted. He leaned toward her. "And I don't, okay? I don't know why I'm so drawn to you. But I am. And not just physically. I have been since that morning in the hospital when I practically begged you to let me come home with you." He lifted a hand as if intending to reach out to her, but let it drop back to his lap. "Are you aware that I've never begged anyone for anything in my life?"

She thought about the pleading tone that had come from him as he'd dreamed about his dad. He may not have begged for anything during his waking hours, but his dreams told another story.

"You *were* enjoying your painkillers quite a bit that morning," she pointed out.

"True. But I didn't beg anyone else."

He hadn't. Nor was she sure what she thought about the idea of her being the only person he'd ever asked anything of.

The knowledge was both sad . . . and a little unnerving.

"It's you," he said again. "I'm drawn to you, and not because you're convenient. Or a stand-in." He did reach out that time, and he put his fingers to her arm. The heat from his skin mingled with hers, and her breathing became shallow. "I'm drawn to your smiles, Arsula. To the fact that you make *me* want to smile. And because when I'm around you, I never know when to be prepared to duck."

This time it was she who laughed. "I'll have you know that I've only contemplated throwing things a couple of times recently."

"Good to hear." His eyes met hers again, and his smile faded. His hand remained on her arm. "You know that Megan stopped by last night?"

190

The ease of the moment shifted until the air seemed strung tight. "I do know that. Do you want to talk about it?" The urge to make the offer had been there last night, but she hadn't been brave enough to hear what he had to say.

What if he still didn't accept that Megan had moved on?

What if that still didn't put a stop to her desire to kiss him again?

He didn't reply at first, clearly slipping back into the conversation from the night before, but after a minute, he gave a self-deprecating shrug. "The thing is, there's not all that much to say. We ended things quite cordially. Or rather, I accepted that things ended a few weeks ago."

A breath tried to whoosh out of her. "And are you okay with that? How does that make you feel?"

Her words had him pulling his hand away. "Come on, Arsula. Don't try to play psychologist on me. You may like to pretend—"

"Stop it," she interrupted him, her tone direct. Why did he always have to toss out an insult? "I'm not trying to play psychologist, Jaden. Nor do I think I'm a counselor who can skirt the rules by not getting an impressive education like you. *Nor* does any of that have a single thing to do with the conversation at hand."

She was angry again. And her voice had risen.

"I'm playing concerned friend, you blasted idiot. As well as a woman who's now kissed you twice."

Her admission wiped the smug look from his face.

"I feel really good about it," he answered immediately. A nod followed his words.

"So you're okay with where things stand?"

You're over her?

She didn't ask the second question out loud, nor did she let herself dwell on her announcement that their kissing played into her concern. Their physical relationship should not come into this part of the conversation.

But she also couldn't hide from the truth. They *did* have a physical relationship. Whether she wanted one or not.

"I actually . . . *am*," he said. "Surprisingly so. But I will admit to getting a bit angry when she showed up."

Arsula snorted sarcastically. "You? Angry?"

"Ha ha." He narrowed his eyes on her, and then the mood in the car shifted once again. This time to something deeper. And possibly more dangerous to her well-being. "You're cute, you know that?"

An unsolicited smile appeared on her face. "Somebody has to be."

"Well, you've mastered it." He reached for her again, and this time he took her hand. He held it between his. "I've been over her for a while, actually. I just didn't fully realize it until last night. I apparently needed to have the conversation in order to get there. But we are going to try the friends thing again. And I'm really happy about that."

A sense of peace that she hadn't felt before wafted from him. "I suspect Megan is happy about that, too. I know she hated the idea of losing your friendship."

He nodded, not saying anything else, but he continued to hold her hand. His thumb began to trace circles over her skin, and Arsula got the urgent feeling that he intended to wrap the conversation back around to where they'd first started. With the kiss.

With wanting more than a kiss.

She'd done all the talking about him and her that she wanted to, though. At least for today. And to be fair, she still wasn't at all sure she even wanted to think about whether there was—or could be—a him and her.

Therefore, she diverted his attention.

"Did I mention"—she turned back to the steering wheel and restarted the car—"that we're also going to your dad's because I feel very strongly that there are unresolved issues between the two of you? *And* that I'm upping my game to help you work through them?"

Jaden didn't speak as Arsula made the turn into the driveway of his family home. Nor did he look at her. In fact, he hadn't said one word—or given her one glance—since she'd driven away from the pull-off.

How dare she?

When she'd first mentioned the outing today, he'd jumped at the chance. He'd been certain this was her way to say that she was ready to talk about things. And he'd hoped the conversation would relay into her being ready to take things to the next level. Because Lord knows, he was ready.

As it turned out, though, she'd essentially been kidnapping him. Due to some harebrained idea she'd conjured up about him and his dad!

What made her actions even worse—aside from letting him get his hopes up even more before she'd dropped her little bomb on him—was that she was also convinced she had the abilities to "help him work through" whatever this mystical issue was that supposedly existed between him and his father. He had news for her, however. Reading dreams couldn't solve the world's problems.

"You're not really going to continue pouting once we get up to the house, are you?"

He fired a glare at her. "I am not pouting."

"Snarling?"

His jaws clenched. "I'm *furious*."

"Ah." She gave a nod, her mood seeming only to elevate the further his went downhill. "Furious isn't a verb, though," she mused. "And that's what I was going for. Maybe the correct word would be—"

"There is no issue with me and my dad."

"Denial." She nodded her head. "There's an excellent word. Though it's not a verb, either."

"Arsula."

193

She shot him an accommodating smile as she continued the trek up the driveway. "Yes, Jaden?"

"You're barking up the wrong tree here, and you need to stop. If there were a problem between my dad and me, don't you think I'd be aware of it?"

"You mean, because you've gone to school for recognizing such things?"

"I mean, because I saw a counselor of my own for years. My father and I are fine."

"Yet your denial is great."

Her calm reply sent his mind into a tailspin, taking it back several years to the time when he had met with someone regularly. When they'd talked about everything under the sun, and "how it had made him feel." And for the life of him, he couldn't recall a specific conversation where they'd traversed the depths of his and his father's relationship.

He was positive they had, though. Everyone in their family had been affected by his mother's behavior. Yet . . .

It didn't matter. He understood himself better than anyone.

"There is no issue," he repeated, this time at a more acceptable range, and then he forced himself to take in the glimpses of the lake the path provided instead of looking at her.

"Then will you prove it to me?"

He gritted his teeth. She never let up.

"Why should I have to?"

"Because I asked you to? Because I worry about you?"

Because she was convinced she could help?

He mulishly kept his gaze focused straight ahead. It wasn't that he was resistant to considering approaches other than those he practiced for solving personal struggles. He was a progressive guy. There was always more than one way to approach a problem. He just didn't happen to buy into her actually being able to "help" people. Just like she couldn't really "read" dreams.

She'd likely studied about dreams, sure. And therefore could pass for someone who had some knowledge on the subject. Because yeah . . . the subconscious worked on issues during sleep. He knew that. He didn't dispute that. He just didn't base his work off it.

His was more a humanistic approach than psychodynamic.

"Will you just humor me?" she asked now. She stopped the car a hundred feet before they got to the house, and she turned in her seat. She faced him, same as she'd done when they'd pulled off the road earlier, and something in her tone made him consider it.

It made him wonder—*briefly*—if she could be onto something.

He refused to accept that as a possibility, though, but he also refused to stay on the subject any longer. So he steered the conversation back to where he wanted it. "If I prove you wrong, you have to agree to kiss me again."

Her shoulders went stiff. "What? No. That has nothing to do with this."

"Yet that's the deal on the table." He eyed her, silently praying she'd say yes. All he'd thought about since she'd run away from his room the other morning was kissing her again.

And maybe doing more.

"But I don't want to kiss . . ." She trailed off as her eyes lowered to his mouth, and he expected the windows to begin to fog over any minute.

"I think you do." He might not believe in intuition, but he could read desire in a woman's eyes. "And possibly you want it as badly as I do."

"Jaden."

He dipped his head and looked over the rim of his glasses at her. *"Arsula."*

She let out a frustrated groan. "You *just* broke up with Megan. Have you forgotten that? More kissing at this point seems like it would be a very bad idea."

"More kissing would *never* be a bad idea," he corrected. "*Ever*. But okay, I can concede your point. So then tell me, what would be an acceptable time frame to wait before I do kiss you again?"

Her throat moved as she swallowed, then she turned away from him and stared in the direction of the lake. "I don't know," she finally answered. "A month, maybe?"

He laughed at that. A full-on, throaty chuckle at the absurdity that he could sit around for the next month and not try to kiss her. "Guess again, Lula-bell."

The corners of her mouth turned down. "I'm just trying to be sensible, Jaden. I'm not sure it would be wise for either one of us. I don't want you to confuse your feelings for Megan—"

"Past feelings."

"—with me."

He reached over and put a finger under her chin when she once again turned away from him, and he brought her face around to his. Her eyes stared back, wide and with more than a hint of fear, and her teeth gnawed at her bottom lip. "I am not confused," he assured her. "You can take that to the bank. I'm okay with the breakup. And I *can* decipher what I'm feeling for you from what I *felt* for her."

The statement was factual. He *could* decipher the difference. He just wasn't yet sure what it was that he felt for her. Attraction, for sure.

Like? He mentally nodded. He definitely liked her.

He also had no doubt that he wanted to better explore whatever this was between them.

"Then maybe I'm just not ready yet," she admitted, and with no hesitation, he accepted her answer.

"Then I'll give you some time."

It went left unsaid how much time or when either of them might know when she *was* ready, and she put the car back into gear. The full expanse of the lake came into view as she rounded the last curve—as well as his dad and Gloria, waiting on the back deck—and Jaden made eye contact with Arsula. "They knew we were coming?"

"Of course. It would be rude not to call first."

"Of course," he muttered.

"Gloria is also feeding us lunch. She insisted, although I assured her Nate has plans for you two to grab something after your appointment with Dr. Wangler."

"I suppose I'll just have to play nice and eat lunch twice, then." And he was surprised to learn that she and Nate had apparently been talking. Was he in on this trip, too?

He didn't say anything else as they pulled to a stop, but he also didn't let it go that Arsula had "forced" him out here. Nor was he fully ready to forgive her yet.

At the same time, he also found himself no longer quite as upset about it.

"Welcome," his dad called out as they opened their doors.

"What a pleasure to have company," Gloria added. She hurried down the steps as he unwedged himself from Arsula's car. "And Jaden"— she held out her hands, as if waiting for him to take them—"it's so good to see you out and about. Your dad is thrilled, too. Aren't you, Max?" She looked back at his dad, who hadn't followed her down the steps.

"Absolutely. Come on up. The both of you."

Jaden had the thought that if his dad was so thrilled to see him, then he could have stopped by over the past two and a half weeks and seen him all he wanted. After all, there had been plenty of chances. Gloria had come by with food no fewer than four times.

They made it to the deck, and Jaden indicated for Arsula to precede him up before he began the battle of cast versus stairs. But instead of immediately following her, he cast a look toward the lake. The view from here was gorgeous. It always took his breath away, no matter how recent or how distant his last visit had been.

He'd been fortunate to have been able to grow up here, he knew. And he was fortunate to have a stake in the business. He understood that, too. *And* he loved coming back to help during the harvest every year. It was one of the few family traditions they'd had before Nick and Dani had begun family dinners and game night a couple of years before. Yet all that being said, he was also the one who'd been most willing to sell when they'd found themselves without a sibling willing to run the orchard. It hadn't been that big a deal to him.

As he stood there taking it all in, though, he understood that to be untrue. Selling off their reason to live in this town would hurt. He fully believed that. So then, why the easy acceptance when it had first come up?

And why had he so adamantly refused to recuperate here when he'd gotten injured?

His brother's prodding on that very subject came to mind. *What was different now?*

Other than a broken ankle, he still had no clear answer to that.

Bringing his attention back to the group, he found three pairs of eyes watching him. His father stood at the railing where he'd been since Jaden had first caught sight of him, Arsula waited at the top of the five steps, seemingly ready to come back down if he needed her, and Gloria remained at his side, a hesitantly expectant smile on her face.

"Would you mind holding these?" he asked, holding his crutches out to Gloria. He hadn't attacked more than a small step up since the accident, but with handrails, the job was handled by hoisting himself up.

They moved into the house, and the feeling of being home washed over him. This was the home he'd grown up in, and though it held plenty of bad memories, it also held good ones. And the only reason he hadn't wanted to stay here was because he hadn't wanted to be a bother. Period.

His brother was wrong. *Arsula* was wrong. There was nothing different this time other than his being hurt.

"How are the trees doing, Max?" Arsula asked as Gloria led them across the room. "Are they going to make it, do you think?"

Jaden looked from Arsula to his dad. What was she talking about?

"If this weather holds, we'll find out soon," his dad replied. The temperatures had hit midsixties the day before and looked to remain there for a while. "Everything will start waking up, probably this week, and then we'll know."

"Why are you worried about the trees?" Jaden asked. They reached the table, and Gloria murmured for them to sit as she continued to the stove. "Isn't it rare that we lose more than a few every year?"

"I'm only worried about the new ones," his dad explained. "The pick-your-own lot."

Gloria cleared her throat as she placed a bowl of potato soup and a sandwich in front of Jaden, and she patted him on the shoulder. "Don't let your dad kid you. He's worried about *every* tree. I wake up alone most mornings these days because your dad is out there before dawn, checking on things."

"What's to check on right now?" Before the trees came out of dormancy, daily inspections would accomplish nothing. "And why go out before daylight at all?"

"Can't be lax, son," his dad chastised. "Got a business to run."

Jaden didn't appreciate the scorn. In fact, the implication that he didn't know how to be responsible flat out pissed him off. He was twenty-five years old. Too old for his father to suddenly want to play father of the year.

He realized that Arsula had grown completely still as he'd sat there and stewed over his father's condescension, and he caught her watching him now. In a way that made him feel she could see things that no one else could. He stared at his bowl of soup, not wanting to even guess at what she might think she saw.

The subject of trees was dropped, and Arsula shifted her attention from him back to his father, while Jaden hung back from the conversation. He wasn't willing to be called on the carpet again, so he took the moments while the other three talked to refamiliarize himself with the changes that had taken place since he'd been a kid. Until Gloria had moved in, the place had remained a shrine to his mother. Carol Wilde had died, Dani had come home from college, and everyone had carried on for years as if the woman herself were still alive and kicking. It had been more than unhealthy as a family unit, but they couldn't go back in time and reverse things.

Thankfully, the error of their ways had finally come to light.

The cane Dani had mentioned caught his eye, propped by the fireplace just as she'd said. As if merely there for décor. He studied it, noting the clear path from it to his dad's favorite chair, and the worry that he'd refused to acknowledge tried to take hold.

"*Max!* Let me—" The crash of a dish interrupted Gloria's words, and Jaden found his dad now out of his seat, one hand grasping the countertop and his empty soup bowl shattered into pieces around his feet. Gloria hurried to his side.

"I'm sorry," his dad said under his breath. "I was just trying to help." Embarrassment seemed to envelop him, making the once strong man seem feeble beyond his years, and his hand shook as he reached down for one of the larger pieces of the bowl.

"*Honey.*" Gloria pulled his dad back upright and gave his arm a reassuring squeeze. "You know I appreciate the help, but you sit. I've got this." She didn't wait for agreement, just helped him back to his seat, while Arsula grabbed a handful of paper towels to sweep up the shards.

Jaden just sat there.

His gaze bounced between his dad and Gloria as she and Arsula worked to clean up the mess. And what he saw was his dad, face drawn and looking far too much like a man needing to be put to bed for a rest, while Gloria tossed more than one worried glance his way. And the *worry* in those glances wasn't something to sneeze at.

Dani had been right. Something was going on with their dad.

But what? And why wouldn't he just tell them about it?

"Are you okay, Dad?"

Arsula and Gloria looked at him.

His dad did *not*. He swiped at a drop of soup he'd discovered on his sleeve. "Why wouldn't I be okay?"

He did sound normal, at least.

"No reason, I suppose." Jaden glanced at the cane once again. It wasn't meant for décor, he was certain. "Just a feeling I had."

The statement earned him a quick smile from Gloria, though he felt the move to be as forced as his dad's intentional avoidance. "I see time spent with Arsula is wearing off on you," she teased. "Here you are, listening to your gut."

"No." He eyed Arsula. "I still listen to facts."

He just wasn't sure what the facts were at the moment.

He also wasn't sure what Arsula seemed to be keying in on as she quietly studied his father. Nor if he wanted to ask her later and find out.

"It's my gut that's talking to me about the trees," his dad added as if they were still on the subject of the orchard, and Jaden decided that whatever had just happened—or not happened, he could totally be blowing it out of proportion—nothing good would come from beating it over the head during lunch.

He dug back into his soup. "Yeah, well the only thing my gut tells me is when it's hungry."

They finished the meal in relative calm and easy conversation, and he and Arsula had barely gotten the doors closed on her car when Jaden turned to her. "Are you happy now? Just as I told you, we're as normal as anyone else. There are no issues between me and my dad, and now you've seen it for yourself."

He puckered his lips on the hope she'd take him up on the kiss. *And* that she wouldn't bring up any concerns about his dad in particular.

She started the engine instead. "Are you sure about that?"

His expression dropped. The woman could certainly dig in her heels. "Yes, I'm sure. I'm *positive*. What could you possibly have seen in there to think I'm wrong?"

"I don't know. It was a feeling mostly."

He groaned in disgust.

She didn't put the car into gear, nor seem to care that they remained within eyesight of his dad. And that was fine with him. He didn't care, either. He wanted to get his point made before she had time to come up with yet another argument to contradict him.

Reaching over, he took her hand in his. "Arsula. *Honey.* You're sweet and well meaning. You are. But I don't believe in 'gifts,' okay? And you're not going to convince me otherwise."

"Honey?" She'd ripped her hand from his the second the word passed his lips.

Clearly, it had hit the mark.

"Then I guess you also wouldn't like hearing that I dreamed about your dad last night?" she spat out. "Or that I'm now certain there's something wrong with him."

He rolled his eyes at her announcement, an action he typically detested. And he didn't bother asking what the dream might have been about. "Would you just stop already? It was just a dream. We all have them. I brought my dad up in conversation the other morning, so he was on your mind. Thus . . . your dream."

"True, he *was* on my mind. And that also likely played into why he showed up. But whether you believe in me or not, I do. And though there is nothing yet concrete enough to point at, it's not uncommon for me to wake from dreams involving those I care about. And those dreams are often warnings of problems to come."

"So now you're a fortune-teller?" He laughed, and he knew the sound came out as cruel—he'd meant for it to—but he felt bad when Arsula jerked back as if struck.

"Something is going on with your dad, Jaden. And you feel it, too. I saw that in there."

"But I don't have to dream it to feel it."

"But it's not wrong if *I* do."

They stared at each other, both in a stalemate, and the thing was, he didn't even know why he was arguing. She was right. He'd felt it. He'd even said he felt it. And that made no sense to him, because he didn't "feel" things. Not like this. Present him with an honest-to-God fact, and he'd be the biggest supporter or defender in the world. But intuition?

Not hardly.

"Back off your refusal to see me as legit for a minute, will you? And hear what I'm about to say." Arsula cocked her head and waited until he nodded in agreement, and then she continued. "I *need* you to stop, Jaden. With all of it. *Today.* And I'm not kidding in the least. I don't run around telling you you're wrong all the time. Laughing in your face. I give your opinions credence and consideration. Always. Even when I also think you're full of crap."

"Either that or you throw things," he muttered, and the heat of her gaze scorched him.

"I am not kidding. Back off. You lash out at people when you feel threatened, and that's what you do to me every time. You're so afraid that my way may top your way, and you can't handle it. It's like you have to be right all the time or you won't be able to pull in your next breath."

"I don't have to be . . ."

He stopped talking as something else his brother had said to him aligned with her words.

You have to be the best.

But he didn't. He just . . .

Well . . . maybe he did. But he didn't know why, exactly.

203

"And while we're on the subject of your bad habits," Arsula went on, "you can be quite selfish."

The attack to his character really should be making him angrier than he was, but instead, her words seemed to be having the opposite effect. "How do you figure that?" He went quiet inside. And he wanted to hear her answer.

"You couldn't believe that Megan might have real concerns about your relationship. You didn't care how your refusal to stay with any of your family might interfere with their lives. You were going to go to a hotel before staying with one of them, Jaden. And that's absurd. It's even more absurd to think that you sitting in a hotel room, hurting and in pain—and not able to take care of yourself—wouldn't have brought them out. They would have been there, checking up on you all the time, staying with you around the clock those first few days, while putting the responsibilities of their own families second. All because you had to have things your way or no way."

She stopped to take a breath, before finishing with, "And I could go on."

He knew she probably could. Hadn't Megan said the same thing about him more than once in the past? Usually the words had come when she'd been mad. Therefore, he'd never really considered them valid. And likely, Arsula was angrier right now than she was letting on. But she had a way of looking at him—of remaining calm when explaining anything she truly thought he needed to hear—that made it almost impossible for him to ignore.

He looked down at the tub of brownies he held clutched in his hands. Gloria had made him a batch of his favorite dessert.

He pried off the lid and held out the bowl. "Another truce?"

"Why?" she asked sarcastically. "Because you don't like me being mad at you?"

Arsula also had a way of calling him out on all his bullshit.

"Something like that," he mumbled. He felt even more like a child right now than when his dad had told him not to "be lax" earlier.

"I am not a joke, Jaden."

"Okay. I agree. You're not a joke." He peered back at her, and he let her see the lack of understanding in his eyes. "But I *don't get* it."

"And you don't have to. You just have to respect. Can you do that at least?"

"Respect our differences?"

"Yes."

He hated when she made it clear what an idiot he was being.

"Fine," he groaned. "I can respect our differences."

"And you won't mock me again?"

"I won't mock you again. And yes, you're right. I'm selfish. I always have been. And I need to work on that."

She didn't respond immediately, and he wouldn't have been surprised to hear her tell him to get out of her car—while she drove off and left him standing alone in the middle of the driveway. She didn't do that, though.

Instead, she took a brownie. "Truce."

Chapter Sixteen

Ursula paced from her kitchen to her living room again, then made a lap into her bedroom and back. She returned to the kitchen, stared down at her closed laptop, then started the journey from kitchen to living room again.

On the next pass back from her bedroom, instead of heading for the hand-me-down kitchen table, she crossed to the living room window and looked out. Foot traffic outside was mostly nonexistent at this point on a Saturday. It wasn't yet dark, but the stores had closed for the weekend, and families had receded to enjoy dinners in their homes. While *she* paced her small apartment due to an email she'd been sitting on all day.

Turning, she remained by the window and eyed the slim piece of technology from across the room. She'd checked her email before heading out to meet with a new client that morning, then had found every excuse under the sun not to come back. It was Saturday, and there were always a million errands to run. Or just a long drive around the lake. She'd done both.

She'd run out of excuses to stay away, though, and the email from Megan still waited. Just under the lid of her laptop.

A noise sounded from below, and she looked toward the open door, almost in relief. She should probably close the door at this point. Jaden hadn't needed her after hours all week, and since Tuesday, she'd even left him to fend for himself in the evenings. Gloria had sent them home with several more containers of food, and now that Jaden was moving around better, he could hop long enough to scoop out his own leftovers and heat his own meals.

She'd still eaten lunch with him the last three days, though. And it wasn't only because she loved Gloria's cooking. It was because she'd sensed that Jaden was honestly trying to make a change. He hadn't handed over any more derisive comments, but more than that, she'd also gotten the sense that he listened when she spoke. Even if she wasn't speaking to him. As if he were hearing the words for what they were instead of behind a veil of doubt.

What sounded like a couple of cabinet doors closing echoed up the stairwell, and she edged over to peek down into the semidarkness. A light came from the direction of the kitchen and another from his bedroom. But Jaden was nowhere to be found.

Satisfaction filled her that he'd improved enough to get along by himself. She was glad he was getting better. Glad she didn't have to wait on him hand and foot.

And she was glad there'd been no more mentions of kissing in the days since they'd cleared the air.

No kissing talk . . . no nothing else. He'd mostly remained holed up in his room, doing his own thing.

She looked toward her bedroom, where her unmade bed could be seen. And she reminded herself that him being self-sufficient was a good thing. That no kissing—and no nothing else—was what she wanted. She didn't make it a habit to sleep with someone who'd been so openly dismissive of her abilities, and she saw no reason to start now.

Even if past events did indicate that said sex could potentially be highly satisfying.

A crash sounded—possibly a pan being dropped onto the floor—and she closed her eyes and told herself to ignore whatever it was he had going on down there. But more than that, to pay attention to what waited on her up here. And that was the email.

The one with the link to her website.

Gaining a backbone, she marched to the kitchen, didn't let herself think about anything other than viewing the pages with an unbiased eye, and sat down in front of her laptop.

The email remained on the screen where she'd left it. She moved the mouse pointer to the link to bring up the site. It wasn't live, of course. The site ran from a temporary server and was accessible only to her. And she suddenly found herself desperate to see what it looked like.

She clicked, and then the back of her nose burned with unshed tears.

Arsula Moretti—Intuitive Life Coach

Take permission to live the life you've always dreamed.

It was her dream. Not one she'd told too many people about, but the one that had been in the back of her mind for years. She'd even gotten certified last year. An intuitive life coach was there to motivate and uplift, but also to help guide others into delving into their minds and hearts. The answers were always in there, but some people needed help in finding them. And the answers were always the keys to lasting changes in life. To not only feeling whole and complete, but to having the confidence to go after all that was sought.

And *that* was what she was good at.

The women in her family had always focused only on their gifts. Therefore, that's what she'd done. She was a dream interpreter. That's how she introduced herself to others, and what initially pulled in clients. But she wanted to be more. And she wanted her family to be proud of her.

With slowed movements, she began to click around to different pages. The initial conversation with Megan had provided several sections that would be needed: resources for yoga, spiritual health, nutrition, and hypnotherapy, as well as information on what an intuitive life coach could do, ways she could be contacted, additional websites and books to check into, and a tab for dreams and what they could mean to a person's life. And as she brought up each page, each revealing a bit more of her own personal hopes and dreams, she couldn't help but think of her family.

Her brother Boyd would love it.

Her father would shake his head and ask if she really thought she was living up to her potential.

And her mother would offer a proud nod of approval.

The ringing of a bell interrupted her thoughts, and when she realized it was coming from directly below the open door, she rose and crossed the room. Standing at the bottom of the stairs, with a light now shining in the stairwell, was Jaden, dressed in a pair of black slacks she hadn't seen before—split at the knee to accommodate the cast—a white button-down shirt, and no expression on his face whatsoever.

The bell kept ringing.

"I take it you need something?" She rested her shoulder against the doorframe and shot him a sarcastic look.

"I do."

"Is that so?" She highly doubted it. She made a show of angling her head in both directions as if checking to see that nothing looked out of place. "You don't look to be in pain of any sort."

He rang the bell harder, but his lack of expression didn't change.

209

"Jaden," she finally yelled out, and his hand quit moving. "I'm busy up here." She thought about the website and had the idea to show it to him. Would that help him to see that she wasn't just a flake?

Did she really care what he thought about her?

She did.

And for some reason, the idea of showing it to him excited her.

The bell started up again, before she could make up her mind to grab the laptop and take it down to him, and as the noise clanged louder, Jaden's expression went from nonexistent to one of mulish intent. He clearly intended to keep ringing the blasted thing until she went down there.

"Stop ringing that bell!" Though she hadn't heard the noise in days, he'd rung it enough the first couple of weeks to make her regret ever giving it to him. And at the moment, she regretted forgetting to take it away.

"Then come down here and see what I want," he yelled back.

"You don't need anything!"

The noise stopped so abruptly that she weaved in place, suddenly off balance. "But I do," he told her, and this time his tone was sincere.

Her shoulders sagged as she fought with herself on whether to go down there or not. He'd been too busy since she'd returned home to ever make her believe he actually needed anything; therefore, she smelled a rat. Or better, a trap.

What was the man up to?

"What do you need, Jaden? I really am in the middle of something."

There was a brief pause as if he were considering whether he really wanted to be a pain in her rear or not, and then he started ringing the bell again.

"I swear to all that's holy, Jaden Wilde." She started down the stairs. "I'm going to take that bell and ram it right up your—"

He waggled a finger back and forth in front of him, tsking as he did, and stopping her two steps before she reached him. "Aunt Sul wouldn't like that swearing," he said.

"I didn't . . ." But she sort of had. Swearing to all that was holy? He was right. Aunt Sul wouldn't like it.

She said her customary sorrys, scowling at Jaden the whole time, then in a quick move, she lunged down the last two steps and reached for the bell. The man was quicker than she gave him credit for. He'd become quite adept at his crutches, and she found herself on the ground floor, with him now four feet away. He held out the bell, as if dangling a carrot as enticement, and rocked it slowly back and forth.

Ding. Ding. Ding.

She lunged again.

He laughed that time and scurried farther away. He'd moved toward the kitchen, and knowing there was no alternate exit to the room, she lunged a third time, intending to trap him inside. Only, as she reached the doorway, he slid unobtrusively to the side. And at the sight that greeted her, she once again swayed as her feet locked in place. The table was set for two. What appeared to be a homemade lasagna and a salad were positioned in the middle of a crisp white tablecloth, an opened bottle of wine sat to one side, and a basket of crusty bread sat off to the other.

She looked up at him.

"I needed you to come down because I cooked dinner for you."

"You cooked for me?" Arsula stared at the table as if she'd never seen one set with place settings before.

"I did."

"Why?" She didn't look away from the meal.

Admitting to faults was a hard thing for Jaden, and he'd messed up with her in a number of ways.

"To say thank you, first of all." Like she'd pointed out, he'd been selfish. It was a bad habit, and one he'd often blamed on lingering effects from his mother. "I've never thanked you for taking me in," he continued. "For putting up with me. I know you didn't have to do that."

She crossed her arms over her chest and dipped her chin.

"I also wanted to apologize."

He'd thought that would bring her gaze to his, but it remained downcast.

"I'm sorry I've disrespected you, Arsula." He still got nothing.

She'd asked him to respect their differences the other day, and what had become instantly clear was what an ass he'd been. Shame choked him for the way he'd treated her. He wouldn't tolerate being made fun of from anyone himself, and he should never have done it to her.

"*And* that I've done it over and over," he added. And the reality was, even while mocking her, respect had already begun to develop. He'd watched people come in here for weeks, anxious to share with her the impact she'd made on their lives. He'd seen their joy and their beliefs that they could accomplish even more, and he'd been jealous. That's what he hoped to do for others someday. As a counselor, results like hers would be proof of success.

So yeah . . . respect. Even if it was hard for him to admit.

And feeling threatened.

She'd hit that one on the head, too, which had been a real eye-opener. He lashed out when he didn't get what he wanted. Or when others had what he desired. She was good with people, and though he had yet to understand it, her ways challenged his beliefs. And he didn't like that.

"And last," he said, his impatience moving him to stand in front of her, "I wanted to let you know that I'll move out if you want me to."

His statement finally pulled her attention to his, and he saw moisture lining her eyes. "You want to leave?" she asked.

Hell no.

He held his immediate response inside, determined to make this her call. "I'm saying that I *will* if you want me to. I realize I'm a little underfoot." With a tilt of his head, he pointed out his plaster-encased leg. "I can get around better now, and there's a spare bedroom on the first floor of the house. I could stay with Dad and Gloria now, without having to rely on them to take care of me."

Pride filled him at the delivery of his speech without showing how he really felt. He *would* stay with his dad and Gloria. And he'd be fine there. But he *wanted* to stay here. With her.

He wanted it to become more than him just staying here.

She nibbled at her lip. "Are you thinking you could stay with them to keep an eye on your dad?"

That would be valid reasoning. And probably he should have thought of it. But he supposed his selfish ways remained. "No, Arsula. Honestly, that thought never crossed my mind. But that's likely because I still like the idea of *you* keeping an eye on *me*." He produced a wayward smile. "I like it here, what can I say? But if it sways you any, I'd be willing to cook dinner again in payment."

Given that she seemed to enjoy his stepmother's cooking so much, and that not once had she brought him a meal prepared by her, he'd concluded she wasn't much of a cook. And food he could do.

He was hoping food impressed her.

Instead of answering, she looked back to the table and seemed to study every detail. The dishes were new and had been delivered the day before, the groceries had come from his sister that morning, and the tablecloth had been an impulse purchase when he'd met up with Megan to look at a location for the store the day before.

"What if your food is subpar?" Arsula looked at him again, and at the teasing note in both her eyes and her words, it finally felt as if he could breathe again.

"Then I'll *buy* you dinner," he said, his voice both lowering and softening. He wanted her to say yes.

He also wanted her to kiss him again.

"You'd buy me dinner . . . As in . . . ?"

"As in a date," he said, making his intentions clear, and her eyes locked on his. "Or a pre-date, if you're not ready yet," he added.

"And what if I never get ready?"

Then he'd die an unhappy man. "Then you'd at least get a few good meals."

That made her laugh, and the sharpness that had been in her shoulders since entering the room eased. Her eyes warmed. "I'm fine with you staying here, Jaden. Of course I am. And when I mentioned you being selfish the other day, I wasn't attempting to imply that you'd taken advantage of me."

"Yet I did."

"I offered." She didn't look away. "And I'm glad I did. But if you feel you need to go home . . ."

He quickly shook his head. "I don't. The offer *is* valid, though. Say the word, and I'll get out of your hair. I'll quit taking advantage of your good nature." He angled his head. "That said . . . I would *prefer* to stay here and keep taking advantage."

She chuckled again, and the smile that accompanied it made his heart sing. "Then the decision is made," she told him. "Stay and take advantage. As long as you want."

The double entendre of her words didn't go unnoticed with either of them, but neither commented. Instead, he pulled out her chair and offered her a seat. "Have dinner with me, Arsula?"

Chapter Seventeen

The man could be a charmer when he wanted to.

And his lasagna was off the charts.

Arsula picked at one of the remaining few bites of pasta on her plate as Jaden relayed the story of how he'd managed to prepare tonight's meal while having only one good foot to stand on, and she found herself giggling at the vision. Lots of hopping, some using a chair to rest his knee on, and a couple of losses of balance resulting in near face-planting against the fridge.

"So," he said after wrapping up his tale. He leaned forward, crossing his arms and resting them on the table. "What do you think, Lula-bell? Was the lasagna good enough to give me another chance to cook for you?"

She poked at a hunk of beef. Did he really want another chance to cook for her?

She'd been replaying their earlier conversation since they'd had it. There'd been talks of dates, pre-dates . . . being "ready." Did she want any of those things?

The better question was, would she allow herself to have those things with him? Because yeah. She wanted them. The man not only wore his creased slacks very well—and yes, they'd been ironed—but he'd apparently made it his mission to impress tonight. And she had news for him. He'd succeeded.

"The lasagna was okay," she replied. "I suppose."

"You suppose?" He chuckled, and she couldn't pull her gaze off the way his eyes looked as they crinkled behind his glasses. He rose and moved to the fridge. "You don't cave easily, do you?"

"I see no reason to."

"Good." He pulled out what looked to be a cheesecake, and she noticed that the platter matched the plates on the table. All of which she hadn't seen in this kitchen before. "Because I don't like easy." He turned back to her and held up the platter. "I also made dessert."

She didn't let on that cheesecake rated right up there with sex for her. "It doesn't look like a cupcake to me."

Laughter filled the room. "You are correct. It's not a cupcake. But then, it's not your birthday, is it?"

"Like you're going to make me a cupcake for my birthday." She eyed the cheesecake. It looked as homemade as the lasagna. "You'll probably be long gone by then. Back in Seattle, terrorizing some other unsuspecting woman with tons of unexpected calories."

"Nah." A contented smile settled onto his mouth as he sliced two slabs and placed them on matching saucers. "The way I see it, there's no point in returning for only a month. I talked to my adviser this week. I'm going to finish out everything here."

"You are?" She'd assumed he'd be leaving by the end of the month. "I guess you're on the hook to make me a cupcake, then."

He looked over his shoulder at her. "I suppose I am."

As he turned with both plates in hand, she rose to get them so he could make it back to the table without hopping. But he shooed her off. "Have a seat, woman. I'm in charge tonight."

"Yes, sir."

A flicker of heat passed through his features, but Arsula didn't let on that she'd noticed. She'd been having flickers herself, ever since she'd walked into the room.

He hopped, performing an excellent balancing routine by not only keeping both slices of cheesecake upright, but also centered on the plates. As he placed hers on the cleared space in front of her, he peeked up, his look saying way more than had been spoken out loud tonight, and all the air seemed to leave the room in a rush. The man had game.

"Tell me about cooking," she said. "Who taught you how to do that?" They'd covered a number of topics tonight, but nothing overtly personal. With a full tummy, though, and way more than cheesecake running through her mind, she wanted to see if they could go deeper.

She wanted to know that he wanted it, too. And not just deeper by getting naked again.

"Ah . . . cooking," he began, and lowered to his seat. He forked up a bite of dessert. "I taught myself, actually. Though not until college. And I did that because I'd grown up watching my sister always handling everything in the kitchen herself. It was my way to appease my conscience, I guess."

"Wait." She sat up from her leaned-back, I-had-two-glasses-of-wine-with-dinner slouch. "It was you, your dad, four additional brothers, and Dani. And Dani was the one who always cooked?"

"And cleaned."

"Wow." For some reason, she wouldn't have assumed that. She knew from Erica that Gabe was a well-rounded twenty-first-century man. As was Nick. "Sexist much?"

She supposed the change was better late than never, but she suddenly hurt for Dani.

"I know." Jaden's gaze strayed to his fork, which no longer had any cheesecake on it, nor did he appear in any hurry to take another bite. In addition, what she'd guess to be grief creased his face. "When our family came close to imploding a few years ago, it was brought to Dani's attention that our mom had used doing the dishes as a way to control her." He shrugged and went on. "We'd all been trained to stand back and wait for her to wait on us."

"And she just went along with it?"

Blue eyes danced over to hers. "That's Dani's story to tell, but yeah. We all went along with all of it. Narcissism isn't pretty, in case you've never experienced it firsthand."

She hadn't. And the sorrow spilling out of him now made her extra glad of the fact.

"Will you tell me about your mom?" she asked.

"How much time do you have?" He smirked. Then he shook off his maudlin thoughts. "My mother is a story that could go on for hours, Lula-bell. Narrow your question."

"Okay." Studying him, she considered what she'd learned about his past. About him. Then she reached over and covered his hand with hers. "Tell me your first memory of her."

His eyelids closed off his thoughts for a full fifteen seconds, but Arsula didn't pull away. She'd felt the muscles under her fingers tense the second she'd made the request, and then she'd watched as he'd meticulously worked from head to toe, forcing every muscle group to relax. She suspected it was a coping technique he'd learned years ago, and she found herself impressed with the ability.

"My first memory," he finally began, "was lying in my bed alone, having peed on myself yet again, and wondering which would happen first. Would my mom come unlock my door and tell me I could come out of my room for the day, or would the school bus drop off my brothers and sister?"

"School bus?" Her hand gripped his. "As in . . . at the *end* of the day?"

"Three o'clock," he confirmed. His jaw grew tight. "Though I didn't know what time the bus showed up back then. I just knew that if

218

she didn't unlock my door before they got home, then either Nick or Nate would show up and do it almost immediately. Usually Nate," he added, his voice now a whisper, and Arsula found herself unable to say anything else.

No wonder the man had gone to a counselor for years.

No wonder that's the field he'd chosen to pursue.

"I'm glad you had your brothers," she whispered.

"Yeah." Jaden nodded. He disappeared into additional memories, but for only a few seconds, before he physically shook it off.

His shoulders rolled under the white shirt, and his lips curved as if trying to recapture the casual charmer he'd been all night. Then he turned his hand under hers and twined their fingers together.

"Enough about me." His eyes roved over her face. "Turn my smile into an authentic one, Arsula. Tell me what you did today. What kept you out of the apartment for most of it?"

She liked that he asked her to make him smile. "Mostly I was avoiding you," she answered drily.

He did smile, and she liked it even more.

But she'd also just fudged the truth. It hadn't been him she'd been avoiding.

"That's a bit of a fib," she admitted. Her heart pounded at the thought of what she *had* been avoiding. "It wasn't *you* I was avoiding so much as it was my laptop."

"Your laptop?" Surprise added to his smile. "What's wrong with it? It doesn't turn into some sort of demonic creature on weekends, does it?"

She liked his sense of humor. "No, but it might turn *me* into one."

One of his fingers slid back and forth where it rested between two of her fingers, and little tingles began to fire up her arm. "So what's the problem with your laptop?"

"It had an email on it that I wasn't ready to look at yet."

His chin angled down as he studied her, and it took all she had not to look away. "You stayed out of the house all day to avoid reading an email?"

"Yes." If she acted like that was a perfectly normal reaction, then maybe he'd believe it. "And before you ask, I also deleted the email app on my phone. That way, I wouldn't be tempted while I was out."

"You deleted the—" He cut off his question and shook his head in wonder. "I swear, Arsula. Some days I still believe you're as loony as I thought you were when I first met you."

"And some days, you probably just wish I was." She wrinkled her nose at him, producing another round of deep laughter, and she noticed that he'd leaned in closer. And possibly so had she. They were both sitting with arms bent and resting on the table, cheesecake pushed to the side and forgotten, and their faces far too close.

"Tell me about this email," he prodded.

"It was from your ex."

His eyes blinked at her answer, but he didn't pull away. "From Megan? About what?"

"About a website."

She didn't say anything more than that. Not at first. Admitting it out loud had made the blood roar in her ears. If she told him about it . . . and especially if she showed it to him . . . the idea of taking that next step would suddenly be all the more real.

"It's a potential website she worked up for me." She forged ahead without letting herself think about it. "For a business venture I've considered."

"A business venture? As in, something different than dream interpretation?"

"As in, a deeper level of something similar. Yet not at all the same. I want to be an intuitive life coach," she admitted. She pressed her lips together the instant the words were out, and then she waited.

She'd said it.

But now, would she do it?

"A life coach?" His thumb slid over hers, and she could see him processing through what that was. As his thoughts returned to the present, his brow furrowed. "Isn't that sort of what you do already?"

He couldn't have asked a better question. She nodded. "Sort of."

He seemed to be figuring her out whether he wanted to or not.

"What I do today is more based upon people coming to me with their dreams," she explained. "Some ask for my help, seeking guidance in their lives whether they realize it or not, and some truly just want to know about an individual dream. I'm always on the lookout for those in need of help, though, and if they're open to working on themselves, I take them under my wing."

"And then they show up here at the office and praise you daily." The statement was meant as praise, and she took it as such.

"Some of those people are just friends, by the way. I'm always talking, always in 'healer mode' internally, and sometimes that slips out in the simplest of forms. Revamping a wardrobe, helping construct a speech asking a boss for a raise. As I told you early on, I'm good with people."

"You certainly are." His other hand closed over the one he already held. "What's the difference in a regular life coach and an intuitive one, though? I've never heard of the latter."

The fact that he was asking questions had a new kind of fire licking deep inside her. One that scared her at the idea of getting burned.

"An intuitive life coach focuses on guiding others to fulfillment from within," she answered, "before then helping them seek the passions that will fuel their life's journeys."

"An intuitive life coach cares about the heart first," he added, and she nodded.

"Always."

Both of his thumbs now slid across her skin. "That's a pretty cool thing to want to do."

She didn't say anything, momentarily unable to speak. Having both his hands touching her at the same time, even with as simple a point of contact as what he provided, was totally playing havoc on her system. Add to that their proximity to each other and the fact that she couldn't get near the man without wanting to be even closer, and suddenly she was not only struggling to speak but to remember what it was they'd been speaking about.

The website.

She nodded again, even though Jaden hadn't said anything else. They'd been talking about the website, and she'd been explaining the differences in the types of life coaches.

"Would you like to see it?" she asked before she could talk herself out of it. Her breathing became labored at the thought. "The website, I mean. It's not complete, nor is it live. But I could show it to you if you wanted."

"I would love to see it."

And she really would love to show it to him.

Excitement growing, she disentangled their fingers and rose from the table. "Then come upstairs with me. I have it loaded on my laptop."

She'd hit the fourth step before clueing in that Jaden hadn't followed her out of the kitchen, and when she turned back, she found him framed by the doorway, his eyes focused beyond her to the narrow set of stairs.

"Oh yeah." She pursed her lips. His incapacitation had slipped from her mind.

Then she realized that he wasn't just *eyeing* the obstacle that would get him through the door of her apartment. He appeared downright scared at the thought.

"Really?" She glanced behind her before continuing. "You're scared of a flight of stairs?"

"I'm not scared," Jaden protested, but there was no heat behind the words.

"You look scared."

"I look *concerned*," he corrected. "Because as you might remember, the last time I went up a flight of stairs, the coming down part didn't end so well."

That didn't make sense. "You went up the steps at your dad's house just the other day."

"There were five steps in total to get to the deck, with a railing on either side." He flexed a bicep. "My arms carried me up. The crutches didn't have to be involved."

She turned again and took in the lone rail running the length of the stairwell. With it positioned on the same side as his injured ankle, he wouldn't even be able to use one crutch while also holding on to the rail with the other hand. Not without easily being thrown off balance.

She could go get the laptop and bring it down, she supposed. That would be the logical thing to do.

Instead, she decided she'd rather make him work for it.

See him want it . . .

And she didn't *even* let herself ask what she thought she might be making him work for . . . or what might be something he wanted.

"Too bad," she murmured. She offered an apologetic smile. "I guess we'll just have to take a rain check." She began backing up the stairs. "I do think I'll go on up, though. Make it an early night."

Crestfallen would describe his look perfectly. "Do you have to? I was enjoying spending time with you."

His words almost changed her mind. Because no, she didn't *have* to go. And because she'd been enjoying spending time with him, too. A lot. She'd enjoyed it so much, in fact, that she'd begun to wonder how the evening might end.

"I think I do have to." Leaving now would be the safe bet. "Thank you for cooking dinner for me, though. I had a lovely time."

His gaze burned into hers, and she thought for a moment he would throw caution to the wind. "And thank you for having dinner with *me*," he said instead.

"Anytime."

He nodded, his eyes once again traversing the stairs, as she reached the top.

"Jaden?" She waited for his gaze to make it to hers, and suddenly, him climbing the flight of stairs was no longer about showing him her website. "It really is too bad you're scared of the stairs."

Jaden forgot to blink as he continued to stare at the empty space where Arsula had been. What had she meant by that?

It really is too bad you're scared of the stairs.

And it really *wasn't* that he was scared of the stairs. He'd just been contemplating how best to get up them. Sort of. Mostly he'd just been hoping she'd go get her computer and bring it down.

But then she'd gone and issued a challenge.

And wouldn't he be a fool if he didn't take her up on it?

Bringing his eyes back to the twelve steps it would take to get him to the top, he determined the time had come for him and his cast to conquer the obstacle before them, and he shifted the crutch under his right arm to settle it in with his left.

The going wasn't actually as tough as he'd expected—once he'd tested out the first few. He found that he could either hop from one step to the next, or he could basically climb up on his knees. He also found that he was glad no one else was around to witness him crawling to get to Arsula. He kept going, though, because as he'd known from day one, he couldn't resist the temptation of being around this woman.

He accidentally thumped his cast on the wall when halfway up and froze as pain reverberated through his ankle, and he told himself to focus on the task at hand instead of what waited at the top. As if that were even possible.

A minute later, he reached the last step, and given that the door remained open—*and* that she was likely waiting just around the corner—he didn't pause before he braced his crutches on the top riser and swung himself up and into her apartment.

He didn't find Arsula waiting for him, though. Instead, he stood alone in a small kitchen.

He took in the scene before him. Laptop on the kitchen table, along with a couple of books and a magazine, and a mug that had, knowing her, contained coffee at one point.

And in the other room, he could hear the shower running.

He peeked around the corner, his heart suddenly racing, until he saw that her bedroom door was closed. And then he looked back down the way he'd come. He'd honestly thought she'd be up here waiting for him. He'd thought . . .

She wasn't hoping he'd join her in the shower, was she?

He looked down at his cast. He couldn't join her if he wanted to. Or if *she* wanted him to. And now that he was here—and she wasn't—he was beginning to think he'd totally misread her intent. She simply liked to tease, so that's what she'd done. And he'd fallen for it. Therefore, the question became, did he to try to get himself back down the stairs in one piece and pretend he'd never intruded into her space to begin with? Or did he stay and prove to her that he *had* made it?

Need to be around Arsula won out, so he poured himself his own cup of coffee, and he settled in at her table to wait. That's when he took a better look at the magazine that lay open in front of him—and discovered it to be a medical journal.

Forgetting the coffee, he flipped through the pages, at a loss as to why she'd have such a thing to begin with. Did this play into being an intuitive life coach somehow? Or was there something within the pages that represented another passion of hers?

Was she attending college online and just not wanting to talk about it?

Wanting to attend classes and eventually get in to medical school?

Or . . . *what?*

He honestly had no idea.

And granted, with the way he'd treated her since they'd met, it came as no surprise that she wouldn't mention it to him. Although, she had told him about the life coach thing.

Which was apparently loaded on her laptop.

He slid his finger across the mouse pad, frowning when the password box popped up instead of a website, while in the other room, the water shut off. Given that it would likely take more than a couple of minutes for her to put on clothes and find him loitering in her kitchen, he decided to peruse the books lining the shelves in her living room. She had a much larger collection than he would have expected, and he found himself more than a little curious what kind of books she might read.

Carrying the medical journal with him, he crossed the room to study the titles. There was quite a bit of fiction in the mix—covering an assortment of genres—along with biographies of historic figures and a handful of nonfiction books on events and places. But there was also a wide selection of college textbooks.

He couldn't figure her out.

He did come to the conclusion, however, that the books she'd provided for him downstairs must have come from the shelves in front of him. Both were equally eclectic.

A noise came from behind him, and he turned, ready to point out how he'd mastered her challenge . . . only to find her standing ten feet away from him, wearing nothing but a towel.

"Jaden!" she screeched when she saw him.

The journal slipped from his hand. "I was . . . I . . . uh"—he pointed to the door—"I conquered the stairs."

"I can see that." Her hand went to the knot at her breast.

"You issued a challenge," he explained. He also forced his eyes to meet hers. "But I didn't expect to find you *naked*."

Her pretty mouth flattened into a line. "That is how I usually take a shower."

He gulped, and then he nodded. "But I didn't know you were taking a shower. I thought . . ."

He quit talking and instructed his feet to move and to get him out of there. It was wrong to walk into a woman's place uninvited—no matter that he had thought he'd *been* invited. The right thing to do would be to go.

Only, to go meant walking away from Arsula.

And to go meant once again facing the stairs.

"Jaden." She said his name calmly but with heavy inflection.

"What?" And he sounded like he was ten years old again.

"Are you just going to keep standing there staring at me like that?"

He was looking at her towel again. "I'm thinking it's what I'll do until you force me to stop."

At that, she busted out laughing, and he said a silent prayer that the up-and-down movements of her chest would cause the towel to fall. He narrowed his eyes into slits and added in a little mental telepathy for good measure, but the towel stayed stubbornly in place.

"I can't help it." He gave up on any thought of having manners and attempted to explain his predicament. He'd been naked with that body three weeks ago, and his worthless memory hadn't been kind enough to hold on to any of it for him. "It's just so much better than I'd imagined. And trust me. My imagination is stellar."

All hints of humor fled, and she dipped down, leaning her head to the side until her eyes met his. "Are you telling me that you don't remember seeing me naked before? At *all*?"

"Disappointingly, no."

"Well, now." Her tone changed instantly to one that was more teasing than laughing. "Doesn't that leave the situation a bit lopsided?" Her grin grew evil, and he was reminded of calling her the devil that first morning. "Because I happen to remember *everything* that I saw."

He swallowed past the lump in his throat. "And what exactly did you see?"

Her smile turned all-knowing. *"Everything."*

"You're right." All blood departed his brain. "That is definitely lopsided."

"I guess that means you should learn to hold your liquor better."

They faced off then, both of them breathing harder than it should take for two people to stand in place, and Jaden did his best to listen with his gut. Just like she was always preaching. Only, he wasn't sure if it was his gut speaking or something about a foot lower.

He did note, however, that she seemed to be waiting for him to make the next move. Because she certainly wasn't running from the room or taking the time to hunt up any clothes.

It really is too bad you're scared of the stairs.

She had to have meant what he'd thought, hadn't she?

And if not . . . he only prayed she might consider changing her mind.

"Arsula?" He kept his voice as neutral as possible.

"Yes, Jaden?"

He brought his eyes back to hers when he realized they'd once again slipped down below, and he knew that the only thing he could do was ask. "Any chance you want to show it to me again now?"

She apparently didn't need long to think about it, because in the next instant, the towel hit the floor.

Chapter Eighteen

Arsula couldn't believe she'd done that.

Then again, wasn't this why she'd taunted him to climb the stairs?

The conversation might have started around showing him the website, but while she'd been in the shower, she'd played out different scenarios for enticing him up. And *not* for the purpose of viewing the website. There had even been one scenario where she'd stood at the top of the stairs, as naked as she was now, encouraging him up each step.

It was simple. She wanted him. And she didn't want to pretend otherwise.

"Jaden?"

He hadn't moved since she'd dropped the towel. He just stood there, staring at her as if he'd never seen a naked woman before.

"You do know what to do next, right?"

His eyes continued to evade hers. "Of course I know what to do. I'm just soaking this in."

A laugh slipped out. "What's the matter? Afraid you might forget again?"

He was seriously too adorable.

"Not a concern this time." He finally moved, the lines of his face going hard and his crutches swinging him closer. "There's been no whiskey in my system since the wedding. This visual isn't going anywhere."

"You did have wine tonight."

"Two glasses. And I promise you"—he landed in front of her, and she found it nearly impossible to breathe—"the picture is set. You also don't have to worry about the effects of a man having too much alcohol."

Her eyes lowered to the front of his trousers to confirm his statement, and she gulped. He remained fully clothed, but she could see his point. Lack of erection would *not* be an issue tonight.

"You ever planning to touch me, then?" she whispered. He was still just standing there, and her danged nipples kept growing harder with every second that ticked off the clock.

"Just as soon as I figure out how to do it without falling on my rear."

"Oh." She came out of her about-to-have-sex fog and realized that he couldn't really do too much while standing up. He still couldn't put his foot down.

She went into action. Hurrying to the kitchen area, she grabbed one of the chairs and brought it over to him, then she thought about the logistics of that. About how it would put his mouth at practically breast level, and she hurried back, thinking she didn't need to be quite that forward. She grabbed the other chair, and when she returned, she realized he was laughing at her.

She dropped the chair. "Why are you laughing?"

"Because you're cute." He leaned forward and pecked her on the mouth. "And very naked," he murmured against her lips. Then he took the kiss deeper.

Arsula stood there, reveling in his touch but unsure what to do to help. She wanted to reach for him. To part him from his clothes, just as she'd done for herself. She also wanted to press forward and devour him with her mouth. But she didn't want to knock him over.

In the end, she lifted her hands to his face, and she showed him with her lips and tongue that she wanted this. That she intended to be a full participant.

He moaned, and she inched forward.

Her chest brushed his, and one of his hands slid over her hip. She undid the buttons of his shirt.

"Arsula?" he whispered a moment later. His mouth was now feasting on her neck, while she'd moved her fingers to his waist and flattened herself to his now-bare chest.

"Yes?" Her palms slid over his back.

"Can we move to the couch?"

Oh, crap. They were still standing up.

She went into action again, nodding like a frantic woman, and hurried to the other side of the sofa. She slid the coffee table out of the way so he could make it to the middle cushion, and then she set his crutches aside and pulled the coffee table back. She waited for him to sit, and after he did, she gently lifted his foot and propped it on the small table.

Then she stared down at him, once again unsure what to do next.

"You're nervous." He spoke from a reclined position, his eyes hot as they watched her and his voice heavy with need.

"Because I don't have a clue as to the best way to do this." She studied him. Should she just climb on top?

But he still had his pants on.

"I don't, either." He reached for her hand. "So let's just take it one step at a time, okay?"

She nodded. She could do that.

"Step one." He grimaced before continuing. "Are you *sure* you want to do this?"

His question was the last thing she'd expected. She held her hands out to her sides. "I'm naked, Jaden. What about that says unsure to you?"

"Yeah, but . . . I'm not entirely certain I took your invitation to come up the right way. We *had* just been talking about websites."

She found the moment to be sweet. Then she straddled his legs, both of her feet remaining on the ground, and prepared to move them beyond sweet. "Not to worry. You read me loud and clear."

"Good to know." His breathing had grown shallow again.

"Step two?"

He lifted off the back of the couch and gripped her behind the knees. "Do as I ask," he informed her, and she nodded immediately. She could absolutely do that. Especially given that her nipples now rested at eye level.

"Got it," she whispered, and he flicked his tongue out and swiped it across one nipple. She braced her hands on his shoulders. "Whatever you ask."

"Excellent." He stroked his tongue over her other nipple. "Then just stand there." His eyes feasted on her again. "And hold *perfectly* still."

She wanted to question his demand. She *wanted* to climb on top of him and ride him like a roller coaster. But instead, she did as he asked. Only, she did let her head drop back.

He used his lips and teeth mostly. Nipping and tugging. Not staying in any one place too long. And every once in a while, he trailed a path over her with his tongue. Or hung around an extra second or two to explore a dip in her skin. His touch was hot as he passed over her, the soft groans coming from him intoxicating, and while his fingers remained firmly gripped behind her knees, he laved over every reachable inch of her body.

Arsula swayed as he made another pass near her breasts, once again not stopping to stick around, and when she felt his lips curve into a smile, she let herself grin in return. She was breathing heavily, ready to go off like a rocket the moment he touched her in just the right spot, but she didn't push for more. She liked what he was doing to her. No man had ever made love to her like this before. With only his mouth, and with her standing so exposed before him. It made the pain of drawing the moment out all the sweeter.

When he finally returned to where he'd started . . . and without making a sound, sucked one nipple deep into his mouth . . . everything inside her tightened.

"Jaden," she whispered. She arched toward him. "When do we get to step three?" she begged.

He smiled around her nipple. Then he released her slowly, keeping the suction going until the last second. "Step three." His hands slid up the backs of her legs, and his mouth dipped to tease at the narrow strip of hair between her thighs. "Climb onto the couch," he instructed, and he looked up at her again, his mouth only inches from her core. "On your feet," he added. "Not your knees."

Her heart thundered. He wanted her to . . .

She climbed onto the couch. Her hands shook as she let him direct her movements. Legs spread, her hands on the top of his head, his hands gripping the rounded curve of her bottom. And her midsection waiting in his direct line of sight.

"Don't fall," he murmured. He licked his lips as he stared at her. "I'm not certain I can catch you if you do."

"Don't fall," she breathed out. "Got it." Her heart might beat out of her chest, though.

He touched her then, his hands stroking softly between her thighs, his knuckles brushing over her dampness. And then his thumbs came up and parted her. She whimpered, her knees threatening to buckle when he blew a hot stream of air over her most sensitive spot, but she caught herself, clasping her hands more securely onto his head. She prayed she didn't leave him bald before this was over, and then he inched ever closer.

He used his tongue again. One tiny flick. Then another. And another.

And before she could even think of trying to control the moment, of not losing all *control* of the moment, Jaden latched on to her, and somehow he seemed to be both holding her up off the couch and devouring her at the same time. It didn't take long until she was on the brink. She wanted to grind down against him, to help the moment along, but in her current position, she didn't have the right foothold to make that happen. So he just kept going. And she just kept writhing.

"Jaden," she finally begged. Everything about her was tight and hard and ready to burst out of her skin.

But Jaden didn't stop, and she climbed even higher.

"I need . . ."

She didn't know what she needed. Her eyes were closed so forcefully that she saw stars, and she knew she had to be hurting him, given that her fingers kept clenching in his hair. But still, he kept going.

Every muscle in her body shook, and at the exact moment she thought she'd pass out from lack of oxygen, she suddenly found her footing on the couch. Jaden's hands were once again clasped on her butt, and he pulled her in tight. She ground herself against him, and then she was flying.

Her release came hard and lasted forever, and when every last inch of her had turned to liquid, she slid slowly down his body. He'd slumped down on the couch previously, in order to get a better angle as his mouth had wrapped around her, and somehow, his pants were now shoved to his knees and his erection strained tall. On her knees now, she positioned him at her opening, but before letting her body sheathe him, common sense prevailed.

"Condom?" she whispered. She dropped her head to his shoulder, while her thighs strained to hold herself aloft. She didn't have any condoms in the apartment, and she feared—

"Right here."

She lifted her head in surprise to find a small packet held between two of his fingers. That first night, he'd said he didn't carry condoms. He'd been monogamous for years.

"I added a box when I ordered the dishes for tonight"—he shrugged—"just in case."

A laugh slipped from her. "Just in case you got me to cave?"

"It wasn't all that hard, you know?" His words were teasing, but the heat in his eyes was not. He cupped her face, and he smoothed both thumbs over her cheeks. "Just in case I got the opportunity of a lifetime," he whispered, and her insides swooned.

"You sure are a smooth talker."

"You do bring out the best in me."

They quit talking then, as both of them waited to see what she'd do. That first night, he'd not only told her he was monogamous, but also that he'd been tested and was clean.

She'd told him she was on the pill—as well as clean.

She'd also never before had a man inside of her without protection.

"It's up to you," Jaden told her. He tucked a strand of hair behind her ear. "I trust you, so I'm good either way."

That was possibly just one more smooth line, but she really did like the sound of it. Also, she trusted him, too.

Making up her mind, she took the condom and tossed it over her shoulder, the move heating his eyes even more. Then she realigned their bodies and looked into his eyes.

She sank onto him in one smooth motion, and both of them gasped in pleasure.

"Arsula." His need was obvious in the vibration of the single word, and she nodded to let him know that her need matched his.

This was good, she tried to tell him, but nothing came out. Whatever this was between them, it was really, really good.

She didn't have the energy to do much more than hold on as Jaden began to move inside her, but she gave it everything she could. He gripped her hips, and she clamped her arms around his neck, and as they moved together, their mouths never broke for air. Not until she felt him begin to peak, and only then did she pull back. As she continued to ride him, he kept his eyes locked on hers, not looking away until the last second, and breaking only as he closed his eyes and threw back his head. And as he emptied himself inside her, Arsula would swear she could feel the strength of the women of her family holding her up.

Whatever this was going on between them . . . it was also very right.

Chapter Nineteen

How about a grilled cheese?" Arsula stared at the inside of her refrigerator—seeing few options to offer the man she'd spent most of the night having sex with—and pulled out the block of cheddar. She held it up in question, but as she did, the overhead light exposed the line of green-and-blue mold running along two sides, and she immediately tossed it in the trash.

She looked sheepishly at Jaden, who sat at her kitchen table in nothing but a pair of black briefs and his cast, and held up her hands in defeat.

"Soup?" she offered. "I think I have a can of chicken noodle. Or I could run downstairs for cheesecake?"

He chuckled. "You're not much of a cook, are you?"

"It's not one of my highlights, no." She pushed the fridge door closed and grabbed a box of crackers off the counter. It was three in the morning, and given the calories they'd burned, both of them were ravenous. She was also too exhausted to run anywhere, cheesecake or not.

"That's okay." Jaden snagged her before she could make it to the vacant seat and pulled her down to his lap. "You have other qualities I like."

His lips nuzzled at her neck, and amazingly, her body once again perked up.

"You've got to stop," she groaned, but she arched her neck, giving him better access for his ministrations. "I'm not going to be able to walk tomorrow."

"Good." His arm circled her, and he squeezed her bare breast. "Because I'm not going to let you get out of bed tomorrow."

"Such big words coming from the man who's made me do all the work."

His hand and mouth stopped moving. "*All* the work?" he questioned. He peeked at her, his face peering over her shoulder and his brows arched high, and she was reminded of how they'd started the evening on her couch . . . and then what he'd done to her on the very table where they now sat.

"Maybe not *all* the work," she conceded.

His thumb stroked down the back of her neck, and she shivered in his lap.

"Probably not even half the work," she corrected on a soft breath, and his returning hot smile did the trick. She was ready again. Just like that.

"That's all right." He nibbled at her earlobe, while his fingers lowered to the juncture at her thighs. "I plan to let you make it up to me tomorrow."

"Just say the word," she whispered. He slipped a finger inside her, and she moaned at his touch. "I'm clearly at your command," she went on. "Tell me what you want"—she angled her hips, reaching for his fingers—"and I'll get right on it."

"I want *you*," he breathed into her ear. "In a way that's both shocking and leaves me in awe."

His other hand sought out her breast, and as she sat cocooned in his arms, he once again sent her soaring.

He stroked her with great care as she came back to earth, his mouth still pressing kisses into her neck and his other hand still cupping her in his palm, and Arsula dropped her head to his shoulder. She breathed heavily, the same contentment she'd awoken with only a week before now shrouding her outside of sleep, and she silently begged that what they were doing wouldn't leave her wounded if it all came crashing down.

"You ruined your cracker," Jaden whispered a few minutes later, and she lifted her hand to find the herb-flavored square ground into dust.

"And you're ruining me," she confessed. She didn't get up and move away, though. She had no strength left in her legs to do so.

Instead, she pulled another cracker from the box and offered it to him. They sat like that, her collapsed in his lap, taking turns feeding each other crackers until the box was empty, and as a car passed on the street down below, indicating early movement on the start of a new day, Jaden pressed a kiss to her ear.

"Can I ask you something?"

Her head was still tucked against his shoulder, and she lifted her gaze to his. "You can ask me anything."

He motioned to the books that had been on her table earlier, before they'd been tossed haphazardly onto her counter. "What are you doing with those?"

She eyed the research tome she'd borrowed from her father's study. It had been sitting on her table for two months. "Bedtime reading," she answered flippantly. "That fattest one was going to put me to sleep tonight before you rang your bell and forced me downstairs."

He pinched her butt. "I didn't force you to do anything." He then pointed at the shelves loaded to the gills on the other side of the room. "And what about those?"

"Those I've already read."

He stared at her, his look indicating that her answer didn't suffice, but she offered nothing else. She wasn't sure she could trust him with these particular thoughts yet. He seemed to have come a long way in accepting who she was, but that could change on a dime.

Jaden shifted her to the chair beside him, then he crossed to the shelves and began reading the titles out loud. He chose only to call out the research books or the college-level course manuals she'd purchased over the years, however, and he didn't stop reading until she grabbed his shirt, where she'd earlier shoved it to the floor, and shrugged into it. He stood there silent. Patiently waiting.

"What?" she finally snapped. "They're books. What's the big deal? I like to read."

"But why read *these* books?"

"Why not these books?" She pulled a horror novel from the top shelf. "I read this one, too. Are you going to make something of that as well?"

"I'm not making something of *these*," he pointed out. "I just want to understand you, Arsula. From what you shared earlier tonight, I thought I was finally beginning to get there. But this changes things. What's going on here? What are you doing with all of these?" He returned the last book he'd picked up.

"I'm thinking about throwing them at you at the moment," she countered, but he didn't back down.

"My question remains. If you're all about being a life coach . . . then what are you doing with these types of books?"

"There's nothing wrong with my books," she argued.

"No. There isn't." He made his way over to her. "Nothing at all. I'd love a house with a huge library, and I'd be thrilled to have half your collection in there."

"But?" she said.

"*But* . . . this seems like you've crossed a line somewhere."

She stared up at him, and she wondered which side of the line he'd fall on. "How do you figure?"

The question was little more than a stall tactic, but she also suspected he wouldn't stop.

He dipped his head to hers when she looked down before he answered, his arms hanging over his crutches and his foot stuck out behind him, and when she once again met his eyes, she saw more than simple curiosity. He cared. How much was still up for debate, but he wasn't just trying to solve a puzzle here. He cared. About *her*.

"What are you looking to learn, Arsula? Are you in school? Hoping to *get* into school?"

"I could get into any school I wanted, *thankyouverymuch*."

He paused at that, and she could see him working through what she'd told him about her family before. They were all doctors. Therefore, they probably had money. They would also have connections. Conclusion: they probably *could* buy her way into whatever school she wished to attend.

"Good grief," she grumbled. Why could men be such idiots? She crossed to the fridge and pulled out a bottle of water, but instead of drinking it, she pointed the mouth of the bottle at him. "I can get into any school I want because my IQ falls into the ninety-eighth percentile, moron. Not because my father would buy my way there."

That had him weaving on his crutches, and she pointed to the chair he'd vacated when he'd first started his interrogation.

"Sit down," she commanded.

He sat.

She handed him the bottle of water and got herself another one, and then she lowered back to the other chair. She scooted it over until it was positioned in front of him, and then she told him more about herself.

"I like to read," she started. "I always have. I soak it in, and I move on to the next book."

"Then why didn't you . . ."

She held up a hand to silence him. "This is my story. Let me tell it."

He nodded, and she went on.

"Why didn't I go to college, right?" Of course that would be the first response from someone like him. "That's a question my father would like answered as well."

She tipped up her bottle and took a drink, and as drink turned to guzzle, her hand began to shake. Jaden reached over and lowered the bottle, as if he'd noticed the same thing, then he set both waters on the table and took her hands in his. He leaned forward, inching her closer at the same time, until they sat elbows on knees, facing each other.

"Switch subjects," he said. "What's the deal with your father?"

A tear slipped down her face.

"Dammit," she muttered. Then she looked up and offered a silent apology. But she hadn't meant to cry. Not about this. It wasn't worth crying over.

Not really.

"Basically," she finally answered, "my father is disappointed in me. I'm smart. I test higher than any of my brothers, and I always have. I could make something great of myself." His exact words when they'd talked over Christmas had been that it was "time to grow up. Time to quit screwing around." "He's 'tolerated my hobby' all these years, but he can't understand why I follow my passion and not his advice."

Jaden's eyes seemed to be looking for more than she was saying. "And his advice would be what?"

She lifted her brows. "Like you can't guess?"

"Okay." He nodded. "I get it. He wants you to go to medical school. That's understandable."

"You would think so." She smirked. "And the thing is, it wouldn't take me the normal four years to get there. I could test out of a chunk of undergraduate classes, go year-round, and load up my schedule. I'd be finished in a couple of years, max. Then it would be on to medical school. To possibly follow in his footsteps as the great neurosurgeon that he is."

Jaden lifted a finger. "Wait a minute. Your father is a neurosurgeon?"

She could see that Jaden had heard of him. "Dr. Donald Moretti. One of the best and most sought after in the country."

He stared in awe.

"I know," she told him. "And his daughter reads dreams for a living. You have to know *that* makes him proud."

Sarcasm dripped heavily from her words.

"But what gets me," she went on, "is the fact that I'm actually considering doing it. Because I want to make him proud. And because I know I could be excellent following in his footsteps. He used to come home from work and share stories of his surgeries. I loved it. In high school, he'd quiz me by relaying symptoms and histories of actual patients, then wait for me to work through a diagnosis. Nine times out of ten, I was spot-on."

"But?" The look Jaden wore was one of utter befuddlement.

"But," she repeated. "He says that a lot, too. But I *love* what I do. And I don't need his idea of more to make me happier. I love meeting people, talking to people. *Helping* people. I love knowing that the gift that was passed to me due to my ancestry isn't being ignored." She stopped for a moment and fought not to hang her head in shame. "But I'm an embarrassment to him," she whispered. "And I really do hate that. He's my idol. He always has been. I couldn't love a parent more than I do my dad. Therefore"—she glanced at her collection of books—"I'm considering it. Only, how do I make both my dad *and* myself happy?"

"What about this one?" Arsula turned in a circle, modeling a royal-blue hat with a white feather sticking out of the top.

"It looks very eighties pimpish."

She giggled and put the hat back. "How do you know anything about eighties pimpish?"

"Netflix. How else?"

"Yeah?" She chuckled. "Somehow I can't picture you sitting around binge-watching anything, but I suppose if I had to choose an era for you, eighties movies would fit the bill. Probably you're a closet *Friends* lover as well."

"Probably. I am full of surprises, you know?"

"You're mostly full of crap." She winked, and he laughed.

They thanked the vendor for letting them look, then moved on. They'd been at the flea market for a couple of hours now, and though he was having a great time, this wasn't where he'd ever have expected to spend a Saturday. They were here because of Arsula, though. She liked flea markets . . . and he was finding that he liked making Arsula happy.

It had been a week since he'd cooked dinner for her, and though they hadn't gone out publicly in that time, they were definitely together. He'd cooked for her once more during the week, and she'd hung out and watched TV in his room a couple of nights. She'd also held him off physically after their marathon thirty-six hours of all-sex-all-the-time the weekend before, citing that she wanted to take things slower than they'd jumped into. But they *had* done a whole lot of making out.

"I want to take a quick look in this one," Arsula said before hurrying into a booth set up with only vintage pieces. The pimp hat she'd previously had on would fit in nicely there, even though most everything else had at least fifty years on it.

"Take a look at these old pocket watches." He stared down into a jewelry case as he stopped beside her. "My dad used to carry one of these."

She looked up. "Yeah?"

"Yeah." The salesperson handed over the one he pointed to, and he pressed the top button to pop it open. "It was very similar to this one. For a period of time when I was a kid, I wanted to be just like my dad, and top on the list of things I'd need to accomplish that had been a gold pocket watch."

She'd gone back to perusing the pieces herself. "Cute. How old were you when you wanted to be like him?"

"I don't know . . . sometime before I was ten, I guess."

He handed the watch back over, and they moved from the counter. "So after your mother died?"

He didn't immediately answer, because he was suddenly reminded of their conversation from the Saturday before. Arsula had asked what his first memory of his mom was, and he'd actually told her. All of it.

In more than three years of dating, he'd never shared that story with Megan, but once the words had come out, he'd been both relieved and terrified. Relieved that he could share something like that with someone other than a paid counselor, and terrified at what else he might decide to tell her next.

He'd also wondered what else he might *want* to tell her next. Because as she liked to point out, she was easy to talk to.

Or maybe it was just that he *liked* talking to her.

"Yeah," he finally responded. "It was after my mother died."

He took her hand and moved to the next booth. He liked doing a lot of things with her.

They browsed in silence for a while, and he let himself think back over the past week, especially about what she'd told him concerning wanting to be a life coach yet feeling like she had to choose between that and her father's wishes. He knew that a lot of females had the tendency to be total daddy's girls. He'd met more than one who would walk over hot coals for her father. But he'd never have guessed Arsula to be hesitant to make life choices for herself. Or *not* to make them, as the case was, due to wanting to keep from letting her dad down. He'd always seen her as more certain of herself than that. And especially after he'd sat beside her earlier in the week and she'd walked him through the proposed website. Arsula Moretti knew what she wanted, and she went after it.

Only, apparently she didn't all the time. And that bothered him.

Bringing the back of her hand to his mouth, he pressed a kiss against it, and even without her looking over at him, he could feel her smile. That's the kind of feeling she should always have. Never any sort of uncertainty.

"How's the website?" he asked. "Did you send that list of changes we came up with to Megan yet?"

A secretive smile played at her lips. "I did. This morning."

"Why the cat-who-ate-the-canary grin on your face, then?" He pulled her to a stop, and he couldn't contain his own excitement. "Did you hear back from her already?"

If she had, he wanted to see the changes now. He didn't want to wait.

"I did hear from her, but it wasn't an updated website that she sent."

"Then what did she send?"

She didn't answer him. Instead, she reached around him and picked up a Halloween nurse costume, and when she held it up in front of her, he joined her in checking it out. It wasn't anywhere close to Halloween, but he could totally see Arsula wearing that. He gulped.

He could also totally see himself taking it off her.

"What did she send?" he asked again, doing his best to keep some of his blood in his head.

"Oh . . . just a mock-up of a book cover."

"What?" He peered down at her. "For whose book?"

Again with the smile, and at the same time, she dug her phone out of her back pocket. "For my book," she announced, and passed her phone over to him. On the screen was a small image, but one that was big enough for him to see her name stamped boldly across the front— and the nurse's uniform was temporarily forgotten.

He looked at her. "You wrote a book?"

"I've written about three-fourths of one. It covers all the things I'm most passionate about. Intuition and how to learn to trust your own, finding your calm even when standing in the middle of a raging storm, and basically . . . living the best you."

She'd written a book. He was amazed. "Do you have someone waiting to publish it?"

"No, but if I decide to finish it, I'll publish it myself. I started it solely for the people I meet or work with on a day-to-day basis, but if I decide to do the website . . ." She trailed off, and his belief in her began to grow even more. He didn't know why the knowledge that she was working on a book helped in that regard, but over the last few days, he'd finally begun to see her as the highly intelligent, über-capable woman that she was.

So if she'd written a book, then it was bound to be excellent.

"Let's get this." She held the uniform up in front of her again. "I have very specific ideas about me wearing this, and you receiving a sponge bath, that I'd like to try out."

Thoughts of the book evaporated. "I do recall mentioning a sponge bath at some point."

"Oh, you mentioned it all right." She handed money for her purchase over to the vendor. "And you're lucky I didn't wake you up in the middle of every night that first week, sponge and warm soapy water in hand. Because I considered it, you know? Just for that one crack alone. And it would have served you right, too."

He suddenly felt as if he'd swallowed a frog. He couldn't get enough of this woman. "I'm quite certain I would have enjoyed it if you had."

"Not the kind of bath I had in mind." She cast a look up at him, and as usual, she had him laughing like a kid.

"I guess that's one thing we'll never know."

She slipped her arms through his. "Never say never, Jaden."

Chapter Twenty

The nurse's uniform from the day before lay in a heap on the bedroom floor, and Arsula had determined it was money well spent. Now they just needed a stethoscope and tongue depressor, and the picture would be complete.

They hadn't actually gotten around to the sponge bath, though. But it was early yet.

"This is a really nice way to wake up." She lifted her head and peered down at Jaden. He was still in his cast, and he was currently on his knees on the floor beside the bed. With her legs wrapped around his shoulders.

Somehow, he'd managed to get her into that position before she'd ever opened her eyes.

"Why are you talking?" His words were muffled by what he was doing with his mouth.

"I'm just saying—"

One hand reached up and closed over her mouth, and she nipped at his fingers. He upped his game then, and she fell back to the bed, and a few minutes later, as she lay in a postorgasmic glow, her cell phone began to ring.

"Don't answer it," Jaden muttered. He'd climbed into the bed and now lay with his nose buried against her neck. "We're sleeping in, remember?"

"Then I guess you shouldn't have woken me up."

She reached over for her phone as Jaden harrumphed about the lack of appreciation of some women, and when she saw that it was her youngest brother calling via video call, she jerked upright.

"It's Boyd," she announced. "He could be calling to tell me the baby is on the way."

Jaden eyed the screen before pushing up. "Then I guess you have to take it."

He kissed the tip of her nose and mumbled about finding them something to eat while she talked to her brother, and she tapped the button to connect the call.

"Is it time?" she asked. Whitney wasn't due for two more weeks, but deliveries happened early all the time.

"Good morning to you, too." Her brother's face appeared on the screen. She could see a very pregnant Whitney moving around easily behind him, so her initial euphoria waned.

"I just thought it might be time."

"I thought you wanted me to hold off a couple of weeks," Whitney said from behind her husband, and Arsula grinned.

"That would be ideal. Could you do that for me?"

She held up a mug, lifting it as if in toast to Arsula, then her easy-going demeanor vanished. "Not on your life, Arsula Moretti. I'm on a countdown to eviction here, and I intend to make the process a short one."

Arsula chuckled, anxious for that eviction process to finish up herself, then after Whitney left the room, Arsula gave her full attention to her brother.

249

"Good morning," she offered, since she hadn't done so before. "It's good to hear from you."

"Drop the bull. I called to tell you that Mom is going crazy down here."

"Why? Is something wrong?"

"Just you." He smiled his thanks off camera as a mug of coffee appeared in front of him, and Arsula glanced through the open bedroom door to where she could hear Jaden in the kitchen. She hoped he remembered to make coffee.

"What's wrong with me?" she asked absentmindedly. Because Jaden had just come into view, and as had happened so often over the past week, she caught her breath at the sight of him.

"Because you haven't called in over a week."

Silence fell in the kitchen as Arsula turned back to the phone. "Oh, crap," she muttered.

She *had* called the week before that, though. She'd called Tuesday night, catching both of her parents at home, and she and her dad had actually had a good conversation. It hadn't been about anything in particular. Just catching up. But he hadn't pushed for information on her decision, and she hadn't brought it up.

She enjoyed talking to her dad like that, but it happened far too rarely these days.

"So what should I tell her about the man in your life?"

Arsula scowled at her brother. "What makes you think I have one?"

"You have sex hair, Arsula Jane."

"I . . ." She lifted a hand to her hair, mortified that he'd noticed. Then when she realized that by lifting her arm he might figure out she was also still naked, she dropped her hand to the bed.

Busted.

"So what's he like?" Boyd asked. He was her champion for all that she did, but he was also her protector.

"He's . . ." She could still see Jaden from where she sat. "I don't know. Kind of like Dad, I guess."

"How so?"

She shrugged before she remembered that her brother couldn't see her shoulders, then she attempted to explain. "Education is important to him. Making something of himself, equally so. He's . . . struggled with who I am, but I think we're getting past it."

"Are we going to get to meet this man anytime soon?"

"I don't know," she admitted. "He won't be coming down for the baby's birth, if that's what you're asking."

"Why not? Can he not get away for a weekend?"

"I . . . haven't asked him to." But now that Boyd had put it out there, she realized that she'd love to take Jaden home and introduce him to her family. And wasn't that a kicker. Not that she hadn't introduced boyfriends before. But usually only after they'd been dating for a few months.

With Jaden, though, one week seemed to be the magic number. She wouldn't bring it up, though. At least not yet. He was busy finishing his degree, and given that they *had* only been together for a week, she wasn't sure either of them was ready for that.

But if Whitney went the full two weeks before delivering . . .

"This one is different, isn't he?" Boyd's question pulled her back. "I can see it on your face."

"He's just a guy, Boyd. No big deal."

"Who is like your hero-worship father."

"Who's like my obstinate, opinionated father."

"Who I sometimes worry you would do anything in the world for." Boyd was referring to the school thing now. They'd had more than one discussion on the subject since she'd moved out of town.

She didn't bother to respond. She wasn't in the mood to talk about their dad.

"Fine. We won't talk about that today. But this man—whom I'm apparently not going to get to meet anytime soon—had better be good enough for you." Boyd offered his words in his big-brother tone of warning. "Don't make me have to come up there."

"Oh, he's definitely *good* enough for me." She waggled her brows teasingly, until her brother groaned in disgust.

"Behave, or I'm calling Mom next and telling her you have a boyfriend."

"Don't you dare."

She loved all her brothers. They each carried a protective streak for her a mile wide. But she loved her youngest brother just a little bit more. Boyd had been closer in age to her, and while the others had been off doing their thing in college, Boyd had been home chauffeuring his eleven-year-old sister wherever she wanted to go.

"I mean it," she said. "Don't tell Mom anything. I don't want to listen to it."

She also didn't want to share her feelings about Jaden yet. Things were too new, and she was too hopeful.

Boyd laughed at her request as if she'd just told the funniest joke. *"Please,"* he choked out. "You know she's going to take one look at me and instantly know."

Arsula did know that. "But how? I don't get it how she always just knows these types of things."

"This question coming from you? The queen of trusting your intuition?"

"I know, but . . ." She shook her head as her words trickled off. "Try not to let her know yet? I really like him, and I'm not ready for an interrogation."

"I know you do, Lula. And that makes me very happy. So yes, I promise. I'll do my best to dodge interrogation from the all-knowing woman who bore us. Before I have to go, though, fill me in on the book. Is it still on hiatus?"

Her mother woes were forgotten as she immediately lit up.

"You've been working on it?" Boyd's surprised tone was edged out only by happiness.

"I haven't yet. I still don't know if I even want to do anything with it. But I have been thinking about it."

She'd actually printed it out earlier in the week, but it had been sitting on the top of her refrigerator since. She wanted to read back through it at some point. To try to see it with an unbiased eye.

Then maybe her decision would come to her.

"Tell him about the cover," Jaden called out from the kitchen, and at the sound of his voice, her brother's interest was piqued.

"Your mystery man is still there?"

"Well"—she pointed to the frizz on her head—"you *did* point out my hair. If he'd left already, I'd probably have combed it."

Boyd laughed again, and this time as the noise died down, he turned serious. "You had a cover made for it? Tell me about it," he said, and she grabbed the piece of paper from the bedside table. The one where she'd printed the cover. Then, tucking a blanket under each arm to provide herself a modicum of modesty, she held the paper up and pulled the phone back for Boyd to see.

"What do you think?" She glanced at it again herself before adding, "I'll text it to you when we get off the phone so you can get a better look. But I'm kind of in love with it."

"Your name needs to be bigger," Boyd told her. "The world needs to know your name."

Any reply she might have given got stuck in her throat. She could always count on Boyd.

"There's a website, too," she said when she managed to speak again. "It's not live. Just an idea I'm playing around with. It would need some work if I ever wanted to do anything with it."

"Send the link along with the cover. I can't wait to see it."

She nodded. She'd send both as soon as they hung up. She'd do it from her laptop, though, and would include the typewritten notes she'd already passed off to Megan.

"Anything I should report in to Dad?" Boyd asked as Whitney returned and sat beside him.

Just that I want to be seen as valuable for myself.

She didn't say the words out loud, though. Nor did she express that she'd like her brother to relay that she didn't want to have to be just like her dad in order to make him proud.

She just wanted to be herself.

"Tell him I'll see him in a couple of weeks." That would sum up her thoughts better than trying to express them. "And that I miss him. I miss everyone."

"Will do."

"And Boyd"—she stopped him before his finger could connect with the "Off" button—"I'm glad you called."

"I'm glad, too. And all of us miss *you* as well."

They hung up, and when she looked back toward the kitchen, she found Jaden propped against her bedroom door, now wearing nothing but navy sweats that dipped low on his hips and holding a steaming mug of coffee. He took a sip, his blue eyes twinkling behind his sexy professor glasses, and a renewed feeling of contentment bloomed.

She could so fall in love with this man.

She was *already* falling in love with this man. And that scared her to death.

"My intuition tells me I'd like your brother, too."

Her intuition told her that she'd better not declare her thoughts out loud. She and Jaden may be having a good time, but there'd been no mention of love yet, nor even anything long-lasting.

She hoped for both of those things, though. The more time she spent around him, the more she liked him.

"You can trust your intuition on *that* for sure." She tucked her feelings back behind the covers for the time being. "Boyd's always been my biggest supporter."

"I gathered as much."

He turned and set down his coffee cup, then, using a rickety metal rolling cart they'd found at the flea market, he rolled their breakfast into the room. She grinned as he pushed the cart out in front of him a few feet, then hobbled up behind it, and then pushed it again. The cart squeaked with every move, and the sound made the moment all the more endearing. They'd had to take the thing apart in order to fit it into her car, but he'd insisted it come home with them for moments like this.

"You think you'll get out of the cast tomorrow?"

Push. Thump-thump. "I sure hope so."

The cart made it to her before he did, and she rolled it out of the way so he could lower to the bed beside her. "You still won't be able to put weight on it, though, right?"

"That's the theory." The bed dipped as he sat. "But I'm hoping my bones have healed faster than the doctor expects. I'm ready to walk on two feet again."

She sipped the coffee he'd included for her. "Got plenty of running around to do, do you?"

He shook his head and leaned over to meld his mouth to hers. "I've only got plans to do you up against a wall."

His words sent a shiver racing over her, and her chest flushed at the thought. She could get down with that.

When he pulled back, he fed her a bite of bacon. "What's going to happen when you go home in a couple of weeks? Are you going to let your dad talk you into moving home and going to school?"

She took another drink of her coffee. "I could go to school up here if I wanted to. Montana has universities."

"It certainly does." He fed her another bite. "But the real question is, do you *want* to go to school?"

Picking up the printout of the book cover she'd just shown to her brother, Jaden held it up for her to see. As she looked back at it—and as she caught the gleam of pride shining in his eyes—she knew one thing to be true.

"What I *want* is to finish my book."

He kissed her again, this time a light tap on her mouth. "Then I say that should be priority number one."

Jaden kept his eyes on the woman sitting across the table from him and did his best to listen to whatever it was she was telling him . . . and *not* to let her see his impatience to be out of there. It had been two and a half weeks since he'd cooked that first dinner for Arsula, and the more he'd gotten to know her, the more he wanted. She was pretty terrific.

She was also sexy as hell.

His gaze drifted to the deep V of her dress. They were just finishing dinner at the Italian restaurant in the hotel where Gabe and Erica's reception had been held, and though he loved taking her on real dates, he'd found that he also appreciated the quiet times they spent together. The evenings he cooked for her.

Those moments made him picture more. A house . . . kids . . .

But then again, every time those types of images floated to mind, he squelched them. He'd been going out with her for less than three weeks. He couldn't be falling for her that fast. Just as he doubted she was falling for him.

"You about ready to go?" he asked during a break in her story about the mother of two she'd helped three years ago.

"Why do I get the feeling you're not listening to me tonight?"

His gaze dipped to the expanse of cleavage he'd been staring at for the past hour and a half. It was somewhat more plumped and pronounced tonight. "I don't know what could possibly have captured my attention," he claimed drily. "Too bad you don't put out any effort when a guy takes you out for the evening."

Appreciation flitted across her face. "Too bad you can't learn to be a tad more subtle."

She put her napkin on the table and scooted to the edge of the booth, as if intending to get up, but made a little "oops" sound at the last minute. She bent down, stretching for some unnamed object, and the top half of her darned near spilled out of her dress.

"Didn't I once call you the devil?" Jaden muttered so only she could hear him. He also sent scowls to every man in the place who'd redirected his attention to Arsula's chest.

She lifted her face from her position near the floor. "And shouldn't you have learned your lesson from that last time?"

As he stared down into the face he was becoming more and more infatuated with, he understood how fast a man could get used to this woman. "Are you saying that you intend to shove me down another flight of stairs tonight?"

"Nope." A hint of the very devil he spoke of showed up as she demurely returned to an upright position. Because at the same time as her back connected with the padded cushion behind her, her foot found his crotch. "I have something entirely different in mind for you tonight."

He pulled out his wallet and tossed down a wad of bills, but before standing, he pressed her foot firmly into his erection. "Then let's get out of here."

She didn't delay, seemingly as invested as he in getting back to the apartment in a hurry, but as they made their way through the crowded dining room, his gaze landed on someone else.

257

"Meg," he said, surprise filling the word.

Arsula stopped in front of him, then she followed his gaze.

"What about her?" Her tone was friendly, but when she saw what he had—Meg on a date of her own—her posture changed. And Jaden knew that *her* change was due to *his* change.

"Nothing," he replied quickly. He motioned with the bottom of one crutch toward the door. "Let's get out of here."

She didn't argue, but neither did she continue moving as if she had somewhere to be. They made their way into the hallway that led to the lobby of the hotel, and as the restaurant doors closed behind them, Jaden didn't let himself look back. He'd seen Megan a few times since that night at the office. They'd met up to look at potential locations for the store, and he, Nate, and Dani had even been with her at the real estate agent's office earlier that day. They'd signed a three-year lease on what each of them felt was the perfect new location.

Additionally, during one of those meetings, he'd shared with Megan that he and Arsula were now dating—he'd felt it the courteous thing to do. Yet Meg hadn't said a word about *her* going out with anyone. And he wasn't sure why that bothered him so much.

Arsula remained silent as they made their way through the historic hotel, not bothering to take in any of the local artifacts serving as décor, and not for the first time, Jaden wished he could put weight on his foot.

At least he was in a boot now. That had happened last week.

But he wanted to be able to take Arsula's hand as they walked. He *wanted* to pull her to the side of the room and talk about what had just happened.

"It's just that I was surprised." He didn't intend to make a big deal about it, but he did feel the need to say something.

"I didn't ask," Arsula replied.

"But you want to know."

She hit the automatic button on the handicapped door, and they stepped from inside to outside. And as had happened almost six weeks before, a sharp wind seemed to snap them in two.

"Good Lord." He hurried up the sidewalk beside her. This time, they'd both come out without their coats.

"Do you want to go back?"

"No." He lowered his head against the wind. He'd known an arctic blast was expected to pass through tonight—every cherry farmer in the area was concerned—but the temperature had remained comfortable when they'd gone in.

"Then let's quit talking and get there as fast as we can."

Arsula's apartment was less than a block away, and it took another ten minutes, but they made it in one piece. He snuck a peek at her as she locked the office door once they got inside, and worry gnawed at him.

"It had nothing to do with her." He stood in the middle of the reception area, determined to have this out before the night went any further downhill. "None of it. Not my desperation to win her back when she first broke up with me, not my drunken behavior afterward and winding up in bed with you, and not my seeming disappointment in seeing her tonight."

He'd figured all of that out as quickly as he'd realized he hadn't actually been jealous to see Megan out with another man.

"Then what, exactly, *did* it have to do with?" Arsula asked. She stood on the other side of her desk, having expertly put a barrier between them.

"It had to do with me," he admitted. He made himself stand tall, even though it was easier to lean on his crutches. It was time to admit a fault he'd known about for some time. "My mother never loved me. Which you know already. But by the time I came along, she'd quit putting out *any* effort. Before she died, I felt like I was on the outside

259

looking in. And afterward . . . I was the little brother my sister had to raise. Dani loved me, of course. And she was great playing the role of mom."

He tried to pace, but doing so in crutches remained a veritable clusterfuck.

"But the thing is, she *wasn't* my mom. And my life has never been what anyone would call normal. That's what Megan represented to me. The normalcy I crave. I want the house, the kids, the white picket fence. And Megan was part of that plan. She was *supposed* to love me. That's why I struggled with the breakup. Why I faltered upon seeing her tonight. My brain hadn't fully reset."

Arsula had grown still as he spoke, and once he ran out of words, his nerves kicked in. He didn't know what else to say. Any other time, he'd expect her to jump in with words meant to coax him through his own thoughts, but he didn't think that would be happening tonight. She remained too quiet.

And she looked too hurt.

"Arsula . . . *please*. I swear to you—"

She held up a hand to stop his words. "What were you thinking when you saw her? Was that really jealousy I saw?"

He nodded, and shame filled him. And he hated that one moment in time would hurt her. "It was at first, but just for a minute. And only because it was startling to see."

"Yet you said you've moved on. You're just friends again. You said I wasn't a stand-in, Jaden." Her voice cracked on his name, and she shook her head with disgust. "And you *know* I wouldn't be with you if—"

"I have moved on," he stressed. He crossed to her and refused to let her push him away. "I'm with you now, and only you. Mind, body, *and* soul. You make me happy in ways I didn't know were possible, Arsula. Don't you know that? In ways I only dreamed about with Megan. I've laughed more since I've known you than I have in a whole year. I open my eyes to a brighter world each day. To a woman who blows my mind with her bravery and refusal to live life any way but her way. I've shared things with you that I never did with her. Do you realize that?" He tilted her face up to his, the thought of losing her terrifying him. "And I *want* to share more. Because you're you, Arsula. And because I'm beginning to think that you *were* sent here for me."

Chapter Twenty-One

Ursula opened her eyes the next morning, and worry roiled inside her. Not for the fact that she'd let Jaden sweet-talk her into bed after he'd gotten jealous of Megan—although that was scary enough on its own—but because she finally got it. She understood what Jaden's problem was.

She rolled to her side, finding him still asleep, and she contemplated the conversation to come. He wouldn't like what she had to say, because it was bound to cut deep. But he needed to hear it. And she knew it had to be now.

She shifted her gaze to the ceiling. The aqua color had a soothing effect, which was why she'd chosen it. So she soaked it in, hoping to even out her energy before having the confrontation that lay ahead. A phone rang in the office below, and she picked up her cell to see what time it was. Still an hour and a half before she had to open the door. It was probably someone on East Coast time, forgetting to account for the time zones.

She put the phone back and returned her focus to the ceiling. She was so Zen as she lay there, she didn't hear Jaden when he moved.

Yet suddenly, he lay propped above her, his blue eyes peering down into hers.

"You're very still," he said.

"I was trying not to wake you."

"No. I mean on the inside." He touched his fingers to her chest. "In here."

She caught her breath at his understanding. "You can tell that?"

"Yeah. I don't know how, but I can. And I have to say, it's not exactly comfort I'm picking up on." He moved his hand higher and traced his fingers over the line of her jaw. "What's wrong, Lula-bell? What can I do to help? You're not still upset about last night, are you?"

He could be very caring at times.

She pressed a kiss to his fingers. "I'm not still upset about last night. And thank you, but I don't need any help. I'm just lying here worrying about you."

His brow furrowed. "What about me?"

"I get it now," she whispered, and his eyes darkened as he stared back.

"You get what now?"

"I understand why you hurt."

Now it was *his* being that went still. "What are you talking about? I thought we'd moved beyond that."

She could hear the trepidation in his voice. "Just because we don't talk about it regularly doesn't mean there's not still an issue. And my subconscious finally worked it out. It's not about your mom, Jaden. Nor is it *just* with your dad. It's with your entire family."

He pushed to a sitting position. "What are you talking about? We both know my mother was the problem."

She didn't know how she'd missed it before. She'd even seen it at the hospital when she'd offered to let him stay with her. In a blink, the discussion had gone from what was best for Jaden to Jaden against his siblings.

Wasn't that part of why she'd stepped in and made the offer? So he'd have someone on his side?

"Yes, your mother *was* the problem. Originally. But after she was gone, why didn't you get the normalcy you craved? Why did Dani have to come home and raise you instead of your dad doing it?"

"Because he's a man," he argued. "That's not so uncommon."

"Isn't it? So you're telling me that if you have kids someday, you won't be there for them if they need you? That you wouldn't play both mom and dad if they didn't have a mother around?"

He'd stopped arguing, but she could see he didn't like where his thoughts had gone.

"Your dad wasn't there for you after your mom died," she continued. "If you were working with a patient, you'd see the same thing I do. He wasn't there for you when you were a kid, so why would you go to his house and risk him not being there for you now?"

"Stop speaking." His words barely made it out, but Arsula heard them loud and clear.

She didn't stop, though. It was time to push. "But there's more to the story." She kept her tone as calm as her insides had previously been. "Because it wasn't just that you wouldn't stay at the house when you broke your ankle. You wouldn't stay with *any* of your family."

A muscle ticked in his jaw.

"Not Dani, not Nick, not Gabe."

He extricated himself and rose from the bed.

"What you fear is that *no one* in your family truly loves you, Jaden. *That's* what Megan represented for you. The one person you could count on to love you for you. Who didn't 'have' to love you."

"I said stop it."

"Therefore, you'd rather let a stranger be there for you than risk staying where you might not be wanted."

He stepped into his jeans, nearly falling as he had to put weight on his ankle. "I didn't ask for your amateur psychoanalysis, Arsula. Nor do I want it."

"But I have valid points, and you know it." She rose to her knees, remaining on the bed. "You spent years working on the knowns of your mother. All of you dealt with her. All of you survived in your own way. But you never faced that *she* wasn't the only one who caused hurts."

His face contorted with anger. "We *did* face it. That's where you're wrong. He hurt Dani. He let her take the brunt of Mom's abuse, and he never once raised a hand to help her out of the situation. We faced it, they both went to therapy to deal with it. You don't have a fucking clue what you're talking about."

"But the same happened with you," she said softly. "And you *didn't* face it."

"I swear, Arsula. You need to pull the fuck back."

"Tossing around curse words isn't going to make me curl up in horror, you know."

He yanked his shirt over his head.

"Nor will it offend me." She rose and went to stand in front of him, and when he looked at her again, she read both anger and fear. She'd nailed it.

All of it.

"Then maybe if I point out what a joke you are, you'll take offense. You don't have any magical gift. Are you kidding me? And the fact that you 'help people'"—he air quoted—"without so much as a lick of education only enhances the lunacy of your actions." He tapped himself on the chest. "I'm the one who knows what he's talking about here. Because *I'm* not the joke. No wonder your own dad is embarrassed by you."

She went quiet. Because yep, he'd offended her. He'd sliced her open.

But she also understood this was part of his lashing-out process. He was hurting. He was scared.

And *she* was pissed.

"Quit channeling your mother, Jaden." She let her own eyes show as much spite as his. "She hurt you, so you think you have some right to hurt others?"

"Do *not* throw my mother back in my face."

"Then don't *act* like her."

He didn't say another word. He turned his back, strapped on his boot, and then he and his crutches hobbled to the inner set of stairs. And when he opened them, while still not so much as saying another word to her, she picked up her cell phone and chunked him in the back of the head.

Thankfully, he didn't fall down the stairs that time, but he did disappear. Probably from her life as well as from her apartment.

Her phone started ringing a couple of minutes later, but she didn't bother to pick it up. Whoever it was could wait. She had to take a shower and wash Jaden Wilde from her body. And she hoped that by the time she had to go downstairs, he'd have found somewhere else to be.

Chapter Twenty-Two

Arsula wheeled into the Cheyenne hospital parking lot around eleven that night, hyped on coffee and adrenaline and twelve hours on the road, and took the first empty parking spot she came to. She had her door open before she'd even stopped and held her arm out behind as she ran from the car, pushing the lock button on the key fob. The car beeped as she hit the brick pavers under the awning, and a few seconds later the automated doors of the emergency room opened in front of her.

She stepped in, catching her breath only long enough to think about the last time she'd been in an ER and how much her life had changed since, then she hurried down the hallway she knew would eventually lead to the elevators to take her to the OB floor. She was at a run by the time she reached the right section of the hospital, and as she waited for the elevator to arrive, she continually jabbed the button.

The steel doors slid open and no one was inside, so she stepped in, hitting both the "Close Door" and "7" buttons at the same time.

"Hurry," she urged, as the elevator began to climb. The call that had come in after Jaden left that morning had been her mother, shrieking about Whitney going into labor. Arsula hadn't heard the message until an hour later, and thankfully, the temp she'd trained to fill in for her had been available to come right in. Arsula had hit the road soon after, and given that no one had updated her in the last two hours, she was now in an all-out panic.

The silence from her family had her flip-flopping on whether the lack of information meant that the baby still wasn't close to being born or that the baby had already been born and no one wanted to tell her she'd missed it. At the moment, though, she'd lay odds she hadn't missed anything. There was too much inside of her, urging her on.

She pressed the "7" button again, not removing her finger as the car ascended, while lecturing herself for not taking the stairs. She knew how slow these elevators could be. Three nephews had already been born here, as well as this being the location where her great-aunt had spent her final days.

The car finally came to a halt, and the second the doors opened wide enough to squeeze through, she burst out of them.

"Arsula!"

Pivoting, she ran for the crowd of Morettis gathered outside one of the rooms. "Is she here?"

"Is *who* here?" asked her oldest brother.

"Baby Arsula." She shot Chris a quit-being-stupid look. "Has she been born yet?"

"How do you know it's a girl?"

Her other brother turned, then, and both of their wives, as well as Arsula's parents, closed around her.

"Did you dream that it's a girl?"

"Did Boyd tell you it is?"

"I always knew Boyd liked you better than us."

"*Boys*, behave yourselves and quit laying into your sister."

Arsula tossed a grateful look to her mother and a quick nod to her dad, who'd stood silent as her brothers had started in on her, then she faced her brothers. "No, morons, Boyd didn't tell me anything. But I have to believe that surely one of you idiots can produce something other than a Y chromosome."

They hated when she called them idiots, because their past grades and current career choices indicated otherwise. However, as she'd shared with Jaden, she tested higher than any of them. Therefore, calling them idiots had been a favorite pastime for years.

"She's pushing right now," one of her sisters-in-law said, but before Arsula could figure out which one, the door to the room behind them opened. They whirled as one to find Boyd standing there, pride on his face, and looking as exhausted as Arsula imagined Whitney must feel.

"She's here," he said, and every one of them cheered. Then he turned to Arsula. "We'd like you to be the first to meet her."

"Really?" Her palms grew sweaty.

Boyd nodded and ushered her in, and the moment she stepped inside the birthing room and saw the tiny baby suckling at her mama's breast, Arsula almost had a breakdown. She'd done her best for the full length of the drive to allow thoughts of the fight with Jaden not to seep into her consciousness, but as she looked upon the love and tenderness in the room—and given that she knew how much Boyd loved and respected his wife—Arsula accepted what she'd known as she'd driven away.

Jaden wasn't the one for her, either. And she'd never have his babies suckling at her breast.

She swallowed past the pain. She hadn't even known she wanted the opportunity to someday have Jaden's babies, but the knowledge rang loud and clear.

"Arsula." When Boyd spoke beside her, she realized she hadn't taken more than a couple of steps into the room.

"I'm sorry," she whispered back. "It's just so moving to feel such love in one space."

He slid an arm around her and hugged her to him, and she laid her head on her brother's shoulder. Then she felt the tears begin.

"Don't cry," he told her. "You haven't even held her yet."

She sniffled. "I know."

But she also knew that her tears were as much for her loss as for her brother's gain.

She finally made herself move forward, and she smiled at her sister-in-law. "How are you, Whitney?"

New-mama love glowed back at her. "My life is complete," she said, and Arsula nodded in understanding. They were more than a couple now. They were a family. And they would be the best thing this tiny baby would ever know.

"Do you want to hold her?" her brother asked, and she jerked her attention back to him.

"Can I?" She took in the baby's soft wisp of dark fuzz covering her head and her four little perfect fingers and thumb resting against Whitney's bare skin. "She's so tiny."

Whitney nodded. "But she's a Moretti, so you know she's going to be tough."

That, Arsula did know.

Medical personnel remaining in the room faded from Arsula's peripheral vision as she stepped to the side of the bed, and her brother reached for his daughter. He pressed a kiss to the baby's head, smiled down in awe at both mother and child, and then held his daughter out for his sister to take.

"Arsula," he said, his voice heavy with emotion, "meet your namesake."

The text message indicator on Jaden's phone displayed a small 4. Four messages he had yet to read. All from Arsula. And all arriving within a thirty-minute span that morning, the first one waking him up. Jaden pressed the button to turn off the display, same as he'd done at least thirty times since he'd arrived at the hospital. Then he shoved the device back into his pocket and pretended it didn't exist.

"He's going to be okay," he heard Gloria saying from her seat a couple of rows behind his. He didn't know who she was talking to because everyone was there. "He's *got* to be okay."

"What was he doing out on the tractor so early this morning?" That came from Cord, who'd just arrived, thanks to Nick's wife flying in her helicopter to pick him up.

"And *why* had he tried to climb a tree with it?" Nick added, his tone morose, and Jaden watched Cord as clarity hit. They hadn't shared that part of the story with him earlier because the scene they'd witnessed when his dad had been found hadn't made sense. But the sheriff had stopped by an hour ago and confirmed it. Their dad's tractor had hit the fifty-year-old birch head-on.

Gloria whimpered, and though Jaden couldn't see her, he imagined her shaking her head at his brothers' questions. But she likely *did* know what their dad had been doing out on a tractor before dawn. Just as Jaden could also guess. Hadn't she been the one to bring it up to him and Arsula when they'd stopped by?

His dad had been worried about losing trees for weeks because his gut had told him he should be. And now, thanks to the extremely fast—and record-breaking—temperature drop of the week before, they'd likely not only lose the pick-your-own section, but chances were good a large percentage of their entire crop wouldn't recover. They'd be out of business. The previously warmer-than-usual temps would have woken many of the trees from dormancy, making them instantly vulnerable to a hard freeze, and then boom, a one-hundred-degree drop in a matter of hours. His dad had probably been out there checking on the trees every morning since. Trying to estimate their losses.

But why had he turned away from the fields and driven into a tree?

He pulled his phone back out of his pocket. He'd heard the notifications when the messages had come in that morning, but he'd ignored them. Because he'd assumed they were about *him*. And because he hadn't wanted to talk to Arsula. It had been five days since their fight, but he was still smarting from her assumption that she knew so much about who he was and how he hurt on the inside.

Or from pretending that some dream had come to her overnight that led her down the path of how to "fix" him. He didn't need fixing, dammit.

And he could hardly tolerate sitting there now, knowing that she'd awoken from another dream that morning, and that if he'd only gotten over himself, his dad might not be on the verge of dying at that very moment.

"Jay."

He looked up to find Megan standing before him, and he rose, letting her wrap her arms around him.

"I got here as soon as I could," she whispered. "I just heard."

Jaden nodded. "I appreciate you coming."

She took his hand, and they lowered to the chairs. Jaden and his family had been there for hours already, with his dad being in surgery for the majority of that.

"How is he?" Megan asked. She leaned in close, friend Megan showing up when he needed her, and Jaden followed his stepmother's lead. He shook his head. He didn't know how his father was.

"He could lose a leg," he finally managed. He wouldn't talk about a worse possibility. His dad couldn't die. Jaden hadn't had a chance to tell him yet how angry he'd been when the man hadn't been there after his mom died. How angry he *still* was.

His father had called in Dani to finish raising him instead of taking it upon himself to do so. But why? He was the parent, not Dani. And he was the parent who *hadn't* had a mental illness.

He was the one who was *supposed* to have loved him.

And dang it, how had Arsula figured that out when he'd never come close to realizing it himself? He was the fucking counselor. Not *her*.

He hadn't wanted to go to the house when he'd broken his ankle—in his time of need—because he hadn't wanted to watch his dad not be there for him again. He *could* be in that house as a grown man standing on his own. But he apparently couldn't do it as a helpless kid.

"Any idea how much longer he'll be in surgery?" Megan asked.

Jaden could tell she was trying to be supportive, and he appreciated it. It was times like this that having someone by your side was important.

It was just . . . he wanted Arsula by his side.

And he hated himself—and her—for wanting that.

He glanced down at the unread message notification again and knew that it was his fault his father hadn't been found until after he'd nearly bled to death. The tractor had hit the tree, rolled, and then pinned his dad underneath. And Arsula had been trying to warn him.

Yet had he read the messages, would he have even responded? That question had bothered him as much as knowing that valuable time had been wasted. But the question *was* a valid one, because he'd never once taken her seriously. Not about that.

"You okay, baby brother?"

Jaden looked up again, realizing that Megan had been replaced with Dani, and he nodded. He was okay. Only, he wasn't.

Arsula had apparently reached out to Dani, Gabe, Nate, Nick, *and* Erica when he hadn't returned any of her messages, and it was thanks to them that their father hadn't died that morning at the very farm that had been their livelihood throughout their childhood years. The place that had meant both family and what a family should and potentially *could* be—as well as what a family wasn't and would *never* be.

And it was thanks to Arsula that they'd even had the opportunity to be able to save him.

"I've had better days," he admitted. He'd been right there, under the same roof as the man. After his argument with Arsula, he'd packed his things and had Nate bring him home. Yet even though all he'd had to do was read his incoming messages, then go outside and save his father's life, he'd let pride and selfishness get in the way.

"How's the ankle, then?" Dani patted his knee, an unsteady smile touching her mouth. "We don't have to talk about Dad right now. We can talk about something else."

"Like my ankle?" He laughed humorlessly.

"It's better than the alternative," Dani said softly, and suddenly Jaden realized how she was being the strong big sister for them again. As she'd always been. Even though she had a husband who could be *her* shoulder in this moment of need.

Ben sat with Haley and Mia, along with the rest of Jaden's family, his gaze on his wife. As Dani sat with Jaden. And it was then that the clouds parted, and the sky began to clear. *He* was the one in need. Out of their entire family, he was the one who couldn't seem to function on his own. He needed to have his hand held. For someone to be there for him.

"I can put weight on it now," he said in answer to his sister's question, terrified at what his realization might mean. "Physical therapy went well enough last week that I've been cleared to use the boot as it was meant to be used."

"So no more crutches?"

"I've already tossed them."

When she opened her mouth to say something else, he put *his* hand on *her* knee. "I'm okay, Dani." He nodded toward her family. "Go be with Ben. Let Ben take care of you. I'm fine."

She hurt for him, he knew. She always had. And he would always love her for that. But it was time to stand on his own and stop whining because no one loved him enough.

Because Arsula had been right.

"Go," he said again. Then he pulled his sister in for hug. "And thank you for everything you've ever done for me," he whispered as he held her tight.

After they parted, she returned to Ben, and Jaden took inventory of the surgery waiting room. There were a couple of other people waiting on news from a loved one, and then there was Jaden's family—along with a handful of friends who'd heard the news and stopped by. And all of them sat with someone else. All holding a hand or offering a touch. All willing to be an emotional rock for whoever needed it.

They were the normal ones. Not him. They were the ones who could function without a crutch.

It made him wonder at the definition of normal. All this time, he'd have sworn he had that one wrapped up. Yet there was Nick with his ex-military, helicopter pilot wife, Gabe and his new family—and *not* his miserable excuse for an ex-wife. There was Cord, the MD and the brother who'd potentially experienced the worst of the mental abuse at the hands of their mother. Nate, the twin who was finally ready to come home and just looking for a reason to do so. Dani and her beautiful family.

And then there was him. He would soon have his master's degree, and like Nate had suggested, he'd likely continue until he earned his PhD. He had a job lined up, money saved for a down payment on a home and to start a family. All "normal," well-thought-out plans that, not long ago, he'd have sworn were on track to happen. Yet he'd lost not one but two women in a matter of weeks, and that was all on him.

He brought his phone up once again, and he finally tapped to read his messages.

Go find your father. Check to make sure he's okay.

Jaden, are you seeing this? I think your father is in real danger.
Please go check.

I know you think I'm crazy, but I'm terrified for your father. My
dream was clear this time. Let me know if he's okay!

Fine. Ignore me. Pretend I'm a joke. You do that so well. I'll let the
rest of your family know your father may be in danger. Maybe
one of them will care more about him than themselves.

He reread the messages. As usual, she was on point.

And as usual, she pulled no punches. That was one of the things
he loved about her.

The thought stopped him cold. He loved Arsula?

But not so long ago, he'd thought he loved Megan. He *had* loved
Megan. Only . . . had he really?

And did he now really love Arsula?

How was he supposed to know?

He read her messages one more time, and though he knew Dani
had updated her after they'd gotten to the hospital, he typed out one
of his own.

Dad is still in surgery. We don't know anything yet. Thank you
for trying to save his life.

A reply immediately followed: Thank you for letting me know. I'm
praying.

Tell Aunt Sul to say a prayer, too, will you?

He held his breath as he waited, and when her next message came,
it was only a small thumbs-up.

His thumbs hovered over the keyboard. He wanted to say more, to tell her that he missed her and that he was sorry he was an ass. But that little thumbs-up felt intentional. And cold.

So he tucked away his phone, and he understood that a person reaped what they sowed. And that Arsula deserved better than him.

"The Wilde family?"

Twelve heads turned to the scrubs-clad surgeon who'd entered the room. Doc Hamm also stood at the man's side, and as Gloria rose, the rest of them silently followed. Friends kept the kids while the adults made their way into a small consultation room, and once the door had been closed, the tension hung heavy.

No one said a word. As if no one could bring themselves to ask.

Finally, the surgeon began to speak. "I'll be honest with you. He was *not* in good shape when he arrived here. Nor is he in great shape now. But he *is* alive."

The entire room let out a collective breath.

"He's going to be okay?" Gloria's words were more plea than question.

"The next forty-eight hours are crucial," the doctor continued. "Your husband lost far more blood than we are comfortable with, Mrs. Wilde. And we did end up having to amputate below the knee."

Gloria whimpered.

"But he is alive. That's the important thing. And while on my watch, I'm going to do everything I can to make sure he stays that way."

Hesitant relief worked its way through the room, and after several questions and answers, the surgeon squeezed Gloria's hands and nodded to each of her stepchildren. "Your dad's a fighter. We're going to be right here, fighting alongside him."

The surgeon left, but Doc Hamm remained, and Jaden watched as the physician looked to Gloria. She gave a small nod, and worry suddenly filled the room again. As if everyone understood there was more to the story. That there was a *reason* their dad had run a tractor into a tree at six o'clock that morning.

"What is it?" Gabe asked. He slipped an arm around Erica's shoulders, while she slid hers behind his waist.

"Your dad is sick," the doctor informed them. "He hasn't wanted you all to worry, but it's time for you to know. He's getting worse faster than we'd expected."

"What's wrong with him?" Dani left Ben's side and ended up standing at the front of the group. "What can we do?"

"You can't *do* anything," Gloria answered, her love for their father evident in the sorrow drawn heavy on her face. "He has a form of rapid-progression Parkinson's."

"And though the meds, for the most part, control his quivers," the doctor explained, "he began experiencing hallucinations recently. We suspect that's what happened this morning. He saw the tree as some sort of threat, perhaps. Hallucinations don't happen with everyone who experiences this disease, but at the rate he's going, I wouldn't be surprised if his becomes severe over time. And if that happens, he'll need to be watched around the clock."

"I'll do it." Jaden spoke up before anyone else could, surprising even himself. His dad might not have been there when Jaden had needed him, but Jaden wanted to do right by him.

"I can take care of him, Jaden." Gloria gave him a patient smile. "But I know he'll appreciate the offer when he hears of it."

"We'll all be there for him," Gabe added.

Jaden fell silent, wondering why he'd made the offer to begin with, and listened to the conversation continuing around him. Cord had most of the questions, going over the treatment plan Doc Hamm had laid out. They also talked about specialists, both who their dad had seen and who he might need to go to in the future, as well as the right approach to take as things progressed. And as Jaden stood there listening, being grateful he hadn't yet lost his dad, he realized that tears had been rolling down his cheeks.

He looked over at Dani, now held tight at her husband's side and who had her own set of tracks marking a path from her eyes, and she reached out a hand to Jaden. He didn't take her hand, though. Instead, he stepped to her other side, and he let her wrap her arm around him. He needed his big sister in that moment, and he wasn't ashamed to admit it.

Chapter Twenty-Three

Arsula settled down in the rocker with baby Arsula Victoria Moretti the following Friday, as amazed now as she'd been right after the tiny beauty had been born at what two people were capable of producing.

"Your mommy and daddy love you so much," Arsula whispered to her niece. "But I promise, if there comes a day when they just don't understand you . . . *I* always will. And I'll always be there for you."

She snuggled the baby close, then she leaned back in the chair and set it in motion. Her brother and sister-in-law granting her the honor of naming the baby after her had been the proudest moment of her life, and she'd make sure never to let her niece down.

She'd also appreciated them letting her stay the week with them. Which hadn't been her *original* intent. She'd gone to her parents' house after leaving the hospital and had settled into her old room as planned. However, over breakfast the following morning, her dad had started in on her. Before she'd been able to swing the conversation into one that two adults might have, her dad had put his foot down with an implied ultimatum—do as I say or lose my respect.

Her mom had been livid—as had *she*—so she'd repacked her bag and offered to help out the new mom and dad to allow them to get a little extra sleep.

That same bag was packed again and ready to be loaded in the car the following morning. It was time she returned to Birch Bay. The only problem was, she was both broken and renewed after this trip, and with her dad so upset with her, she didn't quite know *how* she was going to walk away.

How did one just lose their father like that? And why was it okay for him to do this to her?

As she continued to rock, she noticed a framed photograph sitting on the dresser, and the darned thing brought her instantly to tears. The photo hadn't been there earlier in the week. The picture was one taken when she was just a child, and there had been only three people included in it.

Her, her great-aunt Sul, and her great-great-grandmother Arsula.

She'd had the same photo in her bedroom as a child, and it now was tucked away in an album in her apartment.

She stared at it, her eyes going to the black opal ring that surrounded her much-smaller finger, and the sight made her miss her great-aunt more than ever. Aunt Sul had been married at one time, her husband having died not long into their marriage, and the unconventional ring he'd given her as an engagement ring had always enthralled Arsula. Aunt Sul had let her wear it for the photo that day, promising she'd leave it to her after she passed. But when Arsula and her mother had gone through Aunt Sul's jewelry after the funeral, the ring couldn't be found.

Arsula still kept an eye out for the ring, popping into pawn shops on a regular basis and even going to jewelry shows on occasion. As if expecting it would one day show up.

Looking at it now made her think about the ring she'd woken up wearing almost two months before. There was a world of difference between the two-carat diamond ring Jaden had had made for Megan and anything Arsula might ever want on her finger. She supposed that should have been warning enough about him.

"Isn't she the most beautiful thing?" her mom whispered as she entered the room. She pulled a stool over and sat beside Arsula and the baby, then reached out to stroke her fingers over Baby A's tiny arm. "I love my grandsons dearly, but there's just something about a little girl."

Arsula's mouth curved up. "Especially a little girl who's given the correct family name."

"Very true. I'm proud of Boyd and Whitney for doing that."

"Me too." Arsula pressed a kiss to the baby's head. "I figured you'd be at work today."

"I was, but it's my lunch hour, and I wanted to see you."

"Me, huh?" She peered down into her niece's sweet face. "Something tells me another Arsula was calling your name."

"No, Lula-bell. I came for you."

Arsula looked up in question, and her mother touched a finger to one corner of Arsula's mouth.

"I've seen sadness in your smiles this week," her mother said, "and I don't think your broken heart is completely due to your father. What's happened, baby? Is it about Jaden?"

Arsula gave her mother one of those sad smiles. Her mother had waited exactly one day after Arsula admitted to Boyd that she was seeing someone before she'd called and demanded details. And then she'd even talked Arsula into putting Jaden on the phone.

But Arsula had been back in Cheyenne for a week now, and this was the first time her mother had brought him up. As if she'd known it still hurt too much to talk about.

She nodded. "It is about Jaden. It's over between us."

"Oh." Her mother shook her head. "No. I don't think so."

"Mom." She laughed, her heart breaking even more as a tiny flare of hope tried to fire to life. "You can't say that. You don't even know what happened."

"I don't need to know what happened, Lula. Because I know he's the one."

The words hurt. Because he *wasn't* the one. And her mother wanting love for her wouldn't make it so. She shook her head instead of saying anything else, and she looked back down at Baby A. But as usual, being ignored didn't dissuade Chloe Moretti.

"Let me tell you a story," her mother began. "It's about a girl who was once as beautiful as you, and one who is *not* named Arsula."

Arsula stopped the rocker.

"But one with a special gift nonetheless," her mother continued.

"Mom." Arsula stared at her mother. "What are you talking about? What's this girl's name?"

Her mother caressed the backs of her fingers over Arsula's cheek and nodded. "I do have a gift, sweet child of mine, and it's time to tell you about it. I was born with it, same as you, and though it's very restricted in its usefulness, it does have a great purpose."

Arsula's heart pounded behind her ribcage. "What's its purpose?"

And why was her mother just now telling her about this?

The baby had begun to squirm the moment the rocker stopped, so Arsula pushed off the floor once again. But she didn't take her eyes off her mother.

Her mom's gaze burned steady. "He's the one, honey. Jaden is the man you're meant to be with."

She stopped the rocker again. "What are you talking about?"

"My gift is the ability to watch over my family. To know if they're with the person who'll make them happy for life." She nodded, and the gravity of her words didn't miss Arsula. "He's the one," her mother repeated for the third time. "I knew it the moment he got on the phone."

"He is *not* the one, Mother." She ground out the words. "Your gift is flawed."

"I haven't been wrong yet."

She restarted the rocker. "Well, there's a first for everything."

Kind of like the fact that Jaden was her first broken heart. And he'd broken it into tiny slivers that might never heal.

She rocked without talking for a few minutes, doing her best to ignore everything her mother had said. Jaden was *not* the man for her. He thought she was a joke. He demeaned her life's mission every chance he got.

And the man had more problems than he wanted to admit!

No. Not the one. But that didn't mean she didn't question what her mother said.

Because how could she in good conscience ignore her mother's gift when she wanted to demand respect for her own? She shook her head, unable to put the puzzle pieces together. "He's a pain in the butt, Mom. You're wrong. Jaden isn't the one for me."

"Ah, Lula-bell. What would life be without a daily challenge or two?"

"Or three," Arsula added wryly, then silently adjusted it to one hundred.

Her mother patted her leg. "At least he won't be boring."

At least he wouldn't be her problem.

She went back to ignoring her mother, snuggling her baby niece instead. But her mother—being her mother—wasn't deterred.

"Did I ever tell you the story of your father's and my path to the altar?"

Arsula smelled the top of Baby A's head. "I know how you met. He tripped over you in the hall because he was reading a book instead of watching where he was going."

"That's only the beginning. And I knew he was the man for me the minute I looked up from the floor, by the way. Not that it made me any too happy. I had my eye on the captain of the football team at the time."

Arsula grunted. "I'm glad you chose Dad instead of the jock. I prefer having a brain."

Her mom patted her thigh again. "How can I say no when presented with my reality? So anyway, your dad asked me out after helping me up, and naturally, I said yes. And at the end of the date, he decided he didn't want to see me anymore."

Arsula stiffened. "You never told me that."

"Of course not. Your dad hates it when I share stories of the times he was wrong. And baby girl, he was wrong three times with me. The silly man actually tried to break up with me three times that first year." She shook her head. "I just told him no. That wasn't an option."

"You just told him no?"

"I did. Three times."

That sounded exactly like her mother. "And you've lived happily ever after since?"

"Every day of my life"—her eyes turned hard—"*except* when he tries to do wrong by my daughter."

They grew quiet as they sat there, neither wanting to talk about how unfair her dad was being or how things might truly end up, and baby Arsula started to mewl like a newborn kitten. Watching her, the tug of motherhood began to pull again. And the reminder that she wouldn't be having kids with Jaden.

She dropped her head to the back of her chair. "Why did you never tell me about your gift, Mom? I've gone my whole life feeling bad that you don't have one."

"Because you have to live your life the way it was meant to be. If you knew I could look at a man and say yay or nay, would you have dated all the boys you've gone out with?"

"I'm sure I would . . ." She trailed off as she thought about a couple of the losers she'd spent more than a few dates with. "I don't know," she admitted.

"And would you have behaved differently toward Jaden, even the slightest amount, if you had known?"

She cut her eyes over at her mother. "You mean, as in *not* throwing things at him when he makes me mad?"

"Baby." Her mother touched Arsula's cheeks again. "Really? You still do that?"

"He called me the devil, Momma. And then on the morning I left to come here, he said I was a joke. And he wasn't joking." She shook her head, letting her mother see that he'd crossed the line, and her mother's mama-bear side showed up.

"I assume you informed him that you certainly are not?"

"Of course I did. And I will to anyone else who pulls such crap."

"My point exactly. If you'd known about *my* gift, you might have walked with kid gloves around Jaden. You wouldn't have been you. And he wouldn't have had the pleasure of falling in love with the true beauty that *is* you. My gift has to be protected, Lula-bell. So your dad can hold your hand and walk you down the aisle when the time is right."

"Oh, Mom. Please stop. You know I value the gifts we're born with, but you have it all wrong this time, trust me. Jaden *isn't* the man for me, and at this point, I can't even see Dad walking me down the aisle. Ever."

She was too much of a disappointment.

"He doesn't like having to admit he's wrong, Arsula. That's a fact. But that doesn't mean the day won't come when he does."

When the baby squirmed again, her mother stole her from Arsula's arms.

"My turn to hold my granddaughter," she declared. Then she nodded toward the rocker, indicating that Arsula needed to get up.

As Arsula rose, her gaze fell upon the picture once again, and she picked it up before leaving the room. She carried it with her as she sought out Boyd, and when she found him in the living room, she held the picture in front of him.

He smiled at the sight of it. "I like that one."

"Me too. But I'll admit, I didn't expect to find it in Baby A's room."

He looked at her then, and the love she saw from her brother soothed a little of the hurt from her dad. "I may not be one of you," Boyd said, "but I *do* understand the importance of the women in our family. I want to make sure my daughter always knows that importance as well."

She looked back at the photo. His words meant a lot.

"Thank you," she said, and when he patted the cushion, she sat beside him.

"She's going to need you to teach her the ways, you know?"

Like Aunt Sul had taught her.

She nodded. "You have my promise that I'll do that for her."

"I know you will. Just like you'll also follow your heart." He picked up the iPad he'd been looking at when she'd first come into the room, and she saw her temporary website on the screen.

"What are you doing?" she asked.

"I'm checking to see if there have been any more updates lately."

"You know that updates have been done?"

He nodded. "I pulled it up a couple of days after you first showed it to me, and I noticed that some of the changes you'd mentioned had been made. So I've been keeping an eye on it. It looks really good."

"My web designer has built in everything we've talked about so far."

"So it's ready to launch?"

"I don't know. I may not—"

"I've never seen you so unsure, Arsula. In fact, I can't recall a time that I've seen you unsure at all. And I have to tell you, I don't care for the look."

She sighed. "I can't say that I care for it, either, but you know what Dad wants of me. And you know how strongly he feels about it." All three of her brothers and their mother had heard the argument between them over Christmas.

"And when I look at this website, I know how much you love what *you* do. I'm in awe of you, Arsula. Have I ever mentioned that? You could go to medical school, choose whatever specialty you wanted, and end up flat-out naming your price. You'd be wanted far and wide."

"Kind of like Dad."

"*Better* than Dad."

She looked at him in a new way then. She'd not realized he saw her like that.

"I think that's why it bothers him so much that you don't care," Boyd added, "because he knows you'd be better than him."

Her brother's praise meant a lot.

"But the thing is, Arsula, you *choose* to do something else. You choose to uphold a gift you've been bestowed, and you choose to forgo certain wealth to be a source of *mental* wealth for others."

She'd never thought of it quite like that. "You don't think the fact that I read dreams makes me a loon?" she asked. Her brothers had teased her over the years, but she'd never really thought they considered her ridiculous.

That didn't mean she didn't want Boyd to answer the question, though.

"If I began having recurring dreams," he said, "or struggles that seemed to be playing out during my sleeping hours, you're the *first* person I would call." He squeezed her hand. "You're the *only* person I would call."

She heard nothing but honesty in his words. "I appreciate you saying those things."

"And I'd appreciate it if I never have to see my baby sister looking like she's walking around lost in the world anymore." He angled his chin down and speared her with a look. "Three months now, Arsula. Don't you think that's long enough?"

Her cell dinged with a message before she could figure out how to answer her brother, and as soon as her pulse calmed from hoping the text might be from Jaden, she lifted her phone to check.

Max is going to be okay. He's moving out of ICU and to a regular room today.

The message was from Erica. She'd been keeping Arsula updated on Max's condition.

How is he?

He's good. He'll have to be in a rehab place for a while, and he already has an appointment scheduled with a Parkinson's specialist up in Kalispell. They're hoping to get him on an experimental drug. Also, he'll start physical therapy alongside Jaden as soon as he's able.

Alongside Jaden?

It was Jaden's idea.

Arsula started to ask how Jaden was, but erased the message before sending it. It didn't matter how he was. She may not live her life the way Jaden would choose, but that didn't take anything away from her. And though she did love him, she was also okay walking away from him. Because she loved herself more.

She realized the same could be true of her father. She had to take care of *herself* first. Love *her* more.

And if her father wanted to be a part of her life . . . then he was going to have to love her for who she was, too.

Both relief and pain filled her as her decision became clear. She'd known she would return home tomorrow, but until that moment, she'd still worried she'd someday crumble to her father's wishes. But she wouldn't, she now knew. She would be going home tomorrow, and she would be starting her new life without looking back.

And if her dad ever did change his mind and see her for what she was worth?

Then *maybe* she'd accept his forgiveness.

"You look like you had an epiphany," Boyd observed.

Her heart raced. She had a lot to do with very little time. "I did have an epiphany." And she suddenly didn't have time to be sitting around not doing anything.

"Would you care to share it?"

She picked up the tablet and brought her website back up. Then she tapped to the Resources page and loaded her book cover. She turned the screen toward him. "I finished the book this week," she said. "Did I tell you that?"

He began to smile. "You did not tell me."

She nodded, and the feeling of the world righting itself settled inside her. "I also sent it off to a copy editor to get it proofread."

"You're going to publish it, then?"

She smiled, then she tapped her home page, and her name appeared on the screen. "I'm going to publish *all* of it," she told him. "Wish me luck, brother, because I'm about to stretch my wings to span the world."

His grin overflowed with pride. "You're going to knock 'em dead, Lula."

She headed to her bedroom and grabbed her bag, unwilling to wait until tomorrow to get started, then she popped into the baby's room and hugged her mother goodbye.

She sought out Whitney and Boyd next.

"You're leaving right *now*?" Boyd asked.

"I have too many things to do. I won't be here for Mom to make a fuss for my birthday, so I'm going to make a fuss myself." She kissed her brother on the cheek. "My present to myself will be the launch of my website."

Chapter Twenty-Four

I hate that it's the last day of spring break already." Maggie sighed without looking up. She sat in one of the guest chairs in front of the office's large window, her attention focused on painting her fingernails a bright red.

"And I hate that our favorite restaurant is closed today. It's Arsula's big day. How are we supposed to celebrate correctly without margaritas?"

Arsula looked up from behind her desk and smiled in thanks for her two friends hanging out with her while the rest of the town prepared to party outside. "And I hate that you're both having to miss the fun because of me."

Maggie finally took her focus off her nails, but only long enough to shoot Arsula a look. "No. What you really hate is that you're not out there, too."

"Very true," Arsula conceded, because her friend was spot-on. It was the grand reopening of The Cherry Basket today, and she loved a reason to celebrate. And with it being her birthday and no family celebration lined up? Yeah. She'd like to be out there.

She hadn't heard anything else from Jaden other than that one text while his dad had still been in surgery, though, and when she'd learned that the entire Wilde family—minus Max—would be attending the festivities today, she'd made the decision not to go. She didn't want to risk anything being said between the two of them that might result in awkwardness.

"Can you tell if they've started yet?" Arsula asked, and Erica moved to the door.

As Erica stepped outside to get a better look, Arsula hit refresh on her browser. Her website still wasn't live.

"Doesn't look like," Erica reported as she came back in, "but there's a *huge* crowd gathering. I didn't expect that."

"Good timing with it being during spring break, I guess."

"But poor timing by choosing to do it on your birthday," Maggie added, the twist to her mouth indicating her disapproval.

Arsula wanted to argue that Megan didn't know when her birthday was, so she couldn't have realized that the grand reopening she had planned as store manager would fall on the same day, but that was untrue. Before Arsula had driven out of her brother's driveway the week before, she'd texted her request to launch the site to Megan, and in the subsequent conversation, she'd pointed out that today was her birthday. She'd even shared that due to not being able to be with her family this year, she wanted to make the day special. She'd planned to treat her friends to lunch at their favorite restaurant, then surprise them by showing off her newly launched website.

Instead, she sat trapped inside the office on a beautiful day, while the rest of the town gathered on the opposite side of the square for what seemed to be a fabulous celebration.

"I didn't realize she was going to get the store open so fast," Maggie said. She now craned her neck for a better look. "Didn't they just sign the lease on the place a couple of weeks ago?"

"A little longer than that, I think." But not long enough that Arsula would have thought the store would be opening already. Megan must have produced some serious magic to make that happen.

"There's a fire truck coming," Maggie exclaimed, and Arsula and Erica got up to take a look. It wasn't a fire truck on the way to put out a fire, though. It was one with balloons and streamers covering it.

"What the heck kind of grand openings go on around here?" Arsula muttered. She peered in the direction of where the party would take place. Apparently, when new businesses opened their doors in Birch Bay, they did it in style. Activity had been going on all morning, with two massive screens brought in and set up in the middle of the square, lights strung between the trees, and even a small stage had been erected. She couldn't imagine why cutting one little ribbon involved so much, but she absolutely hated that she couldn't be over there to join in.

"That's it," Maggie said when a bus pulled up and a load of senior citizens began filing out. "All three of us are going over there."

"I still don't think we should," Arsula insisted.

"I don't care what you think," Maggie added. "It's your freaking birthday, Arsula. You're the one who needs to be celebrating around here. Not hiding because you don't want to risk upsetting Jaden. Did he care about upsetting *you* when he told you that you were an embarrassment?"

She'd shared the story of her and Jaden's breakup—as well as her disappointment in her father's stance—with her friends.

"Plus," Erica added, "how would Jaden even see you in this crowd?"

That was a valid point.

"I guess it wouldn't hurt to go over for a few minutes." Without giving it further thought, she shut down her computer and forwarded the phone. But as soon as they stepped outside, she saw Tim heading for the office. At the sight of him, Arsula stopped.

"I just locked up," she explained. Dani had gone over to the party earlier and had told her that if she changed her mind to just lock the doors and put up the "Closed" sign. "I didn't figure you'd be back, but if you need me to do something, I can stay."

"No." Tim held out his hands in a stopping motion. "I was coming to get you. Dani decided she wouldn't feel right if she sat by and let you miss this. We *are* in charge of the promo for the grand opening, after all. The company needs to be represented."

Arsula chuckled. "I suppose that's as good an excuse as any."

She looked up at Tim before heading toward the party, though, her worry apparent.

"Jaden is over there, right? Have you seen him?"

Tim had teased her when he'd first found out she and Jaden were dating, but he'd also wished her luck. He'd thought they made a great couple.

"He is over there." He leaned down to whisper, "But if it makes you feel any better, he looks as miserable as you."

That did help.

She nodded. "Let's go, then. It's my birthday, did I tell you?" She slipped an arm through her friends' arms as Erica and Maggie each moved to her side. "And I intend to party for my birthday."

Tim's smile bordered on mysterious, but he didn't say anything to follow it up.

Jaden watched for Arsula from inside the store, and as he caught his first sight of her, the nerves of the morning calmed. She may not be coming over for him, but at least she *was* coming over. Now it would be up to him to make her stay.

"Your woman awaits, sir," Megan said at his side, and Jaden looked over, realizing, not for the first time, that she'd made the right decision in dumping him. She'd been right, he wasn't the man for her. Just as she wasn't the woman for him.

And if he hadn't been so caught up in making sure that *someone* loved him, he might have even seen that before she had.

He gave her a quick hug. "Thank you for helping me out with this. And for being my friend."

"My pleasure. What are friends for? Plus, when that crowd realizes that we're not just selling cherries around here today, they're going to remember this moment and associate it with the store forever. Big bucks, my friend. And I can't complain about that."

Jaden laughed. "You're an evil genius."

"That I am, and don't forget it."

She nodded toward the mayor, who, with the town's councilmembers, was making his way toward the stage. "Showtime," she said.

Megan exited the store, followed by Jaden and then joined by the rest of his siblings, and as Jaden walked alongside his family, he knew he'd never had a reason to have to prove himself to any of them. All six of them might be a veritable mess, but they were a mess made with love.

Dani gave him a quick hug as she moved to his side on the stage, and then as a group they faced the crowd.

"I want to welcome all of you here today," the mayor started over the intercom, and the chatter immediately died down. "And I especially want to welcome our newest retail store to the downtown area."

Cheers went up as Megan waved to the crowd.

"We're all going to fill up on cherry delectables later, I promise you that. I've seen the inside of the store already, and I'll let you in on a little secret." The mayor smiled, his face friendly and welcoming. "I might have already tried a sample or two," he faux whispered into the microphone, and the crowd laughed. "But before we get to the ribbon cutting—and to those delectables—I hope you'll allow us a few moments first."

Arsula watched the faces around her as Megan stepped to the micro-phone next, seeing that they were as uncertain as she as to what was going on. Since she'd arrived, she'd quickly picked up on the fact that this was definitely *not* a standard grand opening, and everyone knew it. However, special invitations had apparently been sent throughout the town, so many people had closed up shop or been allowed to leave work early to come on out.

"I, too, want to thank you all for coming out," Megan said over the speakers now. "And if you haven't yet met me, I hope that's about to change. I'd like to see each and every one of you in The Cherry Basket every day."

More laughter, and then the crowd quieted.

"I have a friend who has a small presentation to make before we get to the good stuff, and I agreed to hijack you all to allow him to do it."

The hairs on the back of Arsula's arms rose.

Him?

She glanced at Erica and Maggie, but they both seemed as lost as she.

"And don't worry," Megan went on, "I promise the samples the mayor mentioned will be waiting on you. And there *will* be plenty for everyone. But this presentation is really important. You see, this friend of mine means a lot to me. We've known each other for a long time, and he has something he needs to say to a person who means a lot to *him*."

Before Arsula could allow the thought to form, Jaden moved to the front of the stage.

One of the two screens came to life and filled with a picture, and in the next instant, she saw that the picture was actually a live stream. *Of her three brothers, their wives, and their kids.*

She stared at Jaden. What was going on here?

"The thing is," Jaden began, looking toward the middle of the crowd instead of where she stood off to the side, "there are a couple of things I need to say up here today, and one thing leads into the other. So I'll just jump in with number one." The rest of Jaden's family stepped to his side, and they held hands down the line. "My brothers and sister and I want to thank the entire town from the bottoms of our hearts. The love and support that's been heaped onto our dad over this past week and a half has blown us away, and we can't begin to thank you enough."

The crowd cheered, and Jaden went on.

"Dad is doing really great, considering. He is down a leg, and that's put a bit of a crimp in his style, but he's alive. And for that, we're thankful."

Tears threatened at Arsula's eyes as the other screen flickered to life, and in the middle of it, perched on a bed at the rehab center, sat Max and Gloria. Max looked tired, but good. He hadn't felt up to a lot of visitors yet, so she hadn't made it out to see him, so this glimpse of the man soothed a continuing worry in her heart.

Max waved while Gloria thanked everyone as well, and then Max reached for the microphone.

His hand shook as he talked. "I'll eventually get out of this prison they've stuck me in," Max began, his voice weak, but coming across the speakers perfectly, "and when I do, I'll be sure to get by and thank each and every one of you. But today, I need to offer one very personal thanks to one very special person."

Tim appeared at Arsula's side and held a camera phone up in front of her, and the screen up front changed, splitting to show both her and Max.

"This young lady saved my life, folks." Max's words were filled with tears. "She's a special one, and I know I'm not the only one here today who's grateful that she moved to town." More cheers came from those around her. "Thank you, Arsula," Max went on, "for trusting your gut. Thank you for saving my life."

Tears ran unheeded now, and she had the urge to shove Tim's phone out of her face. She didn't need the entire town seeing her blubbering like a baby. But while smiling back at Max, she didn't care who saw her or how bad she looked. She blew the man a kiss, and her heart felt like it increased in size.

"And speaking of that particular lady . . ." The voice changed back to Jaden's, and when she looked back at the stage, he once again stood alone.

Max disappeared from the screen, Tim faded back into the crowd, and Jaden cleared his throat.

"One thing leads into the next," he said, "and my father just told you how. Though I'm sure neither of us needed to introduce her. You've all heard the story of how Arsula Moretti, a beautiful bright light of a woman, saved my dad when she woke up last Tuesday morning, and now I'm hoping she'll consider forgiving some nasty things I've said to her. And maybe saving me, too."

He finally turned and looked directly at her, and when Erica and Maggie shifted as if to move away, Arsula reached out to beg them to stay. Only, in their places she found her parents.

"Mom?" She looked from one to the other. "Dad?"

"You see, this woman," Jaden went on, "is the love of my life."

Arsula jerked her gaze back to Jaden.

"And it's her birthday today." His eyes remained on hers. "And she deserves to have the world handed to her on her birthday."

The screen that had previously shown Max fired back to life, and this time a video began to play. A video she hadn't seen before, but one that started with a shot of her face before morphing into images she and Megan had chosen for her website.

"I had a dream last week." Jaden's voice sounded through the speakers, but he wasn't actively speaking. He'd narrated what Arsula now realized was a commercial for her life coaching business. A commercial no doubt made by her own boss. "And in that dream, I lost my way."

Chills covered Arsula as her mother squeezed her close, and then her dad's voice came though the speakers.

"And in *my* dream, I'd lost *my* way."

She looked at her dad.

"I'm so sorry," he told her. "I . . ."

He lifted the bound copy of the book she'd had printed and left for him before she'd driven away from Cheyenne.

"I don't deserve your forgiveness," he said, "but I do hope you'll give it. I'm so proud of you, Arsula. And whether you can believe it or not, I've always been proud. But I've not always been right."

"Of course I'll forgive you, Dad. I love you." She hugged her dad as Jaden's voice continued from the video.

"But there's a woman who can help you find *your* way. And today, Arsula Moretti isn't just going to be available locally anymore. She's going worldwide."

The video ended, and her website appeared.

"Arsula?" Jaden spoke above the noise of the crowd, and suddenly, a path appeared before her. It stretched from her to the stage, and at the other end of it was Jaden holding out his hand. "Would you please come up here? I have a couple of apologies to make."

She didn't move. She was too afraid to hope.

"Go, Arsula." Her mother let loose her arm. "I told you. He's the one."

She looked at her mom, seeing the assurance in her eyes.

"Go," her father urged. "I've been here talking to everyone all morning. They love you. They're as proud of you as I am." He inclined his head toward Jaden. "And *he* loves you. And I didn't need your mother to tell me that in order to see it."

Her dad hugged her once again, and then Erica and Maggie dragged her away. They were clearly prepared to lead her to Jaden, but they didn't have to. Jaden was the only place she wanted to be.

She was jogging by the time she reached the stage, and as she climbed the steps to the love of *her* life, the crowd behind her cheered. As did her family, grinning back at her from the screen.

"What are you doing?" She stared at Jaden in disbelief.

"I'm trying to prove that I'm not a total jerk." He took her hand in his. "Nor am I unable to learn. You were right. About everything. My dad . . . my family. I'm working on *me* again, and I promise to never stop. But also"—he motioned to the screen where the commercial had played—"I'm behind *you* one hundred percent. You're not an embarrassment, Arsula, nor could you ever be. You're an inspiration. To *everyone*. So no more doubts, and no more lashing out when things scare me."

She found the last one hard to believe. "Never?"

"Well"—he cringed—"how about if I promise to always apologize when I mess up and *do* lash out?"

"That certainly sounds more believable."

He reached for her hand. "I'm so sorry. I've said awful things to you, and there's no excuse. I know that, and I wouldn't blame you for never forgiving me."

"But?" she asked, and he smiled as if he'd seen her question coming.

"But, honey, I'm going to ask your forgiveness anyway. Every day until you give it."

"I give it," she whispered, and she watched love bloom in his eyes.

"I don't deserve you, you know?"

"Kiss her!" someone shouted from the crowd, but Jaden waved them off.

"I haven't gotten to the best part yet."

As he spoke, it occurred to Arsula that his voice still radiated out over the speakers. Which meant that *hers* did, too. Everything they'd said had been witnessed by all.

She turned back to Jaden and didn't worry about the crowd. "What's the best part?" she asked. Because she was ready for the best part.

"That I want to be with you forever."

Someone's hands reached around him and clipped a microphone onto his shirt, and then both of his hands were free to take hers.

301

"I love you, Arsula Jane Moretti. How could I not? You're the only person who's ever thrown things at me, then had me begging for more with only a smile. And not just once, either. Also, I know I'm rushing things—and we both know I should have learned my lesson about rushing already—but I need you to know how I feel. I want to be with you for the rest of my life, Arsula. I'll promise to wait as long as it takes until you feel that way, too. But I didn't want to go another day without telling you—"

"I love you, too."

Relief washed over him at her words.

"Really."

"Good." He nodded, and he squeezed her hands tight. *"Good,"* he said again. "Because I also kind of already got you a ring, too."

The crowd laughed, and Arsula couldn't help but chuckle along with them. She loved this man.

"It doesn't have to be an engagement ring," he told her. "And probably it shouldn't be. Because it's not exactly a conventional ring. But then, this isn't necessarily an engagement either—unless you want it to be."

She decided to remain quiet. The man might as well have to sweat it out a little.

"You don't even have to wear the ring if you don't want to," he went on. "But I saw it, and I knew it would be perfect for you."

She waited for him to hold out this unconventionally perfect ring, but instead, Megan returned to the stage carrying a small white baker's box, while behind her two teenagers sporting The Cherry Basket's logo rolled out massive carts, each covered in white linen.

"Thank you," Jaden said as Megan handed over the box, then faded back into the background.

Jaden turned to Arsula.

"There's one other thing before we get to the ring." He opened the box and lifted out a cupcake sporting a bright-red cherry on top. "I made you a birthday cupcake."

A part sob, part laugh choked out of her. "You made me a cupcake?" she whispered.

The sheer pleasure from the miniature cake now held in the palm of Jaden's hand couldn't be measured.

"I did. And in fact"—he nodded to the two Cherry Basket employees, who whipped the linens from the trays to reveal three tiers of cupcakes on each—"I actually made enough cupcakes for everyone who showed up here today. I've spent the last forty-eight hours baking cupcakes."

Whoops went up through the crowd, and once again Arsula was reminded that they had an audience. But she didn't care. She wouldn't choose to be anywhere but here.

"There is one small difference between your cupcake and everyone else's, though." Jaden leaned toward her, his lips within a breath of being in kissing distance, and he placed the cupcake in her hand. "Yours has your ring in it."

A smile bloomed on her face so wide that she wasn't sure she'd ever be able to get it off. "You baked me a cupcake and put an unconventionally perfect engagement/nonengagement ring inside of it?"

He gave a shrug. "It seemed like the right thing to do."

She couldn't love this man more. "It was the *perfect* thing to do."

Plucking off the muffin top of the cupcake, she carefully set it back inside the box so she could fully enjoy her birthday cupcake later, and then she dug two fingers into the base. It didn't take long to find the ring, and she laughed with the man in front of her as she lifted it up.

Only, then she saw it.

Emotion backed up in her throat as she pressed one hand to her mouth. "Where did you get this ring, Jaden?"

"What?" Desperation crossed his face. "I'm sorry. I told you it was unconventional. Forget this ring." He tried to take it away from her, but she held firm. "I'll buy you a new one," he promised. "A better one."

"*Where* did you get it?"

She knew her demand seemed out of place, but she couldn't yet find the words to explain. She looked out at the crowd and found her mother looking back. Her mother wore the same confused expression as Jaden.

"I found it at the flea market," Jaden finally answered. "I saw this woman with eyes that reminded me of yours. But really . . . I'll get you a new one. Or I'll wait until you're ready to agree to marry me."

She closed her eyes as she began to understand. "Why did you go to the flea market?"

"What? Arsula, why are you asking all these questions? I'm trying to talk to you about forever here." He glanced toward the crowd, where everyone had gone silent.

"Why?" she asked again, her voice now soft and patient. "It's important, Jaden. I need to know why you went."

"But I don't know why." He seemed even more confused than before, but she could see him trying to think through it. "I woke up that morning, and I missed you. I've been freaking missing you since the minute I walked away. And that day . . . I don't know . . . I woke dreaming about you, so I—"

He stopped talking, and she smiled at him as she saw realization dawn.

"You went to the flea market and found *this* ring because you'd dreamed about me?"

He nodded. "I suppose I did."

Then he looked at the ring that was still clutched in her fingers. "Does this particular style of ring mean something to you?"

"You're catching on, sweetheart. But first, what was the dream about?"

"Seriously?" His shoulders slumped. "I don't know. Nothing, really. You were just there. In my head. And you were standing with that cart with the squeaky wheel that we got there."

Her heart began to race.

"So I got up, and I went," he went on. "I was there before they opened. Because I *missed* you. But then I just wandered around. I didn't even stop anywhere until I saw the woman who had your eyes."

Arsula's grin grew even wider, and she silently thanked her great-aunt.

"And then I saw the ring," he told her. "It was just there, and I knew I had to buy it." He took it from her and held it up. "So that's my story. Are you going to say that you'll take me back now and that you'll accept this ring as a promise of my love?"

"Are you going to admit that you listened to your intuition and because of that you found me the perfect ring?"

He sighed, but the smile on his face gave him away. "Are you sure?" His words croaked out. "It really is perfect?"

She nodded. "It really is."

"And I did have that dream . . ."

"Aunt Sul is in your head." She motioned to the screen where her brother was now holding up the picture from Baby A's room. He pushed the photo forward when Jaden turned to look at it, until nothing else could be seen. "Check out the ring in that picture, Jaden. That's Aunt Sul beside me, and that's her ring on my finger. Her ring was supposed to have been mine after she passed, but it wasn't there when we looked for it."

Boyd's finger pointed to the object of discussion, and then Jaden looked down at the matching black opal in his hand. His expression fell. "How did . . ."

"Aunt Sul," she said by way of explanation. "And I have more news for you."

"What's that?"

"That's not a promise ring, dear. That's my *engagement* ring."

About the Author

As a child, award-winning author Kim Law cultivated a love of chocolate, anything purple, and creative writing. She penned her debut work, *The Gigantic Talking Raisin*, in sixth grade and immediately became hooked on the delights of creating stories. Before settling into the writing life, however, she earned a degree in mathematics and worked for years as a computer programmer. Now she's living out her lifelong dream of writing romance novels. She has won the Romance Writers of America (RWA) Golden Heart Award, been a finalist for the prestigious RITA Award, and served in various positions for her local RWA chapter. A Kentucky native, Kim now lives with her husband and an assortment of animals in Middle Tennessee.